The Girl He Left Behind

Flossy Abraham

Copyright: Flossy Abraham 2016

All rights reserved: no reproduction, copy or transmission of this publication may be made without written permission. Copyright theft is stealing. No paragraph or picture of this publication may be reproduced, copied or transmitted save with written permission from the author or in accordance with the provisions of the Copyright, Design and Patents Act 1988, or under the terms of any license permitting limited copying issued by the Copyright Licensing Agency, 90 Tottenham Court Rd, London, W1P 9HE, England.

Any person who does any unauthorised act in relation to this publication may be liable to criminal prosecution and civil claims for damages. The author has asserted her right to be identified as the author of this work in accordance with the Copyright, Design and Patents Act 1988.

Disclaimer: this story is a fantasy from and for the imagination. Any resemblance to persons living or dead is coincidental.

ISBN: 978-1-326-63756-9

Produced by

simonthescribe.co.uk

For my husband –

You will have a special place in my heart forever.

"911, what's your emergency?"

"Hello, my name is Doctor Joseph Barsetti, I live at three thirty-five Marilyn Road, Milton, Norfolk County, Massachusetts and I have an inoperable, terminal brain cancer. I am about to take my own life, so I want you to get here before my wife gets home from work. I do not want my wife to find me, so you need to come now. I feel it's the right thing to do. I do not want to have a long drawn out death with this type of cancer. I do not want to be a burden on my wife. So please tell her I love her and I am sorry.

The sound of one single gunshot rang in the operator's ear; Joseph's telephone fell to the ground.

"Sir……Sir, are you okay, Sir? Doctor Barsetti, can you hear me?"

The operator stayed on the line, he frantically dispatched the police and ambulance whilst he still tried to converse with Joseph. A few moments later, he heard footsteps on a wooden floor and then a woman started to scream hysterically. He could hear the woman's fear in her high pitched screams of horror. Corina Barsetti, seven months pregnant with her first child, had come home from work early as she felt unwell. She manically looked around for the telephone to call for help; she found it amongst the blood and gore on the lounge floor, where Joseph was slumped against the coffee table. She saw a gun, a big gun, which the killer must have left behind; it didn't cross her mind that he had shot himself. Everything was fine when she had left for work this morning. They were happy; they were having a baby together. She shook violently, and as she lifted the telephone to her ear, she could hear a man's voice.

"Ma'am, can you hear me, ma'am?"

"Someone has shot my husband!" she screamed down the phone "Somebody has killed him, he's dead, please help me, somebody has killed my husband!"

Corina wedged the telephone between her shoulder and her right ear, so she could cradle her husband's head in her lap with both hands. He was unrecognisable. As she began to sob she could hear the operator's voice again.

"Ma'am, could you please go outside and wait for an officer? There is help on the way, Ma'am, can you hear me? Could you please do that for me?"

She ignored him; there was no way was she going to leave her husband.

Chapter One

Ten years previously.

Corina Green stood in front of the mirror in her student nurse's uniform, twenty years old and one week off qualifying as a psychiatric nurse.

"Ugh, I look like shit!" she yelled to the other student nurses, with whom she had shared the very cramped accommodation at The Cumberland Infirmary for the past three years.

"You're fucking sexy!" shouted Rebecca from the kitchen "You have the most amazing tits!"

Rebecca was a lesbian and she was very proud of it. She had always quite fancied Corina, but Corina had just shrugged her off and accepted Rebecca for who she was. There wasn't any chance of Corina giving in to her advances. Corina had her eyes on one particular doctor and she couldn't stop thinking about him.

"Jesus Becs, shut up…. We all know Corina is into sexy male doctors!" laughed Hazel, she flicked her long ginger hair behind her and pretended to be a model on a cat walk. "Your father would be proud of you at last if you married a doctor!"

Corina thought of her father, Doctor Henry Green, General Practitioner, who had served the community for nearly thirty years, just like his father had done and his father before that. She remembered his face and the look of disappointment on it, when she announced she was going to leave their family home in Cornwall and travel to Cumbria to train to be a psychiatric nurse.

"A psychiatric nurse?" he had raised his voice at her in disgust "But you can't be a nurse, it's tradition in this family to become a doctor!"

If the truth were to be known, she was clever enough to be a doctor and deep down that's what she really wanted to be, but she had rebelled and it felt good that she knew it annoyed her over powering father. In fact, she had spent most of her childhood annoying him as he took no notice of her, unless he had important company to show her off to, and then he would come across to his guests as the perfect father. She had worked out that if she annoyed him, that was the only way to get any attention from him and she felt that going to Cumbria to be a nurse was the ultimate annoyance. She wondered if he would show up to her graduation with her mother, Matron Penelope Green, The Bitch. The mother who had brought her up so strictly and so harshly, that Corina shuddered when she thought of her. She had more maternal instinct in her little finger than her mother had in her whole body. She hadn't given birth to Corina, she'd had something extracted. She hated her mother with a passion and knew nothing would anger her more than her daughter becoming a psychiatric nurse. They weren't proper nurses after all, not like her; they were just over qualified counsellors. She wondered why they had bothered to have her at all, when they couldn't be bothered with her most of the time. And, when they could be bothered with her, all they wanted to do was control her. Do this, Corina. Don't do that, Corina. Be a doctor, Corina. All the best people become doctors, Corina! Oh, how they annoyed her, so she would continue to annoy them for as long as she possibly could.

"Day dreaming again?" asked Harriet.

"Just thinking about the sperm donor and the surrogate mother" replied Corina; she shrugged off the thought of them ever turning up to see their daughter possibly achieve something.

"At least they didn't send you away to boarding school" whined Harriet.

"Cheer up" shouted Jenny from the sitting room, "I have an idea that will make our last week very memorable at The Cumberland Infirmary!" Jenny always had crazy ideas; she was the one that got them into trouble most of the time. If she wasn't thinking up ridiculous things for them to do, she would be getting them thrown out of pubs and clubs when she had caused an argument, as she didn't know when to keep her mouth shut.

"Uh oh!" joked Hazel "Wait for it!"

"I think in true nursing tradition, we should make a chart of all the departments, bang the consultants and then mark them out of ten for performance!" shrieked Jenny excitedly.

"Fucking hell, Jenny, you are nuts!" shouted Rebecca at her "And any way, what about me? I don't eat sausage, remember? I like to drink from the furry cup!"

"You can do all the woman consultants" laughed Jenny, as she threw herself onto the settee.

"And girls, if you can't get the consultants, go for the house men, or registrars!" she laughed hysterically "I bagsy A and E... Corina, I dare you to ask that American twat out in Oncology" then she faked a bad American accent "Hi there, I'm Doctor Joseph Barsetti, I'm from Boston and I think I am waaaaay better than you!"

"Bloody yanks!" scoffed Harriet "Always up their own arses and so loud!"

"Ahh, he's not loud, he's weird.... quiet and weird!" chipped in Hazel.

"Yeah, but he's handsome, don't you think?" swooned Corina "There's an air of mystery about him and I want to find out what it is"

"Yeah.... He's probably a chick with a dick, there.... mystery solved!" teased Rebecca.

They all laughed hysterically at Corina as she rolled her eyes and then stuck her middle finger up at Rebecca.

"Right, I'm off to do my shift" sighed Corina "You ready, Harriet?"

"I'll draw lots for the departments" shouted Jenny, as Corina and Harriet slammed the door behind them on their way out, "Corina gets most of the 'ology's' though!"

By the time Corina and Harriet had got back from the Psychiatric Ward, the other girls were asleep. There was a big handmade chart sellotaped onto the sitting room wall that was made out of cardboard. All their names were in a column down the left hand side and the departments they were 'covering' were alongside their names.

Corina read out loud her departments "RADIOLOGY, GYNAECOLOGY, ONCOLOGY, OPHTHALMOLOGY and DERMATOLOGY... bloody hell, I won't be able to walk by the end of the week; I noticed nobody has volunteered themselves to shag anyone in the Psychiatry Department!"

She turned to Harriet who had gone as white as a sheet, "What's up, Harry, babe?" Corina gave Harriet a big hug; she had a pretty good idea of what was wrong with her. Harriet started to cry, she was the posh, emotional one and she could cry at the drop of a hat, whereas Corina was more hard faced, just like her mother. She had been brought up to think you were weak if you cried and on many occasions had to fight back the tears so she appeared to be strong.

"I don't want to do this" sniffed Harriet "I'm still a virgin, but I don't want the other girls to know that. I'm saving myself for the right man. Just because I'm a student nurse, they all assume I'm a slut!"

"Hey, listen Harry" Corina stroked Harriet's cheeks with both hands and wiped away the tears in a sideways motion "Just make it up, that's what I'm going to do. They won't have a clue whether you've slept with a doctor or not!"

"Good idea" replied Harriet. She started to blow her nose, she then paused and said "You're such a good friend, Cor, I don't know what I'd do without you... but, what are you going to do about oncology and the weird American, you really like him don't you?"

"Yeah, but he is really weird and I don't think anything's going to happen there!" laughed Corina.

Chapter Two

A week later Corina still hadn't heard from her parents. "Bloody typical" she stated out loud, whilst she pulled her graduation gown down over her head and tried to avoid messing up her freshly styled hair.

"Talking to yourself again?" asked Jenny, as she put her head around the door "How's the 'ology's' going?"

"Well, Radiology gets a seven, but only a two for Gynaecology" Corina lied and gave Harriet a wink as she appeared from out of the bathroom.

"I don't suppose you can expect much more from gynae, I bet he gets fed up looking at vagina's all day!" laughed Jenny "Don't forget to mark it on the chart, slut features!"

Hazel and Rebecca squeezed into the tiny bedroom, Hazel was armed with a camera.

"Don't you just love the eighties!" shouted Rebecca and planted an unexpected slobbery kiss straight onto Corina's lips.

"Get off me, you bloody lezzer!" laughed Corina.... though she was very much used to Rebecca's surprise kisses by now.

Hazel strategically placed the camera on the side board, set the timer, then she lunged into position next to Corina and nearly knocked everyone over like skittles.

"Say cheese" squealed Harriet, as she held onto Corina's arm to stop her from falling over.

"Cheeeeeeeese!" yelled the girls, then they all pouted and did a sexy pose.

....

Corina scanned the congregation at The Carlisle Cathedral to look for her parents. Hundreds of proud parents and family members were sat in the pews, they waited patiently to try and grab a glimpse of their loved ones on their special day. Harriet squeezed Corina's hand as she spotted her parents and then waved frantically at them. Corina could tell instantly who they were; Harriet's mother was sporting the latest Louis Vuitton handbag and tottering around on her Jimmy Choo's, whilst her father looked dashing in his Armani suit. They both waved back as if they were royalty. Corina rolled her eyes and thought they looked ridiculous…but they had showed up, which was more than could be said for her parents.

"At least yours turned up, eh?" said Corina as she patted Harriet on the back, she desperately tried to hide her disappointment and yet again had to fight back the tears, when she noticed a familiar, tall and handsome, blonde haired American Doctor.

Rebecca grabbed Corina's breasts from behind and whispered into her ear "Bloody hell, the weird yank is here!"

Hazel turned to Jenny and muttered out of Corina's ear shot "Imagine him giving you a diagnosis of cancer; he's dead behind the eyes. What Corina see's in him, I just don't know!"

Doctor Joseph Barsetti found himself a seat and half waved at Corina as he sat down. She started to blush and her knees began to shake as the usher shouted for silence. It seemed like forever to get through all the general nurses, the midwifes, the children's nurses, then at last came the psychiatric nurses or 'RMN's'. The official title that the girls were now to be known as – only five of them…. maybe Corina's mother was right, nobody seemed to want to be a mental health nurse anymore. Corina watched as the other girls went up to receive their accolade and of course, she was last.

"CORINA GEORGINA GREEN" bellowed Professor Philip Rushmore "Last, but not least, come on Corina, dear!"

The loudness of the applause startled her to her feet, she quickly lifted her gown up off of the floor and made her way to the stage at the front of the cathedral. She smiled as she took the scroll of honour from the Professor. He was an ageing man and very well respected in medical circles. Her father had often mentioned the Professor to her mother and she wondered to herself, did they take him out of the medical supplies cupboard every year just to do this? Did they dust him off and erect him into position when they put the stage up? She smirked to herself as she shook his hand and then beamed a smile at the camera whilst the photograph was taken by the official photographer. As she made her way back to her seat, she forgot to lift her gown up off of the floor and her feet got tangled in the length of it. She could not stop herself from falling, and she heard the people gasp in horror as her face hit the hard stone floor. She slowly lifted her head up from the floor in a daze and then realised what a fool she must have looked, so scrambled to get up quickly onto her feet. Blood had exploded from her nose, so she covered her face with one hand and pushed Harriet out of the way with the other as she tried to help her. As she rushed towards the entrance, she heard Jenny shout after her.

"Jesus Christ, Cor, take some more water with it next time!"

The Professor glared at Jenny and bellowed again "Could I please remind nurses that we are in a house of God!"

Jenny didn't care, she didn't believe in God anyway, she was only in church to get her qualification and then she was off to pastures new. In fact, she was surprised she hasn't been struck down by lightning just for sitting there in the cathedral.

She mimicked him to Rebecca, who in turn laughed and whispered "Old fart!"

Corina managed to get outside and she thought to herself- thank goodness her parents weren't there to see what an idiot she had just made of herself, she had already embarrassed them enough, so this would be the icing on the cake for them. She leant up against the cold granite wall and then slid down to sit on to her bottom; she put her head between her knees and she started to feel her face and nose begin to swell up. After a few minutes, she could sense someone was stood over her.

"You need a doctor?" asked Doctor Joseph Barsetti, his strong American Boston accent made her stomach flutter. She tried to compose herself and hoped she didn't look like a panda that had just been in a brawl.

"I don't need an oncologist!" she snapped at him, but still tried to act cool.

"I am still a doctor you know, I did my MD before I specialised in oncology, do you want me to take a look or not?"

"I'm not stupid" she snapped again "But, Okay. You can have a look"

"You English girls are a bit uppity, aren't ya!" he laughed, then he started to examine her face.

She stared at him and looked over every inch of his face, she began to note every mark and line as he felt her nose. He didn't seem that weird now; in fact, he actually seemed quite caring. She thought to herself - would it be too forward if she leant in and snogged his face off?

"What ya looking at uppity English girl?" asked the Doctor, cheekily.

Corina hadn't realised he had stopped examining her face a while back, as she had been too busy imagining all sorts.

"Ummm.... Actually, I was wondering what you are doing here.... as it's not normal for an oncologist to attend a psych nurse's graduation" enquired Corina, she desperately tried to hide her embarrassment.

"Oh...well I heard a rumour that the psych nurses were banging their way around the hospital and a little birdy called Harriet told me that I was on your list, so I came here to see if you fancied a pizza before I headed back to Boston"

"Back to Boston?" gasped Corina. She now thought she has no chance with him, so she decided to play hard to get. "Sorry, I don't like pizza, and for your information.... I have NOT been banging my way around the hospital!"

"I know" sniggered Joseph "Harriet told me everything"

"EVERYTHING?" Corina shrieked, she quickly covered her mouth after she realised how loud she must have sounded. She also wondered what else Harriet had told him.

"Yep, I'm only here for one year on sabbatical, done nine months already, so you wanna make these last three months' fun?" he gave her a provocative wink.

Corina didn't know what to say without coming across as too forward and she now began to wonder where the hell her friends were.

"Fun? But I thought I was an uppity English girl?" she playfully tilted her head to one side and smirked at him.

"And you thought I was a weird American guy…. so we're quits" he held out both of his hands for her to hold on to and gently pulled her to her feet "Let's go and clean your face up and then head out for pizza…. I know you like Italian food, it's your favourite!"

Let me guess, Corina thought to herself, HARRIET!

"And by the way, your nose is the best nose I've seen for a while, bloody or not" he seductively whispered into her ear.

For once in her life, Corina was speechless.

Chapter Three

Sat on a plane to Boston just over three months later, Corina couldn't believe how fast their relationship had progressed. But it felt right to her.... it felt good, and she was happy and content. She recalled in her mind how they didn't quite get around to eating pizza on graduation night, as they'd only got as far as ordering the drinks. They had left together to head back to Joseph's flat intent on making love to each other. The love making had gone on for most of the night and in the morning when they awoke, there was no awkwardness or embarrassment; it was like they had been together for ever. She was excited about their future together, but was unsure about what to expect from America, but she didn't care which country she was in, as long as Joseph was beside her. Also, she couldn't believe how much she loved and needed him; he was like her drug, to which she was addicted to.

Her husband was asleep, his head gently rested on her shoulder. She lovingly stroked the side of his face and thought about their wedding at Gretna Green. They had grabbed two strangers off of the street to be their witnesses. She didn't ask her friends to be witnesses, they thought she was making a big mistake, as she'd only been going out with Joseph for six weeks when they decided to tie the knot. Joseph had proposed to her in her favourite Italian restaurant and she remembered how emotional he had got when he had asked her. He had told her that he knew she was going to be his wife the moment he had set eyes on her. He loved the way she was clever, yet stupid, all at the same time. He loved her dry sense of humour and her ability to make him laugh at the most stupid things. He loved her filthy mind and the way in which they made love to each other. She was strong, but vulnerable and he couldn't get enough of her. In fact, he just loved everything about her and nineteen days later they were married.

Corina had phoned her parents after the ceremony, as the champagne had made her feel brave enough to tell them the news. However her mother wouldn't speak to her and handed the phone straight to her father.

"Your daughter is on the phone and she has apparently married that American doctor!"

Her father had screamed down the phone at her "If you've really married that yank, DO NOT ever think about coming back here again. I just can't believe what a disappointment you are to this family, Corina Green!"

The fact that his mother was an American and he had family all over America, really confused her. She couldn't quite fathom out how he could be so understanding and nice to his patients, yet treat his own daughter in such an appalling way. She didn't even receive a card for her twenty first birthday, which happened to be on the same day as their wedding. She would never understand her parents; it was just too difficult to figure out what was going on in their minds and she promised herself she would never treat any child of hers that way.

She had spoken to Joseph's parents on the phone regularly since she had got together with him. His father Alberto, who was a retired orthopaedic surgeon, had originated from Italy and was very much still into carrying on the Italian tradition, this excited Corina as that meant Italian food. Joseph's mother, Mary, was from Boston and she had met Alberto at The Beth Israel Medical Centre, where she had worked as an emergency room nurse. She had told Corina all about their romance and how they had first met, she also told her how she thought Corina had reminded her of herself at that age. She had said to her softly "You make our son happy, so we love you" and it had made her cry, as she had never heard her mother say those words.... well, one night she did... sort of... her mother was drunk and shook her awake in the middle of the night and slurred "You know I love you don't you, Corina?" then stumbled to the door and muttered "Only sometimes though.... when your good" But, she could put that all behind her now, she had her lovely Joseph and she had her new parents, Mary and Alberto. Josephs family were going to throw a party for them next week at The Boston Harbor Hotel in celebration of their marriage, Corina was really looking forward to this and couldn't wait to meet everybody.

First though, they were spending the night at Joseph's parents' apartment before heading off to Vegas for a few days. They had planned to get married again... by someone dressed as Elvis Presley at The Graceland Wedding Chapel. Joseph had laughed uncontrollably when Corina had suggested it, but it was just so typical of Corina. He was in awe of her and he wanted to spend as much time with her as possible before going back to work at The Massachusetts General Hospital in Boston, in a month's time. They still had so much to sort out, including getting a Green Card for Corina. At that moment in time, she only had a temporary visa that allowed her to live and work in the US for six months and he couldn't stand the thought of her being sent back to England after only six months. He wanted her to get a nursing job as soon as possible; they needed to get the money together for a deposit to buy their first home. His apartment in downtown Boston was tiny. It was big enough for a bachelor, but not for Corina as well and all of the children he had planned. He wanted six. Corina had looked shocked when she had found this out...yes, she wanted children, but six...she wasn't sure about six. She had told him she wanted to concentrate on her career first and then they would have babies... when the time was right for the both of them. Joseph's friend Noah, who was a Psychiatrist, had mentioned there was a job going at The Massachusetts State Hospital for a Psychiatric Nurse. His friend treated patients there, so was in the know. Joseph had smirked to himself as he remembered Corina had thought it was a typical hospital, and he wondered what her reaction might be when she found out it was actually a prison for the criminally insane. He wasn't sure about her working in a place like that, but there was no harm in them finding out about it.

Chapter Four

Ten days later and in the car on route to her interview at The Massachusetts State Hospital, Corina felt exhausted, and even though Boston was only five hours behind UK time, she felt jet lagged. So much had gone on since she had arrived in Boston and it was beginning to take its toll on her tired body. They'd had the wedding in Vegas with Elvis Presley, albeit a very poor impersonator of him, but they thought it was so much fun. They had both got themselves so drunk on champagne after the wedding with Elvis Presley, that they couldn't remember the name of the hotel that they were staying in and ended up crashing on Elvis Presley's couch.... Elvis was actually called Roger and they were to stay good friends with him for many years to come.

Then, there was the party thrown for them by Joseph's family and what a party that was, the Barsetti's sure knew how to have a good party. She also got to meet James for the first time there, who was Joseph's friend that he had grown up with. He too, was a doctor and worked with Joseph at The General and Corina thought he was just as handsome. He had treated her like they'd known each other a long time and he was also very tactile with her. Corina noticed that Joseph didn't really seem to like that, and that was the first time Corina had ever seen her husband come across as jealous and over protective.

Corina thought to herself though, that everyone had been amazing and they were so friendly towards her. Not once did she feel out of place or feel unwelcome. The whole family had surrounded her with love and warmth and they made her feel very special. She had never felt special when she lived at home with her parents; she had always felt like the odd one out in her family. She was the disappointment, the accident, the thing that had ruined her mother's figure…and her mother's vagina…. apparently. She tried not to think about her mother's ruined vagina, but then sniggered to herself.... that would be something her mother could remember her by.... onwards and upwards now, she thought to herself and she felt positive that she would no longer feel unwanted and there would be no more doing silly things, just to spite her parents. Boston was her home now and she would make the most of America and all the great things it had to offer.

"Don't fall asleep, Honey" Joseph tapped Corina on her shoulder as she nodded off "We are nearly there"

Corina suddenly felt butterflies in her stomach and she tried to wake herself up; it was going to be her very first job interview. She also felt cross with herself, as she had not had time to research the hospital and feel confident about it. What if they asked her questions that she didn't know the answer to? She felt a wave of panic come over her and she started to feel very nauseous.

"I don't think I'm ready for this, Jo.... I think I'm going to puke" she rushed to open the window "Pull over, Jo; I'm definitely going to throw up!"

Joseph slammed on the brakes "For god's sake, Corina, don't get it on your suit, you'll stink. Turning up like that won't make a good impression, you know!"

As she got out of the car she noticed a big sign that had "Massachusetts State Correctional Services" written on it and a fence.... a very high fence.... with barbed wire. There was lots of barbed wire in a coil on top of the fence. It was all around the huge building that was "The Massachusetts State Hospital".

"What the?" she looked back at Joseph, who tried to hide his laughter, and then up came the water she had drunk on the journey there. She was extremely grateful she hadn't eaten any breakfast. After she wiped her mouth with a tissue, she slowly got back into the car and noticed Joseph was still laughing.

"What's so funny, Joseph?" she glared at him angrily "This is a prison, isn't it!"

"Well, part of it is.... the part that needs a psych nurse.... Sorry, Cor" he suddenly noticed how upset she looked and thought maybe it wasn't so funny after all "We can go home though.... if you want?"

"No, it's fine" she snapped "I obviously need the interview practice!"

They drove another mile or so up the road in silence, then parked up the car in the assigned visitor parking bay once they got through the prison security checkpoint.

"I'll wait in the parking lot for you" said Joseph; he kissed her softly on her cheek.

He felt terrible, as she looked absolutely petrified and he hoped she would be able to cope with the interview, but he thought it didn't matter if she didn't get the job. He wasn't sure her face would fit in a place like that anyway, what was he thinking?

Corina headed towards the visitor's entrance and thought to herself that she would flunk the interview on purpose, as she couldn't picture herself working here......she was a newly qualified, young and inexperienced English psychiatric nurse in an American prison......no way.... She would be eaten alive. She had seen a documentary once about American prisons and it didn't look good. She was ready to make herself look unsuitable for the job and then get out of there as quickly as she could. Her bed in Boston was calling her, and that was the plan for the rest of the day.... sleep......and then possibly something else with her gorgeous husband.

She was shown into the superintendent's office and as she was about to sit, a big fat bald man appeared in the doorway.

"Corina Barsetti, I presume?" he held out his huge sausage like fingers to shake her hand "I'm Robert Jackson, the Superintendent of this shit hole, or Governor, as you English people like to say, but you can call me the Masshole!"

"The Masshole?" Corina questioned, then thought to herself what the hell was she doing there…they should have turned around when they had the chance.

"Yep, I'm from Massachusetts and apparently I'm an asshole, as I don't put up with any of the crap from the scum in this place!" he shook her hand with such vigour that she became unsteady on her feet.

She literally fell back into her seat whilst he headed around the table to sit in his chair. His big, fat, wobbly belly tried to escape out of his shirt and the buttons looked like they were about ready to pop and fly across the table at her. She started to wonder where the panel of people were, that she had expected to interview her, when the Masshole loudly cleared his throat to get her attention.

"Right, Corina. Here's a question for ya…. you've got an inmate on the floor being restrained by two officers, you've sedated him and you all think he's zonko'd, so you go to walk off, but he manages to grab your ankle and tries to get you on the ground…. what do you do?"

Corina thought to herself that the only way to not get this job was to give a stupid answer and say something that would be totally unacceptable to what her psychiatric nurse training in England had taught her. "Kick him in the head with my free foot!" she stated confidently. She grinned from ear to ear and hoped she would definitely be thrown out of the interview.

"Oh my, Corina… correct answer, you've got the job!" shouted the Masshole at her "Come in tomorrow for induction, then you start Monday, Okay?"

"Ummm, Okay" muttered Corina, in a state of disbelief.

SHIT!... She thought. Her mind was in overload; she just wouldn't turn up…. or maybe she would… she would sleep on it and decide in the morning.

"And by the way, English Rose, try not to lose that pretty English accent you've got going on there, they'll respect you more, and make sure your groin and breast areas are well protected at all times.

And, never turn your back on a prisoner. Those are the rules, you got it?"

"I got it" she tried to gulp down the huge lump that had appeared in her throat. Did she though? What the hell was she thinking?

She hot footed it back to the car, where Joseph was pretending to play the drums on the steering wheel. "That was quick, how'd ya get on?" he enquired, he looked at her face intently to try and gauge her mood.

"I got the job, induction tomorrow, start Monday" she reeled it off and gave him a look like a frightened rabbit stuck in the glare of a cars headlight.

"Oh Shit!" they both said together in harmony "Oh Shit!"

On the journey back to Boston, Corina weighed up her options in her mind. There was silence for a good fifteen minutes, before Joseph decided it was time to ask Corina a question.

"Are you mad at me, Honey, for laughing at you?"

"No, not really Jo, I just wasn't expecting a prison and I probably would have done the same thing to you. It is actually quite funny really!"

"Your face, though, Corina. It was a picture!" laughed Joseph.

They both giggled like children after Corina told him that she had tried to flunk the interview with her kick in the head comment. As they pulled up outside of their apartment, Joseph asked "So you gonna go for the induction tomorrow, or what?"

Corina paused for a moment then flicked off her heels into the foot well "I won't need these bloody things at the induction, I'll have to go in looking like a lesbian.... Rebecca would be hot for me...again!"

She remembered her friend and wondered what she was up to. She would have to call the girls back in England soon and catch up, as she hadn't spoken to them since before the wedding.

"I'll see how it goes tomorrow and then make a decision on whether I'll start on Monday or not. Let's go and get some breakfast from Mike and Patty's, to celebrate me being so god damn awesome!" She grabbed her trainers off the back seat and put them on; they really didn't go with her suit and she got a few strange looks whilst she ambled down Church Street hand in hand with Joseph, but it was probably because they both were acting like teenagers and played around with each other, rather than her poor fashion sense.

"You know, Corina, you really must learn to be more lady like now you are married to a doctor" laughed Joseph, he then stuck his hand up her skirt and pinched the top of her thigh.

"And you, Doctor Barsetti, must learn to be more gentlemanly like, now you are married to the Masshole's bitch!" she threw her arms around his neck, then jumped up and tightly wrapped her legs around his waist. He carried her like that to the cafe. They continued to get funny looks from people, but they didn't even notice, because they didn't care. They only cared for each other.

Chapter Five

The next morning, Joseph dropped Corina off at the security gate, she was armed with proof of her nursing qualification and various tops and tights to wear under her uniform. She had assumed she would be given a uniform; but the Masshole hadn't been that informative. She thought to herself that she really must learn to drive, as she couldn't rely on Joseph to run her around all of the time, and it would be difficult when he started back at work.

"Corina, my English rose!" yelled the Masshole from his office, when he noticed her pass with a prison guard, who was taking her to get her photograph taken for her security pass and identification.

"You've decided to come back then? I thought I'd never see you again after the look on your face yesterday!" he chuckled out loud.

"Yes, well I wasn't really expecting such a quick interview, Mr Jackson" she replied politely. She wasn't going to call him the Masshole to his face, even though he had requested it.

"Well, I hope you will enjoy your induction day and I look forward to working with you. We aren't so bad here and I have a feeling you will fit in nicely" he winked at her and then did an about turn back into his office. She could hear him singing as she made her way down the corridor with Pete and she thought to herself that she liked him, he was a bit off the wall, but she liked him.

Pete, the prison guard, was a bit more stand-offish; he didn't really speak to her in a nice way. He grunted a lot and pointed at things that she assumed were important for her to know about. His accent didn't sound like he was from Massachusetts, so she enquired as to where he was from. She thought he said Texas, but she was not sure, so she decided not to try and converse with him anymore. He obviously wasn't in the mood for small talk. After the photographs were done, he took copies of her qualification certificates, then grumbled at her to follow him to the staff room where she was to be handed over to Rory, a much nicer guard with a smiley jovial face.

"Welcome, Corina!" Rory shook her hand and curtsied "It's not often we get to work with such a pretty English girl"

"We never get to work with any nice pretty English girls, ever!" stated Andy, who was another guard, that was sat at the table whilst he smoked a cigarette "You're not one of those lipstick lesbians are you, like you are straight, right? Most of the nurses here are dykes…and I can't tell if they are male or female…you know what I mean?"

"No, I'm not a lipstick lesbian. I am straight, but I am also married, so don't go getting any ideas!" Corina laughed at him.

Rory rolled his eyes at Andy "Really, Andy? It's her first day and you are already sizing her up!"

"Ahh, it's only a bit of fun. She looks like she can take it!" retorted Andy "Anyway, she better be prepared for worse comments than that, she hasn't met the cons yet!"

Corina headed for the woman's changing room with the uniform she'd been given. She put three pairs of tights on the bottom half and a couple of t-shirts on top underneath the uniform.

"Jesus" she griped to herself "I'm going to bloody boil in this!"

She appeared out of the changing room and stood in front of Rory and Andy. She waited for somebody to tell her where to go next.

Andy sighed and turned to Rory and said "Why is it the girls go into that room looking gorgeous and then come out looking like crap? Sorry, Corina, but that uniform does nothing for you!"

"Great!" said Corina sarcastically "But, isn't that the whole point?" she felt they just needed to get on with the induction now and take her to the wing that she would be working on. Rory sensed her impatience and gestured at her to follow him.

She was shown around different parts of the prison before they came to one of the eating areas, where eleven of the inmates were sitting down having their breakfast. It was a very drab and depressed looking place, which was attached to the vulnerable prisoner's unit where she was going to be working. There was silence as she was introduced to staff and then to the prisoners. The medical staff looked pleased to see her, but the prisoners only stared at her, they did not move a muscle or show any interest in her at all. They were used to nurses coming and going, so they didn't expect her to stay long. There was one prisoner that was stood alone at the serving hatch, he had asked politely for his breakfast. It was slopped onto his tray by another prisoner on kitchen duty. The prisoner looked anxious, when Pete suddenly appeared from behind Corina to ask him if he wanted salt. Rory explained to her that they were not allowed to leave salt and pepper pots on the tables as they were usually used as weapons. Corina then overheard Pete ask if the prisoner wanted pepper too, he nodded, so Pete took his pepper spray from his belt and sprayed it all over the prisoner's food. Instantly, the prisoner kicked off and shouted all sorts of expletives as he lunged for Pete. Corina couldn't believe her eyes, as she watched the guards pin the prisoner to the ground, whilst a nurse sedated him. Pete and Rory then dragged him off to his cell, this left Corina feeling shocked by what she has just witnessed. Suddenly, there was a round of applause. It started by a prisoner covered in tattoos, that was sat at the far table on the other side of the dining room.

"Fucking Diaper Sniper, deserves everything he gets!" he shouted to everyone, then banged his fists on the table; he stared at Corina for a moment before he blew her a kiss, then winked at her.

Corina understood now. The sedated prisoner was a paedophile, and even in prison there was disgust for that type of convict. She was soon to find out from staff that he had raped a three-month old baby girl and her four-year-old brother, whilst he babysat for their mother. The mother had been friends with him since high school and she was desperate for a break as her husband had left her, but she had no idea of what he was, so she left the children with him while she went to the mall.

Corina was then shown to the nurse's office. She was told about the daily routine and the prisoner's backgrounds and needs by Britt, a fellow nurse. Britt looked tired and dragged down, but she was very pleased that Corina had been employed to take some of her workload from her. Even though there were only twelve prisoners in the unit, they were hard core criminals, and were very good at manipulating staff to get what they wanted. There was violence almost every day, but staff remained very well trained in restraining techniques. In fact, Britt admitted that it was all too easy to keep them restrained....as a sedated prisoner strapped to their bed, meant a quiet life for staff.

"Have you done any suicide prevention in prisons before, Corina?" asked Britt "Your main role here is to stop the cons from killing themselves. We have had too many suicides on this unit and the Masshole wants to keep the numbers down, as questions have been asked by government officials"

"I did a few placements in our local prison whilst training, but this is my first real job" replied Corina.

"I'm sure you'll be fine, just remember you will have to report to staff psychological services in the main wing at least once a week for supervision, or you will go nuts, just like this lot in here!" laughed Britt "And, another thing, always carry sedation on your person, we don't have time to get it signed off, especially when you have a ten-ton murderer coming towards you angry because his breakfast is late. Sign it off at the end of the day. We all do it, including the doctors"

Jesus, thought Corina. She couldn't imagine the NHS back in England putting up with that, you had to get at least two signatures before you could get it out of the drugs cabinet, then do a pile of paperwork and have a whole bunch of reasons written down why you sedated in the first place.

"If one of them tells you, or acts like they are suicidal, you must assess them straight away, then go and check on them every ten minutes. It's very time consuming, and sometimes I'm tempted just to leave a rope in their cell, BUT that clearly wouldn't be very professional would it!" sniggered Britt.

Corina was not very impressed by this nurse's attitude and she felt she must come back on Monday, so she could make sure that all the prisoners were given the correct care whilst she is on shift. There would be no suicides on her watch.

"Right, Britt. I think I understand everything now" said Corina, in a very matter of fact manner "And, I'm ready to just get on with it now, so if you don't mind, I'll start the next drugs round"

Britt handed Corina pepper spray, cuffs, and a retractable baton, to attach to her belt. She then went to the drugs cabinet and counted out ten epi-pens full of lorazepam, five for each pocket, and handed them over too.

"What you don't use today, put back at the end of your shift, Okay? The drugs for prisoners are given to them through the service hatch. If they are not nice to you, or don't say please or thank you, don't give them their drugs" said Britt, she thought that Corina may possibly be a bit snooty, and that she would soon be put in her place by the Diaper Sniper.

Corina took the drugs list and headed for the service hatch. She could sense that this was going to be a very long day.

Chapter Six

Corina rubbed her huge pregnant stomach whilst she ate her breakfast at the kitchen table and people watched out of her window. She spotted two people jogging together that were headed towards the direction of the park. She never did understand jogging; it looked too much of an effort, especially in the heat of summer.

She only had a few weeks left at work before going on maternity leave and looked forward to meeting their first child. The prison was hard work since she had got bigger in her pregnancy and sometimes she feared for her safety and that of the child she carried, so the Masshole had put her on desk duty.

After eighteen months into her job she was made responsible for the prisons suicide prevention programme. She was very proud of her programme and had worked extremely hard to help maintain the prisoner's good mental health. She had only had one suicide in all the years she'd been there, compared to two a week when she first started her job ten years ago. She rarely had to sedate either, as the Masshole was right, they did respect her more for being English and she had a knack of looking interested in whatever problems they had wanted to talk about, even when some of it was made up just to get attention. She came across as very empathetic and the prisoner's loved that. She had made them feel like they were useful and assured them that when they got out they could make good lives for themselves…. if they behaved. Though, a few of the manipulative cons used to say they were suicidal, just to be able to see her, so they could ogle at her boobs for an hour during the counselling sessions. But she had them sussed straight away and turned the sessions into something deep and boring, so they would think twice about wasting her time again.

She really couldn't believe how lucky she had been in America; she had a wonderful husband and an absolutely stunning seven bedroomed house in Milton. The house was in a prime position situated between the Neponset River and lovely Blue Hills, but not too far from the hustle and bustle of Boston City. There were parks and good schools to send their six children to. Only five more pregnancies to go, she thought to herself, then all her bedrooms would be filled. She was allowed to stay in America, so Joseph's fear of her being sent back to England was unfounded. They had both worked hard over the past ten years to get what they had now and everything was going so smoothly, so she felt nothing could ruin how happy she felt.

....

Joseph didn't feel well, the headaches he'd had lately were so bad that he felt like he couldn't concentrate and sometimes he couldn't see. At times, the left hand side of his body felt tingly and he'd had fits. Luckily, the fits had occurred when he was at work, so Corina had not witnessed them. Being an oncologist, Joseph had a good idea of what was going on and naturally thought the worst, so he confided in his best friend James, who was also a fellow oncologist at the hospital. James had reassured him that it may be something like epilepsy, so there was no need to think the worst just because he was medically trained. He explained that there were many things it could be, but when his blood work came back and it showed he was not healthy, he went on to have neurological tests performed and these were not promising either. Even though James had tried to reassure him, Joseph was sure that something really bad was going on inside of his head and when his brain scan results had shown a massive brain tumour, he was mortified.

James was shocked to see Joseph was still so well in himself after seeing the size of the tumour and he dreaded telling his friend that there was nothing anyone could do for him. They could not operate because of where the tumour was, as he probably wouldn't wake up from the operation anyway. Chemotherapy and radiation therapy would maybe shrink it a little and prolong his life for a few months, but death was inevitable.

"You need to tell Corina, Joseph, you can't hide this from her. Soon your neurological symptoms will become more obvious. She is a nurse and she is not stupid" James had begged Joseph to try and make him see sense.

"I can't tell her just yet; she is so happy. I need to think about what I'm going to do next" Joseph replied. The sound of dread in his voice was too much for James and they had both hugged each other tightly. There was nothing worse than giving a good friend a terrible diagnosis. They may be doctors, but they both had feelings the same as everybody else and it never got any easier when they gave bad news to patients, whomever they were.

Mornings were the worst for Joseph's headaches, so he lay in bed and listened to Corina as she muttered to herself downstairs about people running in the heat. She was good at muttering to herself and coming out with random statements. Sometimes, he would have no clue about what would pop out of her mouth next, as it all depended on what silly thing she had spotted at the time. He thought she was so funny and endearing, that he was sure someone would snap her up when he was gone, but the thought of her being with somebody else made him feel a bit jealous and very sad. He loved her so much, it hurt.

It had been a few weeks since he had got his diagnosis and he still hadn't told Corina. He could not think about telling her. He was worried about Corina coping with him being ill whilst having a new baby to look after. He had seen many a long painful death from brain cancer in his time at the hospital and he could not face going through it.… or putting anybody else through it.

He had made the decision to take his own life that day and nothing would change his mind.

Joseph felt cowardly within himself, but he was spontaneous in most things that he did. His courtship of Corina for instance, he saw her and he wanted her, then he made sure he got her. He loved her so much that he was willing to die to save her from watching him suffer. He knew it was a terrible thing to do to Corina, but he thought it would be better for her to get it over and done with quickly. She would have something left of him in the baby and the baby would help her to get over him. For some reason, he couldn't feel anything for the baby as he loved Corina so much. He didn't think that maybe one day his child may ask about him, like what had happened to him or how he had died. His mind was just so full of Corina, but he hoped the baby would be a useful distraction from what he was about to do. He could hear Corina as she waddled up the stairs to come and say goodbye to him before she went to work. He was grateful that she only had a few weeks left at the prison and then she could relax.

"I think my ankles are swelling, Jo, look at them" puffed the out of breath Corina, as she appeared in the doorway "This heat is killing me!"

"That's because your so god damn fat and beautiful.... lie here with me for a minute and have a cuddle" he patted her side of the bed and Corina clambered onto the bed to lay next to him.

"You know you are the best thing that has ever happened to me, don't you Cor? And, I love you very much" he whispered into her ear after he turned on to his side to hold her in his arms. He nestled down into her neck and smelt the sweetness of her skin. He then kissed her gently along the top of her uncovered shoulder, after undoing her blouse, to reveal her very big and swollen pregnant breasts.

"I love you too, Jo.... bit soppy aren't we this morning. You feeling okay, you do look a bit pale?" she asked him, whilst she cuddled him tight. She placed her nose in the ruffle of his beautiful blonde hair and took in his unique smell. She loved the smell of him, even when he had been working out and was sweaty, he still smelt gorgeous to her.

"I'm just tired; I'm going to lie here for a bit, then head off to the hospital. Will you go and see my parents tonight after work before you come home, honey? They have been asking after you and they want to show you some baby things they have bought" Joseph lied; he wanted her to be out of the house for as long as possible.

"Sure thing.... right, I really must dash Jo; I'm going to be late for work and you know how the Masshole gets if I'm late" she struggled to get up, but Joseph insisted on holding her for a bit longer and snuggled back into her breasts.

"Come on, babe, I really need to go" she kissed the top of his head and then slid down to be level with his face. He kissed her with such passion, she could hardly breathe.

She got up and made herself presentable, then turned to Joseph and said "See you later, sex bomb…we will continue this then" and winked at him as she left the room.

Joseph cried like a baby as he heard her car drive away from the house. He would never see his beautiful uppity English girl again. About two hours later, Joseph woke up and realised he must have had a fit. He felt groggy and could hardly see, his headache had got much worse. He decided to write Corina a note to say goodbye, so he staggered slowly down the stairs to the kitchen to find a pen and a piece of paper. He then sat at the kitchen table to write his suicide note. His hand shook violently as he tried to write, his brain hurt whilst he mentally tried to string the words together so he could write them down.

MY DEAR CORINA

I HAVE DONE THIS BECAUSE I LOVE YOU AND I HOPE YOU CAN UNDERSTAND AND FORGIVE ME ONE DAY.

I DON'T WANT YOU TO SEE ME SUFFER AND I DON'T WANT TO BE A BURDEN TO YOU.

I WANT YOU TO LOOK AFTER OUR BABY AND LIVE LIFE TO THE FULL.

I WANT YOU TO BE HAPPY.

YOU ARE MY BEAUTIFUL UPPITY ENGLISH GIRL AND I WILL ALWAYS BE WITH YOU.

I LOVE YOU COR, MORE THAN YOU WILL EVER KNOW.

JOSEPH

YOUR WEIRD AMERICAN GUY XXXXXXX

It took him a long time to write as his writing hand would not work properly and his sight kept coming and going. He got very angry with himself that he couldn't write properly. He was a doctor and he had studied hard to get where he was today.... how had it come to all of this? Some of the words were wobbly and he hoped Corina would be able to read them. The tears poured down his cheeks as he left the note for Corina, he tucked it into the flowers that he had bought her the previous day. Corina had put them in a vase that his parents had given them for a wedding present. He then thought about his parents for a moment and what wonderful people they were and then wandered slowly through to the lounge. He then took his gun from the safe, which was hidden behind their fake Rembrandt picture that hung on the wall. The gun was there to protect his family; never in a million years did he think he would be using it to end his life. He picked up the phone and sat on the couch. Then, he dialled 911 and spoke clearly and precisely to the operator, so there would be no confusion as to why he was about to take his own life that day.

"Hello, my name is Doctor Joseph Barsetti, I live at three thirty-five Marilyn Road, Milton, Norfolk County, Massachusetts and I have an inoperable, terminal brain cancer. I am about to take my own life, so I want you to get here before my wife gets home from work. I do not want my wife to find me, so you need to come now. I feel it's the right thing to do. I do not want to have a long drawn out death with this type of cancer. I do not want to be a burden on my wife. So please tell her I love her and I am sorry"

He then placed the gun in his mouth, pointed it upwards towards his brain and shot himself.

Chapter Seven

Corina pulled up outside of her home in her SUV. She felt very sick and her ankles had swelled up to almost three times their normal size at work. She also felt dizzy, so she had been sent home. She noticed Joseph's car was still in the drive and thought to herself that it was a bit strange. Maybe he wasn't feeling well either; he did look a bit pale this morning when she had left for work. She struggled to get out of the car as she felt like a beached whale and then slowly made her way up the drive. She thought at any minute she may be sick. She hadn't been sick since the early stages of her pregnancy and up to that point the pregnancy had been a breeze.

As she opened the door she could feel an uneasy atmosphere; she could sense something wasn't quite right and as she entered the lounge she could see Joseph slumped on the floor against the coffee table. She ran across the wooden floor to him to help him, but she could tell instantly that he was dead. Part of his head had been blown away by the gun that was on the rug next to him and there was blood splattered everywhere, even on the high ceiling. She started to scream and scream. Why had somebody killed her husband? Her mind raced with anxiety and the thought of someone murdering her precious Joseph.... Where was the phone? She needed it to call for help. She noticed it was on the floor next to the gun and as she lifted it to her ear she could hear a male voice.

"Ma'am, can you hear me, ma'am?"

"Someone has shot my husband!" she screamed down the phone "Somebody has killed him, he's dead, please help me, somebody has killed my husband!"

She knelt down and placed the phone on to her shoulder so it remained against her ear. She held what remained of Joseph's head in her lap, and continued to cradle him as she sobbed and rocked backwards and forwards, not believing what she had just found. She could hear the operator's voice on the phone again.

"Ma'am, could you please go outside and wait for an officer? There is help on the way, Ma'am, can you hear me? Could you please do that for me?"

She didn't want to leave him and go outside. She dropped the phone as she was violently sick, but still held tight onto Joseph. Her vomit just added to the rest of the blood and gore in the lounge.

She could hear the sound of sirens, and as the emergency vehicles approached, the swirling sound got closer and closer until they were deafening. Suddenly, they stopped as the police pulled up outside of the house. She then heard the police as they shouted and banged on her front door, and then a loud crash as the officers kicked the door in. She suddenly found herself surrounded by police with their guns pointed at her.

"Somebody has killed my husband" she cried at them "Why have they killed my husband?"

The look of desperation on Corina's face made the officers put their guns back into their holsters. They knew it was a suicide call, but they needed to make sure the house was safe before they could disarm. As a female officer approached Corina to help her, she couldn't help but notice Joseph and the state of his face. She couldn't believe the amount of blood and the sight was too much for her. She had to rush out of the room and outside to the garden to be sick. Corina had to be dragged away from her husband. She kicked and screamed at the officers that continued to pull her away, as she desperately didn't want to leave Joseph there alone, but they carried on and then made her sit in the kitchen to wait for an ambulance, so she could be checked over.

Whilst she waited, she spotted a piece of paper that was placed in between the flowers that Joseph had bought her yesterday; they were in her favourite vase on the kitchen table. It was a note and it looked like Joseph's writing, but some of it looked funny. She picked it up and read it before Jane, the female officer, could take it away from her. She could not take in what she had just read.

She turned to the officer and asked quietly, as it hurt to talk from all the screaming she had done earlier.

"What does it mean by I've done this and please forgive me? He couldn't have shot himself.... He wouldn't do that to himself.... he wouldn't want to leave me. He told me he loved me this morning and I was the best thing that had ever happened to him" her voice trailed off, as she recollected in her mind how Joseph had been with her that morning. Now she knew why he was being so soppy and didn't want to let her go. She felt an intense pang of guilt in her stomach; she shouldn't have left him in such a rush.

"Ma'am, your husband called 911 and said he had a terminal brain cancer and that he was going to take his own life. I am so sorry that you have had to witness all of this. He was adamant that he didn't want you to find him" replied Jane; she fought hard to keep her own emotions in check. She could not allow herself to cry in front of Corina.

"Terminal…brain…cancer?" Corina was confused, surely he would have confided in her about having cancer? Why would he have kept that from her and why did she not notice he was suicidal? She must be the worst suicide prevention officer in the whole of Massachusetts. She felt absolutely devastated "I need to phone his parents; I need to see them. They need to come here and get me; I can't stay in this house anymore!"

Suddenly, Corina started to panic and got up to make a run for the front door. Jane grabbed her, but Corina fought hard to get away.

Corina screamed "Get off me; I need to get out of this house. How could he do this to me? He told me he loved me. How could he do this?"

She suddenly turned and changed direction and made her way back to the lounge to shout at Joseph.

"How you could do this? We have a baby coming!"

She tried to get to Joseph, and with her anger that had taken over, she lunged at him to try and hit him on his chest, when she was pulled onto the couch by officers.

"Ma'am, you have to calm down. Think of your baby" Jane tried to reassure her, whilst the officers still held her down on the couch.

"Did Joseph think of our baby when he blew his own fucking head off?" Corina screamed back at her, she hardly ever swore, but she couldn't help her bad language as she felt very angry that he had done this without any warning.

Corina curled up into a ball on the couch and cried. She was covered in blood, and her hands and face had started to feel tight where the blood had dried up on her skin. A big, burly, police officer scooped her up and took her upstairs to her bedroom and placed her gently on her bed. The paramedics had arrived and they tried to get her to go to hospital for a check over, but she refused. She lay on her bed, for what must have been hours, and cried and sobbed into Joseph's pillow until forensics had finished gathering evidence, before Joseph's body was finally removed.

Suddenly, she heard Alberto's voice from downstairs. She could hear him ask the officers where she was and then she heard him make his way slowly upstairs. She sat up in anticipation for his entrance into her bedroom. He stood in the doorway with his arms open; she could tell he had been crying. She walked over to him and they both held each other tight, not wanting to believe what Joseph had done to himself.

"We need to take you to the hospital for a check-up, Corina dear" Alberto told her quietly, he still had a hint of an Italian accent, as his voice wobbled with emotion. "Mary will be with you there. Now come on, we will all get through this if we remain strong. We have the baby to consider"

Corina looked into his big blue eyes and she could see his pain. The pain that was so evident after he had just lost his only son to suicide. She also felt his pain. She just couldn't believe this had happened. The love of her life had gone and left her in the most horrific way.

She was heartbroken.

Chapter Eight

Three days later, Corina sat and stared at a picture of Joseph that was on his parent's wall in their sitting room, he was about ten years old in it and she thought he looked adorable. He had a mass of blonde hair and she hoped her baby would have his hair or at least something that would remind her of him. He was flying a kite in the picture and he looked so innocent and happy. She wondered if her tears would ever stop, but they just kept on coming. She could not speak to anyone without breaking down and she could not get Joseph's blown off face out of her mind. Even when she tried to sleep, the image would pop into her head and it would wake her up. She couldn't actually remember what he looked like without having to look at a recent photo of him, as the horrible image kept appearing and the feelings of guilt and heartache consumed her. She felt guilty that she had rushed away on the morning of his death, just to be on time for work. Why didn't she stay a bit longer and cuddle him for longer? Why did she put the Masshole before her precious husband? Her mind kept going over and over that day and she wished she could turn back the time. She wondered if she had stayed with him, he may have confided in her and she would have persuaded him not to do it. She would've looked after him; she would've done anything for him. He was her life, her everything. Her weird American Guy.

She heard Mary as she pottered around in the kitchen and wanted to go and give her a hug. Mary must be devastated, thought Corina, but she was acting like nothing had happened. She was carrying on as normal and running around after everyone. It must have been her way of coping, but Corina did think it strange that she had not seen Mary shed a tear. As Corina stood up she could hear a small popping sound and a sudden gush of waters started to pour down her legs onto the sitting room carpet. Then, she felt an awful pain, it was a sudden sharp pain that seared through her womb and into her vagina.

It was so painful that it took her breath away and made her fall onto her knees.

"Mary, please can you come here quickly" she shouted "I think my waters have broken"

Mary rushed through from the kitchen "But, you're only seven months pregnant, it's too soon!" Mary was flustered as she started to look for the car keys "Let's drive straight to the general, Corina, can you stand up?"

The pain wasn't going away, it was constant. Corina had expected contractions with breaks in between, not one long pain that was relentless. Then, she noticed the blood that was running down her legs, it was a bright red, fresh stream of blood, with no sign of stopping.

"Oh my God, Mary, what's happening?" she started to panic and instinctively knew that something was terribly wrong.

"Let's just get in the car, it'll be quicker than calling for an ambulance. Lean on me, Corina. Everything will be fine, Honey. Now let's get going" said Mary, she was very concerned with the amount of blood Corina was losing from between her legs.

Within fifteen minutes they were at The General. Mary had found a wheel chair for Corina and shouted for an orderly to help push Corina to the Obstetrics ward. The corridors seemed endless and Corina's pain was getting worse. She felt very weak and found it difficult to stay awake.

"We are here Corina, try and stay with us" Mary was worried as Corina didn't look very well at all.

A resident doctor took one look at Corina and shouted to the theatre nurses to prepare the operating room, they were going to do an emergency Caesarean section. Corina was experiencing a placental abruption and both she and the baby were in a serious condition. Mary watched helplessly as Corina disappeared into the operating room and she began to pray that both Corina and the baby would be okay. The nurses showed her into the family room and there she stayed until the nurse had called Alberto and he finally showed up around half an hour later. Alberto entered the family room to find Mary crying, he was relieved that she had finally let go of her tears as he was getting concerned that she hadn't cried for Joseph yet. He held her tight until she had composed herself enough to tell him what had happened to Corina.

Just over an hour later, the doctor who had performed Corina's Caesarean Section came into the family room to speak to Alberto and Mary. They both stood up quickly when they saw him enter the room, but knew by the look on his face that the news he was about to tell them was not going to be good.

"Mr and Mrs Barsetti, please sit down" the doctor gestured for them to sit next to him "As you know Corina has suffered a placental abruption. The placenta had completely detached itself away from Corina's womb causing her to bleed heavily. We have had to give her a blood transfusion as she has lost a huge amount of blood. Once the placenta had come away there was no way the baby could survive whilst still in the womb, so I am very sorry to tell you that the baby was stillborn. I have managed to save her womb though, so she can go on to have other children"

"Oh...well that's alright then!" Mary exclaimed sarcastically "I don't think Corina will be worried about having other children at this moment in time, she has just lost her husband and now her baby!"

"I didn't mean to sound flippant" the doctor replied quietly "But, sometimes we have to remove the womb if the bleeding won't stop and that would mean......"

"It's okay, doctor" interrupted Alberto "We understand, it's just been a very hard few days for all of us and we are all very upset. Please can I ask what sex the baby is?"

"A little boy.... would you like me to tell Corina what's happened when she comes around from the anaesthetic or would you like to tell her?"

"We will tell her if you don't mind, thank you" said Alberto, the tears welled up in his eyes; he thought it would be best if it came from them. But, he knew she would be devastated whom ever told her. Mary felt so sad that the baby too had died; and she could not believe this had happened to Corina so close after losing Joseph. The poor girl would be beside herself, she thought. Then the tears came again. Alberto held out his hand to her and led her towards the recovery room, they had the worst news to tell Corina and they were both dreading it.

....

Later that day, Corina cradled her baby son in her arms, the tears poured down and fell heavily like rain drops onto the blue fleece blanket that he was wrapped in. She had stared at Alberto and Mary in disbelief when they had told her that her baby was dead too and she could not understand why all this had happened to her. How someone's life could change in a matter of days, from complete happiness to a horrible nightmare, it was beyond her and she could not figure it out. She looked down at her precious son and studied his tiny face. He looked like her and he had a head of thick brown hair, just like her hair. But, she felt disappointed that she couldn't see any part of Joseph in him, he just looked like her. She opened up the blanket and examined every part of his body to try to find something that reminded her of Joseph, when suddenly she spotted a small mark on his back. The mark was shaped like a crescent moon.... exactly like Joseph's birthmark on his back and in exactly the same place. She felt relieved that there was something; even a small birthmark meant the world to her.

In the few hours she had left with her baby, she spent the time cuddling him and talking to him. She told him all about his daddy and what a wonderful doctor he was. A nurse also helped her to take his hand and footprints as a keepsake. Then, she dressed him in a little blue baby grow and took photographs of him, before they took him away to the morgue. She had decided to call him 'Joseph Alberto Barsetti', and he was going to be buried with his daddy in Milton Cemetery. Alberto and Mary also joined her for some quality time with their grandson and there were lots of tears, but the room was also filled with love for this little child that never took a breath outside of his mother's womb.

Chapter Nine

Corina was still waiting for Joseph's body to be released; she couldn't understand why the coroner had taken so long with his investigations. It had been proved without a doubt that it was suicide and it had been over a week, so what was the hold up? She had started to feel more and more hopeless and depressed within herself, and the ever decreasing pregnancy hormones didn't help her either. Her breasts were like rock where the milk had built up because she had no baby to feed. She felt sore from the caesarean too. She had the same thought over and over again in her head…what was the point of being in America without Joseph and the baby? She was pretty sure Alberto and Mary were just putting up with her until after the funerals and then she would be made to move on. They wouldn't want her in their lives anymore. She couldn't even give them a grandson. She felt like a failure as a mother and a wife. She felt useless.

"I'm going out for a walk, Mary" Corina called to Mary from the massive foyer, she looked up at the huge chandelier that hung from the ceiling and wondered why she had never noticed it there before. The sun that shone through the window made it glisten and leave spectacular shapes on the walls, she stood there for a few seconds to watch the shapes as they moved around.

It was only eight in the morning and Mary was getting dressed in her room. Alberto was still in the shower.

"You really shouldn't be doing much, dear" Mary didn't want her to go out alone "If you wait a moment, I'll come with you"

Corina hadn't heard her, she had already made her way out through the front door and was headed for the elevator. Joseph's parents lived in The Four Seasons Condominiums; they had a lovely twelfth floor south facing apartment right opposite the public gardens and the public gardens were Corina's most favourite place in Boston. As she got out of the elevator, the concierge in reception gave her a pitying look and nodded his head at her in acknowledgement. All of the staff there had heard about her husband and she was sure everyone would look at her and wonder who was to blame. She stood for a moment at the elevator entrance to get her bearings and then walked through reception and out onto the street, she crossed Boylston Road and headed straight into the gardens.

It was a lovely sunny morning and as Corina sat on her special bench in front of The Lagoon she noticed a family of ducks as they headed for the water. The ducklings waddled along behind their mother; sometimes they fell over, but quickly regained their balance and quickly caught up to her again. The mother looked proud of herself and Corina watched in awe as they all made it safely to the water. The swan boats on the lagoon were all empty at this time of the morning, but there would soon be holiday makers that would fill them up to enjoy the lake and the Victorian feel of the gardens with its magnificent statues, the monuments, and also the huge fountains. She loved the "make way for the ducklings" statues; they use to be Joseph's favourite too. He used to kiss Mrs Mallard on her head and then pat the eight ducklings in turn as he walked past. Corina used to laugh at him every time and call him an idiot.

The smell of exotic flowers wafted her way, she began to reminisce back to when she and Joseph had sat on the exact same bench on the evening of their arrival in Boston. She remembered how excited they both were to travel to Las Vegas the following day. Then, she thought about Roger their Elvis impersonator friend, and that she must tell him about Joseph, so maybe he would come to the funeral. She suddenly thought about organising the funeral. The thought of it made her heart jump into her mouth. She couldn't bear the thought of it and she didn't even know when it was going to be, thanks to the coroner dragging his feet. A sudden wave of anger came over her and she felt like she wanted to scream out loud. She suddenly felt frustrated that Joseph had left her in the way that he did and she couldn't cope with the terrible feelings of rejection. She hated being alone and he knew this. He was just plain selfish, and with that thought she got up and headed out of the gardens. She was going to go to the hospital to see James.

....

"Mrs Barsetti, you can't just walk in, Doctor Patton has a patient with him" Rachael, James' secretary, followed her into his office "I'm sorry Doctor Patton, but I couldn't stop her!"

The look of guilt on James' face said it all to Corina.... he must have known something.

Corina turned to the patient and shouted "Get out!"

"Do you want me to call security, Doctor Patton?" his secretary was worried, she had never experienced that sort of behaviour in the oncology department before. When she was down in the Emergency Room, it was common place. But, she had been in the oncology department for a few years now and she liked how oncology was quiet and calm, but this was making her feel very uneasy.

"It's Okay, Rachael. Could you please take my patient to the waiting room and sit with her, while I speak to Mrs Barsetti?"

"Certainly, Doctor Patton" Rachael glanced over to Corina and made sure she gave her the dirtiest of looks. She then led the patient gently by the arm into the waiting room.

James looked at Corina; he noticed she was shaking with anger "Please take a seat, Corina. You are looking pale; you shouldn't have come here so soon after having a caesarean. You need to be resting"

"Shut up James! I want to know why you didn't tell me Joseph had planned to kill himself" her anger had made her lose control and she couldn't stand still, let alone sit. She started to pace the office up and down like a mad woman. This made James feel very threatened and uncomfortable.

"Corina, I promise you I didn't know he was going to do that, otherwise I would've tried to stop him. I begged him to tell you about the cancer, as I couldn't tell you what was going on because of patient confidentiality. As soon as he asked me to do the tests, he became my patient and you know I can't betray a patient's trust"

The tears welled up in his eyes, he felt terrible that Joseph had taken his own life. But on the other hand, he tried to understand why he had done it, he knew Joseph must have been in turmoil about not wanting a slow painful death and putting Corina through that too. He didn't think this would be a wise thing to tell Corina his thoughts at that present time though.

"Bullshit! You fucking Doctors always stick together and he always told you everything.... EVERYTHING!" Corina knew that once she had started to swear, she had lost it "You should be ashamed of yourself, James. You're an asshole.... a big headed American asshole!"

"Corina, please calm down. I know you are upset, but you can't be here in this state. I'm going to phone Alberto to come and get you. If you could kindly just sit down and try and get yourself together, I'll give him a call now"

"Fuck you, James!"

Corina couldn't take any more of what she thought was a patronising attitude and walked out. She was adamant he must have known something and this angered her so much that she slammed the door very hard on the way out. The force of the door as it slammed, cracked the glass and it shattered and fell to the floor. She made sure she gave Rachael the filthiest of looks as she passed her and then on the way past Joseph's office she kicked the door and slid out his "Doctor Joseph Barsetti" sign, held it up in the air and stated very loudly to the patient, who looked very afraid... "Doctor Joseph Barsetti. COWARD!" she then threw it on the ground in front of them before she left. She headed for the nearest ladies' toilet, locked herself in a cubicle, and cried. She didn't feel any better for her outburst, in fact she felt worse. The feelings of guilt had started to build up again and she felt awful. She felt absolutely exhausted and didn't think she could move to walk anywhere else, so she stayed in the cubicle until she heard Rachael's voice call her name about ten minutes later.

"Mrs Barsetti, are you in here?" Rachael was very wary that Corina may still be angry, so put on her best sympathetic voice "Doctor Patton has asked me to see if you are okay and wants me to take you back to his office"

Corina was still crying and tried to speak to Rachael in a controlled manner, but her emotional state was evident as she spoke "I can't actually move, could you please come in and help me? I am so sorry for my outburst; I don't know what came over me"

Rachael slowly put her head around the cubicle door after she had unlocked it from the outside and held out her hand to Corina to help her up. She couldn't help but offer to give her a cuddle, Corina looked broken and she wished she hadn't looked at her in such an offish way.

"There there, it will all be okay, Mrs Barsetti" she said softly as she held Corina in her arms and gently patted her on the back "I promise you will get over this one day and be happy again"

Corina didn't believe her. How would she ever get over this? She knew there was only one option left and she knew what she had to do. She would soon be with Joseph again.

…..

James had sent for a cab to take Corina back to Alberto and Mary's apartment as he couldn't get hold of Alberto to come and get her. He waited outside the hospital with her to make sure that she got in the cab safely.

"Please go home and rest, Corina. You will feel much better after a good rest, so try and get a good night's sleep. There will be a lot to do once Joseph's body is released, so you need to keep your strength up" he kissed the top of her head as she got in the cab and stayed and watched until she had disappeared out of view.

Corina didn't say a word to him and didn't look back as she left the hospital in the cab. She felt numb towards him, she didn't care about him, or what he thought she should do, as she was still adamant he knew far more than he had let on. She had cried so much in his office that her head pounded and she was sure her tears had now dried up forever.

"Please could you take me to three thirty-five Marilyn Road, Milton?" she leant over and asked the cab driver through the hole in the protective glass.

The cab driver nodded, but didn't mention the fact that he was told to take her straight to The Four Seasons. He didn't care where she wanted to go as long as he was paid. As the cab pulled up outside of her house, Corina could see the front door had been mended from where the police had kicked it in on the day Joseph died. It felt strange as she looked at the house again and she felt very wary about going inside. It was hard to believe that just over a week ago she had been sat in the kitchen and had felt thankful for what she had got; she had thought it was the best house ever. Now, she didn't care much for the house, she just wanted her husband and baby to be alive and with her again.

"You gonna pay me or what?" snapped the cab driver "Fifteen dollars, yeah?"

She gave him a twenty-dollar bill and mumbled "Asshole" under her breath as she struggled to get out of the cab. She stood and watched as he pulled away. She rolled her eyes as he screeched his tyres like a boy racer so he could get away quickly. She then made her way up the drive; she fumbled for her keys in her hand bag. She dropped the keys three times whilst she tried to put the key in the lock as her hands shook so much. Once she had managed to unlock the door, she pushed the door wide open and stood motionless in the doorway and thought twice about entering. She noticed there were lots of mail on the floor and she assumed they were sympathy cards, but didn't bother to pick them up. She could see straight through to the kitchen and up the spiral stairs from the hallway. Nothing had changed since that day. She stepped in and looked to her right so she could see into the lounge and a flash back of Joseph's blown off face greeted her.

"No, no, no!" she screamed, whilst she banged both sides of her head with the palms of her hands. She had to get the horrible image of Joseph out of her head. She couldn't stand it. She wanted to see his beautiful smile again and his gorgeous thick, curly, blonde hair. It didn't matter how many times he brushed his hair, he still had the bed head look whatever he tried to do to it, but Corina had loved it. She got up the courage to go into the lounge and find a photograph of him. Once inside the lounge she tried to avoid the blood stains, but to no avail, as they were everywhere. The couch was covered in stains and she didn't think anyone had even attempted to clean the coffee table. They certainly hadn't cleaned the ceiling, as the splattered blood was still there as a reminder of what Joseph had done to himself. She slowly made her way to the sideboard to take their wedding picture off the top, when she noticed a piece of Josephs tooth was on the floor beside her shoe.

"My poor Jo" she cried, her tears hadn't dried up like she had previously thought. She grabbed the picture and left the lounge as quickly as her sore stomach would allow her and headed to the kitchen to get a sharp knife and a glass. She searched through the cupboards for some alcohol and came across a bottle of Moonshine; it had ninety per cent alcohol content, so she knew that would probably knock her out quickly as she generally didn't drink much alcohol at all. Afterwards, she slowly climbed the stairs and went into the bathroom and opened up the medicine cabinet. There wasn't much there to kill her instantly, but she grabbed all the Tylenol she could find and ibuprofen. There were also sleeping tablets that she used to use to help her sleep when she was on nights before she got pregnant. She also remembered that there was some lorazepam in her work uniform that she had forgotten to put back when she worked at the prison. She then thought about the prison and the fact that the diaper sniper would probably rub his hands in glee over the demise of the prisons suicide prevention officer, especially when he heard she had killed herself after she failed to notice her husband was suicidal.

In the bedroom, she found the lorazepam in her uniform pocket and then sat down on the bed. She poured the moonshine into the glass and raised it high up to the ceiling and said "See you soon, Joseph, my darling"

She nearly threw up with the taste of the moonshine, but managed to swallow down all the tablets that she had gathered from the medicine cabinet. She took the knife and did several sweeping cuts across both wrists, but she didn't feel a thing. Her head had started to swirl, so she got into the bed and gave herself the shot of lorazepam. She snuggled deep under the covers with her head on Joseph's pillow and their wedding picture next to her; she could still smell Joseph's unique smell on the pillow and felt at ease within herself as she knew she would soon be with him again. She then fell asleep and it wasn't long before she was in a state of total unconsciousness.

....

The phone rang at Alberto and Mary's apartment. It was three thirty in the afternoon and Corina still hadn't returned from her walk and they felt very worried about her.

"Maybe this is her" said Alberto to Mary "Hello, Doctor Alberto Barsetti speaking"

"Hello Alberto, this is James here, I was just wondering if Corina had got back okay. I sent her home in a cab after she came to the hospital this morning in a very distressed state. I would have phoned earlier, but I have had patients to see and I have only just got away"

Alberto suddenly had a bad feeling in his stomach about Corina and why she had not shown up yet, so he expressed his concerns to James.

"Where do you think she would go, Alberto?" asked James "She seemed very fragile and I think we really need to find her soon".

"She would either go to the gardens or back home to Milton. I can't think of anywhere else she would go as she's not come back here, so I will check the gardens, if you could go to the house, James, I would appreciate it. I'm not really ready to go back to the house yet"

"Of course I will, Alberto. I will phone you as soon as I've found her and then bring her back to you"

After he had finished the call, James got straight in his car, but struggled to get to Milton quickly. The traffic was a nightmare at that time of day and after an hour of nose to tail traffic, he felt frustrated and shouted obscenities at other drivers when they drove badly or too slow. Eventually, he got to the house and as he walked up the drive he noticed the front door was open; as he entered he stepped over the big pile of mail on the floor and looked around for Corina. He called her name over and over again, but received no answer. He went through to the lounge and saw the blood stains everywhere from Joseph's suicide.

"Jesus Jo, you must have been desperate!" he whispered to himself, then left the lounge as quickly as he had gone in.

There was no sign of Corina downstairs, so he ran upstairs and frantically looked in every room for her. He called out her name over and over again, but there was still no answer. He opened the door to the master bedroom and saw that Corina was fast asleep in the bed. He gently shook her to try and wake her up, but she felt very cold. He knew something wasn't right with her, so he felt for a pulse in her neck and found it was very faint, and she was breathing, so she was still alive. There was an empty glass on her bedside table and lots of empty packets of pills strewn around on the floor, along with a bloodied knife and a used epi-pen injection of lorazepam. He feared the worst as he pulled back the covers and then noticed her wrists were cut. He quickly wrapped them in a couple of t-shirts, that he managed to find in one of the drawers, to help stem the bleeding. He then grabbed the telephone off of the bedside table and dialled 911 to get some medical help, after which he phoned Alberto to tell him that he had found Corina and to meet him at the hospital as soon as possible. He was determined not to let Corina die; he wasn't going to lose her too. It would be more than Alberto and Mary could take.

It would be more than he could take.

Chapter Ten

The next morning Corina awoke and felt very confused; she had no idea of where she was. The room she was in was not familiar to her. She guessed it was a hospital, as she was attached to drips and monitors and a nurse was hovering over her as she checked the machines, but it was not The General. The nurse gave Corina a sweet smile when she noticed Corina was awake and was looking at her in a very confused way.

"Good morning Mrs Barsetti, can I get you some breakfast?" the nurse asked quietly, so not to wake Mary who was asleep in the chair next to the bed.

"Not for a moment, thank you, I'm not feeling too hungry yet...could you please tell me which hospital I'm in?"

"You are in the Beth Israel Deaconess Medical Centre, Honey. Doctor Michaud will be in to see you soon and he will explain everything" The nurse gently raised the head of Corina's bed and made her feel comfortable "I'll get health care to bring you in some breakfast, then you can eat it at your leisure"

Corina noticed Mary had stirred from her sleep and she felt a huge surge of guilt come over her. Poor Mary, she must be in turmoil herself, Corina thought. She really felt sorry for what she had done. Mary's son and Grandson were both dead and now she had to deal with her attempted suicide drama.

"How are you feeling, dear?" Mary asked, as she came closer to the bed to hold Corina's hand.

"Not too bad, thank you" Corina then started to garble words about being sorry and that she only wanted to be with Joseph and how could Joseph do this to them?

"It's Okay, dear" Mary interrupted "Don't fret yourself, I understand. I'm just glad you are alive. Alberto will be here to get me soon, so I can go home for a freshen up and then I'll come back after you have seen the doctor"

Alberto had decided not to stay with Mary and Corina last night; instead he left and went home. He needed to be by himself to get his head straight. He couldn't cope with everything that had gone on, but he would pay for Corina's medical care at the hospital as a token of his love for her. Alberto had to remain strong, he was the head of the family after all and he mustn't show any more weakness at this point. He had already cried in front of Corina on the day his son had died and then again on the day his grandson was stillborn, but he had to try and be strong for her sake. Too much emotion could send her over the edge and he was desperate that she didn't hurt herself again. Alberto knocked quietly on Corina's room door and he slowly entered. He could not speak to Corina for fear of the emotion that he felt was about to overwhelm him, so he just stood there and smiled at her.

"I'm sorry" Corina mouthed to him, so he blew her a kiss from across the room to reassure her. Corina blew a kiss back and felt relieved that Alberto didn't seem too cross with her. She respected Alberto and what he thought meant a lot to her. Mary leant over and kissed Corina on the head "I'm so glad you are alive, my dear. I do love you, you know. You are still my daughter, even though Joseph isn't here. You don't have to feel alone" the tears welled up in both their eyes and Mary squeezed Corina's hand again, she then left with Alberto.

Corina felt very guilty for disregarding their feelings to do what she had done, but it was a decision that she would have to live with for the rest of her life and the scars on her wrists would be a constant reminder of the day she hurt herself to be with Joseph. At that moment, she actually felt very numb about what Joseph had done. Her emotions were like a rollercoaster and were very up and down. One minute she loved him and the next, she hated him. But, she really wished that it would all go away. She wanted to start her life over again and forget everything that had happened. A knock on the door startled Corina out of her daydream.

Doctor Noah Michaud put his head around the door and asked "Is it okay if I come in, Corina?"

"Of course, Noah" she recognised him from when she first came to Boston, but she hadn't seen him since. He was Joseph's friend that had given them the heads up about the job at the prison, but he had left his post before she had started working there.

"How are you feeling?" he enquired "It's been a while since I saw you" he pulled the chair up to the side of the bed and sat down on it so he was close to Corina.

"I'm feeling pretty stupid" Corina looked sheepish as she tried to explain her feelings to Noah "I got myself into such a state; I didn't know what else to do, but seeing Alberto and Mary has made me feel very glad to still be alive"

"That's good to hear, Corina. I would have been very concerned if I had come here this morning and you were still intent on taking your own life. You have all been through a great deal this past week or so, and finding Joseph like that must have traumatised you immensely. I do understand why you would feel the need to be with Joseph, but we are all grateful that your suicide attempt failed"

Corina studied him closely. He was a strange looking man and his fashion sense was almost non-existent. He looked like he had been dragged through a hedge backwards. In fact, he looked a tad crazy and pretty much suited his job. Corina remembered how she used to laugh with the girls back at The Cumberland Infirmary about psychiatrists and how they all seemed to come across as nuts. The girls always thought that's why they were so good at their jobs; they must have extreme empathy….as they knew how their patients felt most of the time.

"You have lost your husband and child within three days of each other and that is enough to push anyone over the edge" continued Noah "So I am going to put you in touch with psychological services, so they can work with you to get through this hard time. It will take a while for you to feel normal again, Corina, but you must take this opportunity to talk to somebody"

Not likely, thought Corina to herself, she would never speak of this again. She did not want people to know what had happened and she didn't want people to judge her and think she wasn't right in the head. She already knew she was the talk of Milton, as nobody could believe Joseph was capable of suicide and she obviously must have done something to drive him to it.

"We will keep you in for another night, just to keep an eye on you. Luckily, you were found before the tablets could do any real damage. You may feel groggy for a day or two, but that will pass. Your wrists are dressed with steri-strips, apart from the one cut that was deep enough to require stitching. Unfortunately, there will be scars, but hopefully in time they will fade and be less noticeable"

He got up from the chair and paused before he said "There is just one more thing to tell you before I go. I wanted to tell you this before you left the hospital as I didn't want it to come as a shock later"

Corina's heart began to race with anticipation. She started to panic about what he was about to tell her.

"I'm afraid you won't be able to return to the prison in your role as suicide prevention officer and I expect you will have your American mental health nursing registration taken away until you can prove you have good mental health yourself. I know it's probably another blow to you at this time in your life, but it's probably for the best that you don't go back there"

Corina shrugged, she couldn't imagine ever going back to that place anyway. She didn't actually care and it was one less thing for her to worry about. She needed to get her life back together again and not worry about the likes of The Diaper Sniper. Thankfully, he would not be part of her life anymore. She felt like he should be dead instead of Joseph. But life was unfair.... she felt she had to get used to the bad people being on the earth, whilst the good people were taken before their time.

"Now, you get some rest, Corina. I will pop in and see you in the morning before we discharge you"

Corina nodded and nestled down into the bed. She felt very tired and soon she was fast asleep again.

Chapter Eleven

Back home at The Four Seasons, Corina sat with Alberto and Mary as they ate their dinner. It was a hot and sticky evening, so they had opened the patio doors to the veranda to let some air blow through. Corina pushed her food around the plate as she did not feel very hungry. She still felt tired and drained and her wrists stung underneath the bandages. She glanced over at Alberto who looked uncomfortable as he cleared his throat to talk.

"Corina, they will be releasing Joseph's body tomorrow, so he will be sent with the baby to the Dolan funeral home in Milton. Is that okay with you?"

"Yes, why wouldn't it be? He was your son, so you can put him where you like" Corina suddenly realised that she had sounded awfully abrupt and there was an awkward silence between them all which lasted for at least a few minutes.

Finally, Alberto said "Yes, we know he was our son, but he was also your husband and we wanted you to have a say in the funeral arrangements!"

Corina didn't know what to do about funeral arrangements, she had never organised a funeral before, so she didn't have a clue where to start. She began to feel uncomfortable and didn't want to have the conversation about bodies and funeral arrangements.

"I'm going to see Joseph and the baby tomorrow, Corina" said Mary. She sensed that Corina might be finding the conversation very difficult "Would you like to come with me? We could talk to the people at the funeral home and discuss the arrangements together"

"What do you mean SEE Joseph? How can you see him? You do know you won't be able to actually see his face, don't you? His face was blown away…. REMEMBER?" Corina felt a strong upsurge of anger that had begun to rise from the pit of her stomach "I've already seen that disgusting sight, why would I want to see that again? And, I have already said goodbye to my baby at the hospital.... Are you deliberately trying to upset me?" Corina continued to rant on until Alberto snapped and shouted at her.

"Right, that is enough.... whether you see your husband and baby or not is up to you, but you WILL go with Mary to the funeral home and you WILL make arrangements for the funerals. It's about time you faced up to your responsibilities as a wife and a mother, instead of trying to run away from everything. No wonder Joseph confided in his mother and not you before........." his voice trailed off as he realised he had said too much. The look of horror on Corina's face was too much for Mary, so she quickly got up to try and leave the room.

"WHAT?" screamed Corina at Mary "You knew? I don't believe this…. which part did you know about, that he had cancer or that he was going to kill himself?"

Corina felt totally enraged, so she went to grab Mary to try and stop her as she continued to try and leave the room. Alberto had to get in between them to protect his wife from Corina's violent outburst. Corina punched his chest and screamed in his face with temper, she was determined to get to Mary. Mary hid behind Alberto, who fought with all his strength to stop Corina from attacking her. Mary hoped she would calm down for a minute so she could talk to her. The tears poured down Mary's face and she shook with the emotion and the horrible feelings of guilt that had overcome her.

Mary looked out from behind Alberto and tried to get Corina to listen "He asked me to help him end his life when he found out about the cancer, but I said I couldn't. I tried to talk him out of it…honestly I did, but he was adamant" she could no longer talk and held on to Alberto to steady herself. He helped her to sit down, but continued to shield her from Corina's anger.

"Oh my God Mary, that's pathetic. Why didn't you tell me? I could have stopped him…I would have done anything for him; I would have nursed him while he was sick. I would have preferred that than finding him like I did. I can't believe this; why would you keep that from me?" Corina shouted so loud at Mary that she had to cover her ears.

"I want you to stop this now, Corina. It's too late to do anything about this now. My wife is distraught; can't you see she feels bad enough already?"

"Now I know why you didn't cry; you were expecting it. What sort of mother allows her son to kill himself and not tell anyone... did you know too, Alberto?" she seethed with the continued anger that had engulfed her and she didn't know what to do with herself. She could feel her heartbeat as it pounded in her chest and in the sides of her head, and she couldn't stop the urge to want to punch Mary hard in the face.

"No, I only found out this morning. And, he only kept it from you because he loved you so much. But, this has to end now Corina, before you say something you will regret. I suggest you go to your room and calm down. We will talk about this again calmly in the morning"

Alberto helped Mary to stand and took her to their bedroom. Corina could hear Mary's sobs in her bedroom from where she was stood in the dining room, but she felt no sorrow for Mary, she was just too angry with her. Corina also felt angry with Joseph as well. It felt unbearable; she couldn't stay there with the knowledge that Mary knew he was suicidal. She felt she had to leave, and soon. Corina walked down the hallway and stood outside of their bedroom door and called to Joseph's parents.

"Alberto, I'm going back to the house in Milton. Tell Mary I will meet her at the funeral home tomorrow at two o clock. Is it okay if I take your car?"

Alberto paused for a second before he answered as he wondered if she was doing the right thing by leaving, but he felt he couldn't stop her and he didn't have the strength to stop her anyway, so he opened the door and handed her the keys.

"Drive carefully please, Corina, we will see you tomorrow" he kissed her on both cheeks, then disappeared back into the bedroom. He really hoped she wouldn't do anything to harm herself again, he also wished his temper hadn't made him tell her that Mary knew that Joseph wanted to end his life.

Corina gathered up some of her clothes to take with her and then drove to her home in Milton. She dreaded spending the night in the house alone, but she couldn't stay with Mary and Alberto as she was too angry with them. She felt betrayed, and she also felt responsible for Joseph's death because he couldn't confide in her. She felt dreadful that she knew Joseph must have felt very desperate and alone.... just like she did at that present moment in time.

......

Corina sat in the kitchen of her home in Milton, she felt deflated as she looked at the cards that had been left on the kitchen table. James must have put them there, she thought.... James....she suddenly remembered his face when she had shouted at him at the hospital. She had treated him badly and he had saved her life by coming to find her. She knew she must call him later to apologise. Corina started to open the cards and read the sympathy comments. "We are so sorry" and "Thinking of you at this hard time" from people she didn't even know. Who were these people that were thinking of her? She didn't feel anything but anger, so she ripped them up and threw them straight into the bin. She got up from her chair and went into the lounge. She had decided that she was going to sit there amongst the blood stains and the mess and try to explain to Joseph why she wouldn't be going to his and their baby's funeral. She suddenly felt close to Joseph there. She could feel him and it was the place his soul had left the earth to go to where ever it was going.

"Joseph, if you can hear me, I want you to know that I loved you so much and I thought we were happy. You said you loved me, yet you couldn't confide in me, instead you have humiliated me. In your letter you asked me to understand, but I do not understand. I will never understand how you could love someone so much, yet not give them any sort of chance to help you. I would have helped you, I would have done anything for you, but you ruined everything when you pulled that trigger and put yourself first. I hope you are with our son and that you are happy, because I have nothing now and that is why I cannot go to the funeral and have everyone point the finger of blame at me.... and they will blame me.... they will blame me because I am the wife you couldn't talk to and I am the wife that wasn't good enough to bring a baby into this world alive. I am the wife who still loves you with all my heart, but I feel now that I possibly meant nothing to you at all because you have left me in such a horrible and cowardly way. You also asked me in your letter to forgive you...." Corina paused to weep as she sat on the couch, the vision of Joseph's blown off face appeared and she shook her head vigorously to try and get rid of the horrific picture "I DO NOT FORGIVE YOU, DOCTOR JOSEPH BARSETTI, AND I WILL NEVER UNDERSTAND!" she shouted "GOOD BYE JOSEPH, I HOPE YOU CAN REST IN PEACE"

Corina got up from the couch and walked over to the door; she turned around and had one final look around at the carnage that Joseph had left behind. She walked out and closed the door behind her. She would never sit in that lounge again and she hoped she would never have to return to the house in Milton ever again. She went upstairs and packed a suitcase full of clothes, found her passport, then got into Alberto's car and set off to drive to the airport. She was going back home to England and nothing was going to stop her.

During her drive to The Boston Logan International Airport, she felt extremely sad and alone. She felt devastated that Joseph had confided in Mary and worst of all Mary didn't try to warn her. She could not understand why Mary had not wanted to try and stop him and was confused that she just waited for him kill himself. She wondered what Alberto thought of it all, but she knew Alberto would think she was running away again...She was fully aware that she was running away, but she didn't know what else to do. She was going back to England for a fresh start; there was no reason to stay in Boston with the people that she felt she couldn't trust. She knew she would not see her husband and son being buried, but she felt they wouldn't be there anyway; they would just be empty shells in their coffins and she couldn't cope with people crying and looking at her. Anyway, Joseph said he would be with her always, so if this was true, what did it matter if she was in England or Boston. There was no difference to her. It was her turn to be a coward. After she parked the car, she made her way inside the airport to try and book herself a seat on the next plane out to London. She noticed a British Airways desk so wandered over to get a ticket.

"The next flight to London Gatwick is at five-forty tomorrow morning, would you like me to book you a seat, Madam?" asked a very pretty desk attendant, she too was English and Corina was very pleased to hear a familiar accent "Which class would you like to sit in, please?"

"First class please" Corina thought about being able to get some rest on the way to London, so she thought first class would be better, especially as she had started to feel uncomfortable where her stitches were from the caesarean. She handed the girl her credit card and waited for the ticket to be printed out. She felt embarrassed about her bandaged wrists and hoped the girl wouldn't realise what she had done to herself, she tried to cover them up with her cardigan sleeves, so she pulled them down and stretched the sleeves until they reached her knuckles.

"You must check in by three-forty Madam, check in is just around the corner. Thank you for flying British Airways" she smiled at Corina as she passed the ticket and credit card back to her. She hadn't noticed her wrists, but she could tell that Corina had been crying.

It was only eleven forty-five, so Corina decided to try and find a telephone to call James. She had a few hours to spare before she could check in, so she would call him and then find somewhere to sit and have a coffee.

"James, its Corina. I'm sorry for calling so late"

"Hi Corina, how are you?"

"I'm fine, thank you. Listen, James, I just wanted to say thank you for helping me and I also wanted to apologise for what happened at the hospital the other day. I shouldn't have accused you and I'm really sorry. It turns out Mary knew about Jo wanting to kill himself and she did nothing about it, so I'm heading back to England. I cannot stay here, so please don't try and stop me" Corina started to cry again, she was worn out with the constant tears, but she just couldn't help it and they continued to flow.

"But, Corina, are you sure you are doing the right thing. What about the funeral? Joseph and the baby will be at the funeral home tomorrow; you should really stay here and say goodbye" James did not want her to leave; he felt she would regret it for the rest of her life.

"James, I have said goodbye in my own way. Please try to understand that I feel humiliated that Mary knew and I am also very angry with Joseph. I would be very grateful if you could speak on my behalf at the funeral, say something nice, tell people I'm ill, tell them whatever, but I am not going to attend. I am supposed to be meeting Mary at two o clock tomorrow at Dolan's, so if you could meet her there for me and help her to arrange the funeral, that would be great"

"Sure Corina, But…"

"James, please, I am not going to the funeral, I cannot stay. I cannot face Mary again; I am scared of what I will do. I just cannot believe my life has turned upside down like this. I miss Joseph so much, but I am so angry with him. Please try to understand, please!" Corina's voice was filled with emotion and it had started to become too much for James. He tried to understand, but he knew she was making a big mistake.

"Ok Corina, calm down…"

"And, I don't want you to give them the heads up about me leaving, I am going and that is final. I will call you after I have landed in London. You meant a lot to Joseph, so it's only fitting that you represent me at the funeral. I have to go now. I love you, James, and thank you" Corina then hung up. She didn't have any intention of calling James when she landed; she had decided she would cut all the things to do with Joseph out of her life.

Chapter Twelve

James left it until the morning to phone Alberto to tell him that Corina had gone; he knew she would be well on the way to London by the time he phoned.

"Do you think she will come back, James?" asked Alberto, he was very shocked when he found out Corina had gone in the night "And, do you know what she has done with my car?"

That was so typical of Alberto, thought James, worrying about a car rather than what Corina was going through "I'm assuming the car is at the airport, Alberto. And, I honestly think she is not coming back. She was very upset and has asked me to meet Mary at the funeral home to help her with funeral arrangements"

"Oh, well how selfish of her, but I will tell Mary to expect you"

James felt he should stick up for Corina and even though she had called him a big headed American asshole in his office, he liked her, he liked her a lot, and he felt sorry for her. He had thought about it overnight and could see why she was extremely upset and angry. He thought that her going back to England was a bit extreme, but there was no use in trying to stop her last night.

"Corina feels like she is doing the right thing, Alberto. Just like Joseph felt he was doing the right thing to protect Corina. She is very angry with Mary and does not want to be around her at the moment. I am hoping that when she gets to England, she will regret leaving and come back to Boston. She has lost a great deal in a short amount of time and she feels let down by the people closest to her"

"Actually, James, I think I would prefer it if you didn't meet with Mary today. I think we will sort out the funeral together instead" Alberto didn't want to hear James try to explain Corina's selfishness and took umbrage in the fact that he had defended her "We would all like to run away and hide and pretend this didn't happen, James. But, the fact is, it has happened and it is now left to Mary and I to pick up the pieces. Have a nice day and I will be in touch about the funeral soon" continued Alberto and then he abruptly put the phone down on James.

"Jesus Christ!" exclaimed James "Hung up on again. That family is hard work!"

He too found it strange that Mary had not asked for help from anyone when Joseph had told her of his plans. No wonder Corina had found it hard to stay. The whole scenario could have been a lot different if she had just told someone. He had to go to work, but he decided he would pack up Joseph's office whilst he was there and keep his personal things safe at his house for when Corina was ready to come back and get it.

Alberto couldn't believe James had stuck up for Corina, he also wondered why he had not tried to talk her out of going back to England. He thought she should have stayed and talked it over with Mary. He felt extremely tired as he had been up with Mary all night comforting her. She was beside herself with guilt and was desperate to talk to Corina about Joseph. She would be very upset to find out Corina had gone and he felt anxious about telling her. He also felt disappointed in his only son, he felt he shouldn't have put the burden onto his mother to try and protect Corina. It was all such a nightmare and he wished Joseph had not been so rash in his decision to end it all. He missed his son and he missed the happy family life they had all had together. In fact, he missed the old Corina; the happy go lucky Corina, the fun Corina with her warped sense of humour and her ability to make everyone laugh. She had changed for the worst since Joseph and the baby had died and although he knew it wasn't her fault, he felt she had turned into an angry selfish monster. He hoped that when she had chance to sort herself out in England, she would come back and be his sweet Corina again.

"Is everything alright, Alberto? I heard you talking on the phone" Mary had wandered through into the lounge from her bedroom. She looked terrible; her eyes were swollen and puffy from crying all night.

"No, Mary, everything has just gotten a whole lot worse. Corina has flown back to England and it doesn't look like she is coming back. So, it looks like we are alone to deal with everything. But, don't worry dear, we can do this. We are strong"

Alberto hugged his wife as she had started to cry again. She didn't feel very strong, she wished she had told Corina what Joseph had planned, but there was nothing she could do about it now. She would have to live with her guilt forever.

"Let's go and get dressed Mary, then we can get a cab to the airport to pick up my car. Then, later we will go and see Joseph and the baby. The sooner we get things done and organised, the sooner we can get on with our lives.... with or without Corina"

Mary nodded to him as she was unable to speak. They both made their way to the bedroom, holding on to each other tightly as they really didn't want to let go of each other. They had an emotional time ahead of them and desperately needed one another to help them both get through it. Mary couldn't imagine life without Alberto and would be devastated if she lost him. She knew Corina must be feeling heartbroken and wanted to be with her, so she could help her through the grieving process.

Chapter Thirteen

Corina had landed in London and suddenly realised she only had dollars in her purse, so she had to go and find a money exchange bureau. Once she had got her money sorted, she sat in the airport café with a coffee and people watched. She tried to figure out what she was going to do next. She had no idea of where she was going to go, but had no intention of going back to her parents' house, just to be lectured by them. She felt nothing for them and she couldn't care less if they had dropped off the face of the earth. She suddenly thought about her friends that she had trained with in Cumbria, so she decided to give Harriet a call and hoped that she still had the same number. She made her way to the public telephone that was beside the café, she fumbled around with some loose change and fed the telephone the right amount to make the call.

"Hi, could I please speak to Harriet?" she asked the man who had answered the phone.

"Just a minute, please…. Harriet, there is an American lady on the phone for you!" he shouted to Harriet.

Corina was a bit shocked that he thought she was an American. She hadn't realised that she had picked up the accent at all as she was so used to hearing American people speak. She had been in Boston for ten years though, and hardly ever came across an English person, so she couldn't really compare, especially when she spent most of those years behind bars as she had worked at the prison.

"Hello" Harriet still had her posh accent "Harriet Richardson, speaking"

"Harriet Richardson…Did you finally get married and lose your virginity?" joked Corina.

"Oh my goodness, CORINA, Arrrggggghhhhhh!" she screamed hysterically down the phone "What's happened to your voice?"

"Boston happened, that's what! Could I please come and see you, and maybe stay for a couple of days?"

"Of course, I'm still in Carlisle in the same house.... won't Joseph be coming with you?" Harriet enquired, she sensed something was wrong with Corina and hoped they hadn't split up.

"No, he's dead" Corina started to cry.

"Oh my Goodness, I'm so sorry, Corina.... But, how?" Harriet wasn't expecting Corina to say that he had died, she wasn't expecting that at all and felt shocked.

"I'll explain properly when I see you, but it's been so awful, Harriet, I can't believe he's gone" Corina tried to compose herself, but the tears continued to flow down her cheeks "I'm going to try and catch a train up to you, so I may be a while yet"

"Okay, Corina, try not to upset yourself too much. If you call when you get to Carlisle station, I'll come and pick you up. Looking forward to seeing you"

Corina put down the receiver and turned to find a queue of people that were waiting to use the telephone. They all stared at her and this made her feel very uncomfortable, as she felt very conscious of her tears. She made her way to outside of the airport and got in a taxi to take her to Paddington station.

....

Alberto was in his bedroom and as he got changed he started to think about Corina again. He wished she hadn't gone back to England, so he was going to go and see James. He wanted to talk to him to see if they could come up with a solution to try and get Corina to come back to Boston for the funeral. He had been to the funeral home the day before with Mary and they had both arranged the funeral service and burials for ten days' time, in the hope that he could get Corina to come back in time to see her husband and son put to rest. The telephone started to ring, which startled Alberto as he was in deep thought. Mary had answered it in the lounge and he could hear her as she talked. It sounded like she was arguing with someone and she had started to get upset, so he went to see what was going on.

"No, Corina, please don't do this. He is my son and I want him near me" Mary wept as she spoke. Alberto took the telephone away from Mary and listened to Corina as she raged on the other end. He didn't recognise the person she had become, but he knew grief could do terrible things to a person, so he tried to remain calm.

"Corina, where are you?" Alberto asked calmly "Are you feeling Okay?"

"I am staying at Harriet's in Carlisle and no, I'm not bloody okay! I am trying to explain to Mary that I have decided I want Joseph and my son flown over here to England, I am his next of kin and I want him here with me. I want their funeral here and I want them buried together here in England, because I have no intention of ever returning to Boston again"

"Corina, please, that is not a very nice thing to do to us. We are grieving too you know, they are our son and grandchild and they belong here in Boston. Joseph was born here and so was your son. Joseph's life was here; please rethink as I don't think Mary can take much more" Alberto pleaded with her.

"Do you know what Alberto? I couldn't care less about what Mary can take, or what Mary wants; she didn't deserve a son like him. She let her son kill himself and didn't even ask for help or try to stop him, she should have told me what he was thinking. WHY DIDN'T SHE TELL ME? I DON'T UNDERSTAND!" Corina started to yell down the telephone at Alberto, he could hear Harriet in the background as she tried to calm her down.

"You are just trying to blame someone, Corina. Joseph would have done it whether Mary had gotten some help or not. He was intent on ending his life. I wish you would just come home and talk it over with Mary; she is desperate to see you again and talk to you. Please, Corina, I am begging you not to do this. If you can't feel sorry for Mary, then feel sorry for me. You said I was like a father to you and you have called me Dad for ten years, but since Joseph has died you have called me Alberto and it's upsetting me. I am grieving for

Joseph too, you know, and I want him to stay in Boston where he belongs. And, Boston is where you belong. Please let me come and get you and bring you back home, please"

"Which part of, I WILL NEVER RETURN TO BOSTON AGAIN, do you not understand? He was MY husband; did you not hear me? MY HUSBAND, and I want him here with me!" Corina could not talk anymore; the emotion had taken her over again. Harriet had to take the telephone from her and talk to Alberto.

Alberto started to cry as he heard Harriet's posh English accent, it reminded him of the Corina he had first met all those years ago. The lovely English Corina, sweet and polite, and happy. She was so excited to be in Boston, he never thought the day would come when he would hear her say that she didn't want to be there anymore. She spoke to him with such venom in her voice, that it scared him; he knew he would have to handle her differently from now on. Obviously she didn't feel sorry for him or Mary; as she was so caught up in her own grief that she would do anything to hurt them and that included taking Joseph and the baby back to England. There was no way he would allow her to do that, so he asked Harriet for her help.

"Harriet, do you think Corina is doing the right thing here?" he wanted her opinion before he asked for her address to go and see Corina in England.

"No, I absolutely do not and I have told her so. I am so worried about her; I don't know what to do. She is not the Corina I know and it's frightening me. I am trying to get her to see a Doctor, but she won't go. She will need her stitches taken out soon too, but she won't even let me take a look"

Corina shouted at Harriet "I don't want this on my medical records in England, Harriet, that's why I won't go to the doctors. They will judge me and I am quite capable of taking my own stitches out!"

"You see, Alberto" Harriet had started to cry as well "She's only been here a day, but I can't cope with her. She was up all night last night having nightmares about Joseph and screaming about seeing his face. I love her to bits, but she needs some help and I am not able to give it to her. My husband wants her to go as she is upsetting the children. They are only young and they don't understand"

"It's okay Harriet, you give me your address and I will get on a plane as soon as I can and come and get her"

As soon as Alberto got off the phone to Harriet, he reassured Mary that he would not let Corina take Joseph and their grandchild's bodies to England. He made sure she was happy and settled, then he left the apartment and headed off to the general to see James. Once he had met James and discussed what they were going to do to get Corina to come back to Boston, it was decided that James would go and get her and Alberto would stay home with Mary, as he didn't want to leave her alone at this time. James was happy to go; he had thought more and more about Corina's wellbeing and was determined to bring her back to Boston.

He would not return without her.

Chapter Fourteen

Harriet had got even more concerned about Corina in the couple of days that she had to wait for James to come and get her. Corina had gone from being angry and vocal, to being very quiet and she just sat in her room and avoided everyone. She would just stare at Harriet when she tried to speak to her.

"Corina, sweetie" Harriet knelt in front of Corina and held her hand, she spoke to her tenderly and hoped Corina would listen.

"Corina, James will be arriving soon. I have booked you both rooms at The Warwick Hotel, so you need to try and talk to him. Please, for my sake. I hate seeing you like this and I want you to let him help you. Are you listening, Corina?"

Corina didn't say a word, but nodded. Harriet felt relieved that she had acknowledged her and gave her a hug. But there was no hug back from Corina, she felt limp and she didn't bother to lift her arms up to hold Harriet.

"Oh, Corina, what Joseph did has broken you, hasn't it?" Harriet still hoped for some sort of response "I am so sorry you are going through this and I promise I will always be here for you, where ever you are, you only have to call" Harriet felt so sad that her friend had left England, so in love and happy, only to return ten years later in a complete mess. She began to cry for her, but Corina continued to stare into space like Harriet wasn't there.

"I will let you know when James arrives; can I get you a cup of tea or something?"

Still there was nothing, no reply and no movement. Corina stared with her eyes fixated on the wall. She looked straight ahead as though Harriet wasn't there. Harriet quietly left the room feeling forlorn. She hoped James would arrive soon, for Corina's sake.

....

"Could you please take me to twenty-seven St Georges Crescent, Carlisle?" James asked a taxi driver outside of Carlisle railway station.

"Aye" the taxi driver replied and laughed "Yank are you, boy? I charge double for yanks"

"I sure am" James found the driver's accent hilarious. It was very different to Corina's accent when she had first arrived in Boston and he was intrigued to hear the driver talk about his life. He found out the driver was a poor sheep farmer from just outside of Carlisle. He came to the city each day with his taxi to earn extra money, so he could afford to feed his sheep.

"Why don't you just get rid of the sheep?" asked James, he thought that would be a simple solution to the taxi driver's problem.

This question was not taken lightly by the driver and James was forced to sit through the next twenty minutes of the journey being told about the taxi driver's family history. James heard all about their sheep farm and how it dated back to the early 1800's and his father would turn in his grave if he ever sold the sheep.

"Okay, yank boy, we have arrived at your destination. That'll be twenty-one pounds fifty please" the taxi driver held out his hand for the money.

James gave him thirty pounds and told him to keep the change.

"Thanks for the tip, but here's a tip for you... never tell a sheep farmer to get rid of his sheep in these parts.... you might find yourself walking home next time!"

James sniggered to himself and said "Have a nice day!" in true American style.

"Aye, good day to you, yank boy" the taxi driver tilted his cap at James and then drove off at speed.

A bemused James looked up at Harriet's house; he stood there for a minute and took it all in. It looked very big and Victorian and very different to his house in Quincy. He wandered up the steps to the front door and rang the bell. He could see a petite lady through the coloured glass in the door as she came down the hall. She was very smartly dressed and her long blonde hair was swept neatly up off of her face. She was very pretty and James thought to himself that Joseph had done the right thing by marrying an English girl. James had found the Boston girls he had dated too hard to handle, he also hated the way they thought they were above everybody else and that the world revolved around them. English girls seemed much more easy going and relaxed, but then he thought maybe he had just picked the wrong type of Boston girl.

"James?" asked Harriet as she opened the door. She held out her hand to welcome him.

"Harriet, I have heard so much about you over the years" James ignored her hand and went straight in for a hug "Good to meet you at last"

"Do come in James, Corina is upstairs in her room. Would you like to go straight up, or have a cup of tea and some cake first? You must be very tired, but you will need some energy to deal with Corina!" Harriet looked worried and she hoped James would be able to convince Corina to go back to Boston.

"Tea and cake would be nice, thank you, Harriet. You can tell me what's been happening before I get Corina. Did you manage to book us a hotel?"

"Yes, I've booked you rooms at The Warwick Hotel, just outside Carlisle, its lovely there. I have told Corina, but I'm not quite sure that she has taken that information in. She has been in her room since she called Mary and Alberto to tell them about bringing the bodies back here" Harriet started to cry "I'm sorry, James, but I am so worried about her. I hope you can get through to her, because I am seriously considering calling the psych team out to assess her"

"There is no need for that now, Harriet. I am here, and I will do my best to sort this all out" James hugged her again to reassure her and then they both went to the kitchen for tea and cake.

....

Upstairs, Corina had heard the doorbell ring so she slowly got up to start to pack her things. Resistance was futile, she really couldn't be bothered to fight any more. She knew James was there to take her back to Boston, so she would just go. She would show her face at the funeral and then she would come back to England afterwards. She didn't really know why she had demanded that the bodies should come to England, as where would she bury them? She didn't have a base in the UK and she didn't have any family to turn to, so the best thing to do was let them be buried in Milton Cemetery, as she had originally planned. At least Alberto, and the sad excuse of a mother Mary, could visit them and tend to the graves when she wasn't there. She thought about Mary again and still wondered why she had kept Joseph's plan quiet. She was going to have it out with her when she got back to Boston and she expected a damn good reason why she had kept it to herself for so long.

After she had packed her belongings she made her way downstairs. She could hear James' voice and his Boston accent reminded her of Joseph, so she stood outside of the kitchen and listened to him for a few moments. She listened to Harriet tell him what she had done with her life since she had qualified as a psychiatric nurse. Corina felt proud of Harriet, she had done well in her career as she was now running the psychiatric unit at The Cumberland Infirmary. It was a big responsibility for her, but she found the job very fulfilling. She had also met her husband there, Doctor Andrew Richardson, a psychiatrist, and they now had two beautiful children together, Alicia and Isabella. When she finally went into the kitchen she headed straight for Harriet and returned the hug that Harriet had given her earlier.

"I am so sorry that I have put you through all of this, Harriet, and I am really sorry that I blanked you, but I just needed time alone to figure things out" She then turned to James "I know you are here to take me back to Boston, James. Although, I am not very happy about it as I do not really want to go, but I do not want to upset Alberto any more than I already have. I want you both to know, that as soon as the funeral is over, I will be returning to England to start afresh. I will probably start my life again in the Lake District, that way I will be close to Harriet and my friends, so I don't want you trying to change my mind, James. Returning to Boston is a temporary thing, Okay?"

"Okay, Corina" James got up from his chair and hugged her, he was just glad that she was agreeing to return for the funeral.

"I think you are doing the right thing, Corina" Harriet was relieved Corina didn't have to be forced to return to Boston "I'll give you both a lift to the Hotel; it'll save you getting a taxi again"

"Thank God" laughed James "I think I've had my fill of Cumbrian taxi drivers today; I think I insulted my driver by telling him to get rid of his sheep!"

Corina looked at Harriet and smirked.

"Never tell a sheep farmer to get rid of his sheep in these parts, sweetie" Harriet giggled at James "I'm surprised he didn't make you get out and walk!"

James looked at Corina, who had actually cracked a smile. It was good to see her smile, even if it was just for a fleeting second.

Chapter Fifteen

In her room at The Warwick Hotel, Corina had made herself comfortable on the settee in front of the television. She was wrapped in a bath robe after she had got out of the shower; her hair was still wet and uncombed and the water dripped down the back of her robe. She flicked the channels over; UK television didn't have that many channels, so it was easy to choose what she wanted to watch. She came across a programme called Prisoner Cell Block H on channel 4 and got into the storyline straight away. America had many channels to choose from, but this had always made it very difficult for her to make an easy choice when she was in Boston and she usually ended up turning it off after she got frustrated with too much choice. But she found Prisoner Cell Block H was quite amusing to watch, especially when she noticed the scenery had wobbled on occasion. There was a gentle knock on the door and she could hear James ask if he could come in. Corina got up and let him in. She thought he looked very smart and that he also smelt lovely, as she got a waft of his Chanel aftershave when he entered the room. She had always been a Chanel girl and would wear no other perfume. She watched him as he came and stood beside her. He was tall and very handsome and his jet black hair was pruned to perfection. He had obviously made an effort for her.

"You fancy going out for something to eat, Corina? I figured I no longer have to persuade you to come back to Boston, as you have already made your own mind up, so why don't we try and make the most of Carlisle while we are here. We are flying back tomorrow night, so tonight we can relax a little" James looked at her and patiently waited for her reply.

"Can I just finish watching Prisoner Cell Block H first, it's hilarious!" Corina sat down again and patted the seat next to her for James to join her.

Corina was right, the Prisoner programme was funny, though James thought the producers hadn't really realised how lame it looked and that it must have had a very low budget.

"Look, James" Corina laughed "There's Vinegar Tits, that's what they used to call me at work!"

"Vinegar Tits? But, she is a hard faced screw. You don't look anything like that!" James looked closely at the screen "Did that wall just wobble then?"

"Yes!" Corina giggled loudly, but then stopped abruptly and began to look very uncomfortable.

"What's up, Corina?" asked James. He watched her get up and head towards the bathroom.

"I shouldn't be having so much fun, its disrespectful to Joseph to be laughing with his best friend like this" explained Corina, nervously.

"Corina, I know its early days, but you are allowed to have some fun…what are you going to do, wear black and mourn for the rest of your life? Just relax; nobody can expect you not to laugh when you find something funny. It's good to see you laugh. Come and sit back down and we will finish watching it"

"No, I'm just going to get dressed and dry my hair, then we can go out. You stay and watch it if you like" Corina quickly disappeared into the bathroom with her clothes and shut the door.

James sighed and carried on watching the programme.

The programme had been finished for fifteen minutes before James thought to himself…how long does it take for her to put some clothes on and dry her hair?

"Are you nearly ready, Corina? I'm starving!" he shouted to Corina.

The door opened and out came Corina. She was dressed in a short and very tight black dress, along with high heels. The dress accentuated her attractive figure and her legs looked in great shape in the high heels. For someone who had just had a baby, James thought she looked gorgeous, so much so he had to stop looking at her and make himself think about something else. The huge erection he had made his pants feel too tight and he was sure Corina would notice.

"Shall we just eat in the hotel, James? It doesn't feel right that we may end up going to a place that I used to go with Joseph"

"Sure, anywhere you want, Corina" James replied quickly whilst he covered his erection with a cushion.

"Come on then, let's go" Corina thought James looked a bit uncomfortable and gave him a curious look.

"Ladies first" James let Corina pass him before he got up, he was pretty sure she hadn't noticed anything.

Corina was pretty sure James had got an erection and tried to avert her eyes as he got up.

'I've still got it' she thought to herself, as she walked down the corridor to the lift. She still had that certain something that doctors couldn't resist when she was a student nurse. She had no idea what it was, but she could have had a different doctor every night at The Cumberland Infirmary, if she had wanted to. But, she had chosen not to sleep with every man that tried to get her in bed and was very picky about which doctor she had shared her bed with. She only had eyes for Joseph.

James chose a table in a quiet corner, so he could talk to Corina about what he had found in Joseph's office when he had cleared out Joseph's things from his desk. They both ordered their choice of food and started to drink the bottle of wine that had just arrived. James thought Corina looked relaxed and she looked like she was enjoying herself, though she was drinking the wine a bit too quickly for his liking.

"Slow down, Corina, drinking that much on an empty stomach will get you drunk before the food comes out!"

"That's the whole point, James" Corina winked at him and she knew by his uncomfortable look that he had just got another erection.

James decided there and then that he wouldn't tell her about what he had found in Joseph's office, he would leave it until they were both safely back in Boston. If she was going to get drunk, he didn't want her to make a scene in the restaurant. He also wished his penis would behave, but he found her extremely attractive tonight and couldn't help but get aroused.

"Soooooo, James" said Corina playfully "Why hasn't a handsome doctor like you got a girlfriend yet?"

"I've been concentrating on my career.... and the girl I really like was already taken"

"Well, Doctor Patton, life is too short to be concentrating on your career, you need to get out there and find yourself a wife. You should have some fun, while you still have your good looks and you don't need Viagra.... if you know what I mean?" Corina winked at him again, she could tell he still had his erection.

He wished she would stop winking at him, it was driving him wild.

The food arrived and James sincerely hoped it would soak up some of the alcohol that Corina had thrown down her throat.

"Could we please have another bottle of whatever that was?" Corina asked the waitress.

James hadn't even finished his first glass yet, but Corina had drunk the rest. He gave the waitress a 'Please, take your time' look. She immediately understood and served the other tables before she bought the wine over. By which time Corina had finished her food.

"I'm stuffed" she sat back and rubbed her stomach "That reminds me, could you please take my stitches out tonight, James? I'm all healed now"

"Well...."

"You do know how to take stitches out, right? You haven't forgotten, since you became a high ranking oncologist at The Massachusetts General Hospital?" she accentuated her Boston accent to tease him.

"I haven't got anything here to take them out with, Corina. That's why I paused"

She leant over the table to James; he got a glimpse of her cleavage as she whispered seductively into his ear "You could always take them out with your teeth while you're down there"

"Corina, I......"

"Oh, come on, James! Are you coming back to my room with me or not? I know it's me you have fancied all of these years. I'm not stupid.... and anyway, Joseph told me years ago. I need some male company and I haven't had sex for ages. So, I figured its better the devil you know, so come on let's go upstairs...... that erection you've had all night tells me you're gagging for it" she played footsie with him under the table and ran her foot up into his crotch area. It may him feel very aroused and he couldn't resist her.

James thought he might as well make the most of her, as he knew once she found out what he had found hidden in Joseph's office, he would probably never see her again.

....

It was four-thirty in the morning and James was still awake, he watched Corina while she slept. He didn't feel guilty that he had slept with his best friend's wife, as he had waited a long time for that to happen.... almost ten years in fact. There certainly was no guilt when he thought about what they had done with each other, because he had never had sex like it. It was mind blowing and he wanted more. Corina looked so beautiful to him just lying there and he thought her naked body was so sexy. One of her arms was above her head, so he could see the cuts on her wrist. The steri strips had closed the wounds up nicely, but they were still red and he thought they must still feel sore. He wished she hadn't mutilated her own body because of what Joseph did and he knew she must be embarrassed about the scars as she was constantly trying to cover them up. He ran his finger gently over the scars and down her arm into her armpit, he then followed the curves with his finger over her breast and down along her tummy to her caesarean scar. He had managed to take the stitches out quite easily....and he hadn't needed to use his teeth. Corina stirred and slowly opened her eyes; she looked curiously at James when she noticed he was staring at her.

"What's up, James.... are you feeling guilty about having sex with your best friend's wife?" she teased him. Her voice sounded sultry as she was still sleepy.

"No, not at all.... are you feeling any pangs of guilt?" he tickled her armpit and this made her squirm.

"Nope, but it looks like I picked the wrong doctor for the best bedroom fun.... I mean, Joseph was good.... but bloody hell James, you were amazing!"

Corina pulled back the sheets and then climbed on top of him to straddle him.

"You wanna do it again, Doc?" Corina lent over and teased him with her lips; she hovered her mouth above his, as if she was going to kiss him, but then pulled away. Her long, brunette, wavy hair covered both of her breasts and as she sat up again, he pushed her hair out of the way to behind her shoulders, so he could caress her erect nipples.

"Oh my God, Corina, you drive me wild" he flung her back over onto the bed and covered her with his naked body, he pushed her legs apart with his foot and entered her with his big throbbing penis "Of course, I wanna do it again" he whispered into her ear "I've wanted to do this for years!"

Chapter Sixteen

"You okay, James? You're looking a bit thoughtful" Corina asked James, as they sat and ate their breakfast together in the hotel restaurant. James was thoughtful, he was thinking about what he had found in Joseph's office and wondered if he should tell Corina or not.

"You're not feeling guilty about what we did are you, James? Because there's really no need, we were both consenting adults and technically we are both single. And, I actually don't feel guilty one little bit as I really needed those orgasms!" she giggled at him whilst she ran her hand down towards the inside of his thigh. James looked at her, he wondered how she could be so blasé about it all. Only yesterday morning, she had sat and stared at Harriet's wall in her bedroom and wouldn't speak to anyone. Then, last night she was worried about having a laugh over a television programme. The day before, she had ranted and raved like a mad thing when she threatened to have the bodies flown back to England. Now, she was acting like nothing had happened over the past few weeks and last night she had basically seduced him. Not that he minded the being seduced part, but he didn't want it to all end in tears.

"No, I'm not feeling guilty, but I am worried about what Alberto will say when he finds out about what we've done. He sent me over here to bring you back to Boston, not to fuck your brains out!"

Corina giggled again "He is never going to find out, how would he? I'm not going to tell him…. are you? Come on, James; let's make the most of it here. It will soon be all doom and gloom again, when we get back to Boston" She stabbed a sausage with her fork and shoved it into James mouth "Eat up; I'm just going to call a taxi to take us to the station. We need to get back to London in good time to catch the flight tonight to good 'ol Boston town!"

Corina got up and took a few steps to leave, but then walked back to James' side of the table and whispered seductively in his ear "If you play your cards right, big boy, you may get to become a fully paid up member of the mile-high club!" she placed her hand on his crotch and gently caressed him until he got another erection. Then stopped, kissed him, and walked away again.

James watched her walk away and thought she looked hot in her short skirt, blouse, and flip flops. He wondered if she had realised it was pouring with rain outside and he hoped she was going to change her footwear before leaving for the station. He had no idea how it was going to pan out with Corina back in Boston. Would she still try to get in his pants or would she suddenly come hurtling back to earth with a bang when she had to deal with the aftermath of Joseph's suicide?

In the meantime, he was going to make the most of Corina wanting him. He had wanted her for a long time, so he was going to savour every last minute of her affections towards him.

After she had ordered the taxi, Corina phoned Harriet and said her goodbyes again, she told her she would be back in a couple of weeks and could she please keep an eye out for somewhere for her to live. She would also need a new job. She thought that would be interesting trying to find one if her registration had been taken away in America. She wondered if it counted in England…she would have to find out, and quick, or she would soon run out of money once she had found herself somewhere to live. Corina went up to her hotel room and lay down on the bed for a sneaky rest before James came up to find her. She started to think about James and began to feel turned on by him again. The thought of sex with James also made her feel a bit shocked that she had feelings for him so close after Joseph's death, but it surprised her that she hadn't felt any guilt. Though, she did feel like she had got back at Joseph by sleeping with his best friend, as she knew Joseph would have hated it if he was still alive, but she felt Joseph had betrayed her by killing himself. She hoped he had seen it all from where ever he was and he would feel jealous. Then, she realised that was a ridiculous thing to think, as she had no idea where he was.... but she felt smug anyway.... that she might still have upset Joseph after his death.

Anyway, sex with James had taken her mind off of things to come, like facing Mary and Alberto....and the funeral. She was dreading the funeral.

"I've paid the bill, Corina, and the taxi is outside. You ready?" James popped his head around the door "You're not sleeping are you? Can't take the pace, huh?"

"Oh, I can take the pace alright. It's you yanks that can't keep up!" Corina rolled off the bed and slid her feet into her flip flops.

"Corina, it's pouring down outside, why don't you change your shoes!" James laughed at her.

"Naaaaaa, its summer, I'm wearing my flip flops. Now, let's go before I get you on that bed again, I am feeling incredibly horny again for some reason!"

James hoped her good mood would carry on when they arrived back in Boston. He wanted to make love to her again and he was definitely enjoying her playfulness. No wonder Joseph had fallen in love with her, she was insatiable. Alberto and Mary might think it a bit strange though, as she really was acting like she didn't have a care in the world.

To James' amusement, the same taxi driver that took him to Harriet's house was waiting outside of the hotel to take them to the station.

"Good Morning, Yank Boy!" he yelled from the open window of the taxi "I see you've pulled, aye?"

Corina giggled and got into the back of the taxi with James. She cuddled up to him and tickled him on the stomach. He put his arm around her and kissed her cheek. They looked like any other happy couple to an outsider; no one would know that Corina was recently widowed or that she had just lost her baby. It was like they were in another world; a parallel universe, pretending to be happy and not have a single thing to worry about.

"No snogging in the back of the taxi, please, Yank Boy" the taxi driver winked into the rear view mirror at Corina.

"How's your sheep?" asked Corina, as she threw James a naughty look. She knew he would talk for hours about his sheep. James was not amused; he had heard it all before. This was going to be a long, boring journey to the station for James, but Corina found it hilarious.

Chapter Seventeen

Corina was in her bed back at The Four Seasons and she felt exhausted after her flight back to Boston with James. All that travelling in a short space of time, back and forth to countries with different time zones, had taken it out of her. They had both joined the Mile High Club and that part of the journey had made the tiredness worthwhile. Making love in an airplane toilet was not one of her finest moments and she was pretty sure everyone knew what they were up to, especially when James had to cover her mouth to stop her from making too much noise at climax. She couldn't wait to see James again and had arranged to meet him at his house, once they had both got some well-earned sleep. He said he had wanted to show her something, but she had no idea of what it might be. With that thought, she began to doze off again.

"Corina, dear" she could just about hear Mary in her sleepy state, as she knocked on her bedroom door "Can I come in and see you?"

Corina thought she would be mad when she saw Mary again, but in fact, she felt absolutely nothing. It was weird to her that she'd had so much emotion and anger when she found out that Mary knew about Joseph's plan, yet now she felt numb. She had switched off to everything and all she could think about was James. Mary came in and sat on the bed. She looked very uncomfortable and paused for a moment before she began to open up to Corina.

"Corina, I have regretted not telling you what I knew every day since Joseph died and I hope you can please try to forgive me now. I really didn't think he would do it so quickly, I thought I would have had time to talk him out of it" Mary started to cry. She felt vulnerable, as Corina just stared at her and her eyes seemed to glaze over almost instantly. She expected Corina to show some sort of emotion, to cry, or even shout at her. But, there was nothing, not even a reassuring touch on her hand that she normally gave her if she was ever upset about anything "I know you may not agree with me, but he loved you very much, and he begged me not to tell you. He felt he was doing the right thing; he obviously wasn't expecting you to come home from work so early to find him. He would never have wanted you to see him like that" Mary began to get herself into an emotional state and she could barely get the words out "Please Corina, I need you to understand"

"Yeah, whatever, Mary"

Corina shrugged her shoulders and rolled back over on to her other side, so her back faced Mary. Corina had thought in England that she was going to have it out with Mary and wanted a good reason why she had kept it quiet. But, now she just couldn't be bothered, so she went straight back to sleep, leaving Mary gob smacked that she had got nothing back from her. Not one single flicker of emotion and not one single tear. Mary quickly left the room and headed straight to the kitchen to tell Alberto.

"Alberto, Corina has gone from being emotional and unreasonable, to not showing anything at all. She didn't even shout at me, she just shrugged and then turned over and went straight back to sleep!" Mary cuddled Alberto and cried onto his shoulder, making his shirt soggy with her tears.

"Mary, my dear" he tried to reassure her "She is grieving and she probably can't cope with anymore, so she has switched off. It's quite normal after having such a traumatic experience. I'm sure it won't be long before she kicks off again, so let's just leave her to sleep and we can make the most of the peace and quiet"

Mary hoped that was the case, but she wasn't looking forward to seeing the angry, unreasonable Corina again. Corina had almost seemed happy when they had picked her up from the airport this morning, she had a spring in her step as she laughed and joked with James. Mary couldn't take it in and thought it was very strange, so she would keep a close eye on Corina.

……

Later that day, when Corina had finally got herself up and organised, Alberto agreed to take her over to James' house in his car.

"How are you feeling, Corina?" Alberto enquired, as they drove along the highway to Quincy.

"You know, there's no reason why I can't use my own car whilst I'm back in Boston, Dad" Corina ignored his question "You could drop me over to my house to get it, then I could drive to Quincy myself"

"We are nearly at James' house now, Corina. And, I just asked you a question!" he was surprised that all of a sudden she had started to call him Dad again.

"I'm fine, Dad. Don't worry about me. You just look after yourself and Mary. James is being good to me, so really, don't worry" Corina sounded flippant and this annoyed Alberto slightly. She seemed very robotic to him and he felt like he was being fobbed off.

"How can you possibly be fine, Corina? Now, that's just silly!" he pulled over into a safe zone, as he could feel the anger as it started to bubble up inside of him "How do you expect me not to worry about you? You find your husband dead, your baby dies, then you try to kill yourself and now you are acting like you don't have a care in the world. You haven't mentioned Joseph once since you got back and you haven't shed a tear. I expected you to still be upset with Mary, but you have just blanked her!"

He knew it was probably grief and possibly her way of coping, but he needed for his own peace of mind for her to show him some sort of emotion. He pulled out of the safe zone and he carried on driving in silence. There was still no reaction from Corina, she didn't even flinch, she just stared out of the window and ignored him.

As they pulled up outside of James' house, Alberto decided to ask her about James and whether or not he was coping okay with the death of his best friend and work colleague.

"Is James okay, Corina? He must be finding it very difficult too, after knowing Joseph for most of his life"

"Oh, he's great. Especially now he gets to fuck me whenever he feels like it!" Corina got out of the car and began to walk briskly up the drive, leaving Alberto reeling with anger. He quickly got out of the car to follow her, then ran to catch her up. He felt enraged with what Corina had just said.

"Corina, I want you to get back in the car. We need to talk about this" he grabbed her arm and tried to pull her back towards the car.

"There's nothing to talk about. Your son blew his own fucking head off, so James is picking up the pieces. I felt lonely; so I banged him.... I needed to feel loved, I needed some dishy male company. I don't need your sort of old man company, now get off of me!" she struggled to get away from him, but he wouldn't let go.

"But, with Joseph's best friend? Now, that's pretty low, Corina! I'm not going to allow this to happen. You are coming back with me, whether you like it or not!" he shouted loudly at her, he hoped she would snap out of her ridiculous need to be with James.

James had opened his front door, he had heard the commotion from inside of his house and he wondered what was going on. He started to walk down the drive towards them.

"Get back inside, James, I'm taking Corina home with me" Alberto yelled at James.

"What the hell is going on, Alberto? You can't force her like that. Let her go!"

Corina fought hard to get away, but Alberto had no intention of letting her stay with James and held her tighter, so she could not release his grip on her.

"I trusted you, James. I sent you to England to bring her back, not make a move on your best friends' wife. You disgust me, you both disgust me. I didn't realise my son had married a whore and a heartless one at that!"

"Let me go, please, you're hurting me!" Corina pleaded "I'm sorry, please let me go!"

"I've had enough of this, Alberto" James shouted "You have to let her go. Your son was no angel, I can assure you!" he waved a large brown envelope in front of Alberto's face, the envelope that had been hidden in a draw back in Joseph's office "Now, please calm down and let her go. We need to go inside and talk about what I've found"

Corina and Alberto looked at each other with curiosity in their eyes; they both wondered what was in the envelope. Alberto let go of her arm and rubbed it gently with the palm of his hand. He could see he had bruised it as there were finger marks imprinted on her skin. She gave him a loathing look when she noticed the bruises had appeared, then turned away in a huff and followed James up the drive and into the house. Once inside, James offered them a coffee but they both refused. They both just wanted to know what was inside the envelope.

"Come on, James. Let's see what's inside the envelope" Alberto was getting impatient with James and his stalling.

James handed him the envelope, he then took a step back and held his breath in anticipation of Alberto's reaction. He knew Alberto was not going to take lightly what he was about to see. Alberto went pale after he had pulled out the two big photographs that were inside, he then looked at the letter that was with them. It soon became apparent to him that his son was being blackmailed. He quickly put them back into the envelope so Corina could not see them and handed it back to James. James stared at Alberto and thought he was being very calm about what he had just seen; he hadn't expected him to be as cool as that.

"What is it? I want to see" asked Corina, curious as to why the colour had drained from Alberto's face so quickly.

"I don't think that's a good idea, Corina" Alberto looked at her with tears in his eyes. What he had just seen disgusted him more than the thought of Corina and James sleeping together.

"James, just give it to me, I want to see" she snatched it out of his hand and quickly ran to the downstairs bathroom. She locked herself in, so both men could not stop her from looking at the contents of the envelope.

Once inside the bathroom she stared at the photographs in astonishment. She wished she had taken Alberto's advice and not looked at them. She couldn't believe what she was looking at. The photographs were of Joseph and another man. In one, they were kissing and in another they were in a very compromising position. Her husband had been sleeping with a man. Her stomach turned and she started to cry. She looked at the letter and read the demands on it. Whoever was blackmailing him had wanted money and also drugs from the hospital. They wanted it quickly or they were going to send copies of the pictures to her and Alberto. She suddenly realised this would have pushed Joseph over the edge, no wonder he had wanted to end his life so quickly. She thought the whole story about him loving her so much and not wanting her to see him die was bullshit.

She unlocked the door and went back into the lounge. She threw the envelope onto the table in disgust and turned to look at Alberto. Alberto looked noticeably upset and shaken, she could tell he was trying to hold back his tears. She felt angry again, she needed to get out of James' house and back to the Four Seasons before she exploded with emotion.

"I would like to go home now" she said quietly to Alberto.

"Corina, you shouldn't have looked at those" Alberto got up off of the couch and moved towards her. He held out his arms and gestured at her to hug him.

"Get off me, don't even touch me!" she pushed his arms away from her and then quickly left the house to go and sit in the car. She patiently waited for Alberto in the car so he could drive her home. He took a while to come out and when he finally appeared, she noticed he didn't have the envelope with him. He must have left it with James to sort out; James was good at sorting problems out, she thought to herself.

The journey home felt awkward and was in complete silence. They had no idea of what to say to each other or what they were going to do about the letter and the photographs. They were both in complete shock and Corina's anger swirled around inside of her, ready to burst out at any moment. Nothing was said about the photographs when they got back home either. They both went straight to their bedrooms and hid themselves away. Corina threw herself onto her bed, buried her face into her pillow and screamed into it; in the hope it would make her feel better. It didn't. She wondered if Alberto would tell Mary. Then, she thought that Mary probably knew already. Joseph had probably told her when he told her of his plans to kill himself. It was probably another secret that Mary had kept to herself. She could not hear Alberto talking to Mary in their bedroom. In fact, there was an unusual silence. She got up off of the bed and wandered quietly back out of her bedroom and into the kitchen. She found Mary doing a crossword puzzle at the kitchen table. She had already sneaked Alberto's car keys, which were on the kitchen worktop, into her handbag on the way into the kitchen to see Mary.

"Would you like a coffee, dear? I've just been in to see Alberto and he is having a lie down; he said he's not feeling well"

"No thanks, Mary. I think I'm going to go for a walk in the gardens" Corina wasn't surprised he had gone to lie down; he was probably feeling as sick and angry as she was.

"You are coming back again, right?" Mary gave Corina a concerned look "You are not planning to disappear again…. are you?"

"No, Mary, I just need to stretch my legs and get some fresh air. I promise I will come back"

Corina put her hand on Mary's shoulder and Mary lowered her cheek and snuggled into it. Mary was pleased she had shown her some sort of affection; she couldn't stand it if Corina hated her.

Corina didn't go to the gardens; she went straight to reception and used the phone to call James.

"James, I need to see you. We need to talk about those photographs. I'm going to drive over to see you. Okay?"

"Okay, Corina" He felt excited that she was coming over, even though it was in unusual circumstances, but he just needed to see her. He couldn't get what had happened between them in England and on the plane, out of his mind.

It took her about thirty minutes to get to James' house in Quincy. She parked the car on his drive and waved to James, who had come outside to greet her. They both went inside and sat in the lounge. James had already made a pot of coffee, which he had placed on the coffee table alongside the brown envelope. James sat close to Corina, he went to put his arm around her so they could kiss, but she refused his advances. Instead, she picked up the envelope and took out the photograph of her husband and the mystery man kissing. She held it up to show James.

"Do you know who this is James? We have to find out who it is.... I need to speak to him. I want to know what has been going on and for how long."

James looked at the picture; it was obvious that it had been taken from afar. It was also obvious that Joseph had no idea that it had been taken of him.

"Look, James, I don't care about who the blackmailer was, he can't do anything to us now, as Joseph is dead. I just want to know if my husband was really gay. None of this makes any sense. We were so in love and had a healthy sex life. We never argued.... yes, we had our little disagreements, but there was never a raised voice in our house. Look at the picture again and see if you recognise the other man...please!"

James felt very uneasy, he knew exactly who the man was. He was an intern at the hospital. An intern that was addicted to amphetamines. An intern that would do anything to get his fix and that included sleeping with a fellow doctor, especially when he had been paid by somebody else to do it. The promise of a regular flow of drugs was a big incentive and James knew this. That's why James had paid him and that's why James had arranged with the intern to meet Joseph in a certain place, so he could take the photographs without Joseph's knowledge. And, that's why he had made the story up about finding the envelope in Joseph's office. James had always wanted Corina for himself, but he wanted to hurt Joseph more. He had taken advantage of the time they'd had a drunken boy's night out. Joseph had confided in him that sleeping with a man was on his bucket list. Not because he was gay, but because he just wanted to try it. Joseph had a very high sex drive and always wanted to try new sexual experiences to satisfy his needs. He had told him that Corina had talked about the time she had slept with a woman consultant whilst doing her nurse training, she had done it just to find out what all the lesbian fuss was about…so what was the difference? Once Joseph got ill and had his cancer diagnosed, James had encouraged him to do it. But, little did Joseph know that his bucket list experience had all been photographed without his knowledge. He also wanted Joseph to know he was sleeping with his wife; he wanted to make Joseph suffer before he died of cancer. Joseph had always got want he wanted. Joseph had always made a move on James' girlfriends, every girlfriend he had would always end up sleeping with Joseph. Then, he would dump them and move on to the next girl that fell for his good looks and charm. He was surprised that Corina had lasted so long. Joseph had obviously really loved her, that's why James had taken the perfect opportunity to blackmail his friend. But, James didn't know Joseph was going to kill himself, so things hadn't gone to plan. Joseph had never actually seen the photographs or the note; he'd killed himself before he had got the chance to read it.

"Sorry, I have no idea who it is" James told Corina coldly and poured himself a coffee. He didn't bother to look up at her.

"How will I find out who it is then, maybe I could hire a private detective or something? This is all so bizarre, James. I don't believe for one minute that Joseph was really gay. What shall I do?" Corina was confused as she looked at the photos again. Joseph didn't look like he was enjoying it. Something wasn't quite right.

"I think you should try and put this out of your mind now, Corina"

James knew Corina wasn't stupid and he didn't want her to start to dig about and find out it was him who had instigated the whole thing. Before he had got close to her, he had only wanted to sleep with her to hurt Joseph; he wanted to use her like Joseph had used his girlfriends. But, he had real feelings for her now and he didn't want to lose her. He was cross with himself that he had shown everything to Alberto and Corina, but Alberto had made him mad by hurting Corina and trying to force her back into his car. He knew he should have kept it to himself as he didn't want to ruin everything now.

"How can I put this out of my mind, James? I've seen it now. I just want to know who he is!"

"Leave it with me, Corina, I will see what I can find out" he moved closer to her and gave her a comforting cuddle. Again, he tried to kiss her, but she moved away from his face and wouldn't allow him to kiss her.

"James, you know I am still going back to England, don't you? I hope you don't think that our relationship is going to progress any further, as I can't stay in Boston. Once the funeral is over I will be gone" she at looked him straight in the eye "It was only sex…. you do understand that, right?"

Corina did have real feelings for James, but she couldn't carry on any relationship there in Boston. She could not stay there to be reminded daily of her husband's betrayal and she couldn't upset Alberto any more than he already was.

"James, you do understand, don't you?" she stared at him and wondered what was going through his mind.

James understood, alright. He understood that Joseph and Corina were made for each other. They were exactly the same type of person, in the fact that they both knew how to play people to get what they wanted sexually. James looked at Corina and gave her a wry smile.

"I understand, Corina. I understand perfectly"

Chapter Eighteen

The morning of the funeral had arrived and Corina absolutely dreaded what the day had to bring. Alberto had avoided Corina for days since they had found out about the photographs, but Corina didn't want to broach the subject with him either, so she was happy to be avoided. She assumed that if he wanted to talk about it, he would come to her. Corina was also too scared to ask Mary if she knew, in case she didn't know and if she did know, Corina would most definitely feel betrayed again, so either way it was a catch twenty-two situation. Corina could hear all of Joseph's family in the lounge as they talked amongst themselves; some even laughed and joked around. This made Corina feel rather uneasy. Why were they laughing when they were about to go to a funeral? She thought it was very disrespectful to her when they knew she was in the apartment. But then, this was the family that she hadn't seen since Joseph had died, they hadn't bothered with her, so she had gone out of her way not to come in contact with any of them. She felt they would blame her anyway, so she was relieved she hadn't seen them. When she entered the lounge with her head down, there was an awkward silence.

"It's okay, you don't have to stop talking and laughing on my account" mumbled Corina. She felt uncomfortable because she could sense them studying her as she walked across the room. When she finally looked up to see them looking at her, some of them looked sympathetic, others looked blank and tried to avoid eye contact with her. She ignored them and went over to the sideboard and poured herself a very large brandy. Alberto came up behind her and whispered in her ear.

"I need a word please, Corina. Outside"

She followed him out into the foyer, swallowed the brandy down in one gulp, then waited for him to speak.

"Now, Corina, I've been meaning to speak with you about what happened at James' house the other day"

Corina looked at him defiantly and shrugged. She knew what was coming, so went to walk off. She didn't want to listen to him if he was going to slate her and James for sleeping together. It was old news as far as she was concerned.

"Don't you dare walk away, Corina" he snarled in her ear "This is important" He held onto her arm and forcibly directed her out of the front door and into the hallway.

"What is it with you, Dad? Don't you think you've bruised my arms enough?"

"I just want to talk to you. Now, please listen. I do not want those photographs mentioned today; in fact, I never want them mentioned again, EVER. Do you understand me, Corina?"

"Why are you so cross with me? I didn't know anything about the photographs and I'm just as shocked as you are about them"

"I am not cross with you, Corina. I am just feeling very stressed and I don't want my family in there finding out about the photographs.... or about you sleeping with James. I am sorry if I have hurt you, but I am burying my only son and grandchild today, so I want it all to go smoothly. There must be no shame brought upon this family today. Do you understand me, Corina?"

"Yes, but...."

"Corina, why are you wearing black?" Alberto interrupted "I thought we agreed we would all wear bright colours, so we could celebrate Joseph's life"

"Let me think.... oh yes.... probably because I am in mourning, my husband and baby are dead.... remember?" Corina snarled back at him, sarcastically "And, anyway, you never told me about that, because you haven't spoken to me for days. I'm not a mind reader!" The brandy had made her feel very brave, but when she saw the reaction on Alberto's face, she realised she probably shouldn't push him any further.

"Please go and change, Corina. Before the cars get here" he pointed at the door to try and will her to go back and change.

"No, I will not. Why would I want to celebrate the fact that my husband killed himself?" she put her face right up to his "I am Joseph's wife and I will be wearing black. If you don't like it…. tough!"

"You gave up the right to call yourself my son's wife the day you started sleeping with James"

Corina didn't show any remorse as she walked away from Alberto. She would not let that comment upset her today. Today was not a good day to justify her actions with James to Alberto. Alberto's face was red with anger. He didn't want his feisty Italian temper to get the better of him, so he decided to let Corina walk away.

….

Corina had felt pretty much okay within herself, until she entered the huge room where the coffins were stood at the end of the aisle. There were lots of seats either side of the aisle that were filled with people that wanted to pay their last respects to Joseph. He was a well-respected Doctor, so many of his patients had come to say goodbye. She noticed Noah was there and Roger from Vegas. The Masshole had turned up and he squeezed her hand and smiled at her as she passed him. He had brought Rory and Andy with him, and Britt. Britt gave her a supportive smile and then burst into tears. She felt so sorry for Corina; she couldn't help but cry, she had really liked Joseph. She thought they were the perfect couple and was very shocked to hear about what had happened to Joseph and then to the baby.

The coffins were both matching. There was a big white coffin for Joseph, his picture was placed on top and was surrounded by white lilies. Baby Joseph was laid inside a tiny white coffin, there was a blue teddy bear on top and daisies were placed around the teddy bear. Suddenly, Corina realised that she was about to say goodbye to her husband and baby for the last time and she felt like she had been punched in the heart. She was so overcome with emotion that she could not stand up. She collapsed in a heap on the ground and Joseph's Uncle Giuseppe rushed over to help her up. She managed to get to her seat with his help and she sat down, but she could not stop the loudness of her sobs. The mourners looked at her in sympathy and she tried with all her might to cry quietly, but she just could not stop. She wished she had stayed in England; she didn't want to face burying the husband and baby that she loved so much.

"Corina, where are you going?" Alberto tried to attract her attention without having to raise his voice. She was headed towards the coffins at great speed. He watched helplessly as she threw herself at Joseph's coffin and tried to hug it.

"I'm so sorry, Joseph. Really I am, please forgive me"

Corina tried to hug his coffin. Her arms could not fit all the way across it, so this made her slide onto her knees. All of a sudden, she felt extremely guilty that she had slept with James. She also felt bad that she had shouted at Joseph, back at the house in Milton, that she didn't understand or forgive him for ending his life.

"I love you, Joseph, I do understand and I do forgive you"

Everyone looked at her in complete shock, most people found it too difficult to watch, so broke down in tears. Alberto struggled to pull her away. She grabbed Joseph's picture and held it close to her chest as she chanted that she was sorry, over and over again.

"Corina, please...Everybody is looking at you. Please, stop this now" Alberto whispered into her ear "He knows you are sorry, now come and sit down" He was worried that she might mention the photographs, but he managed to get her to go back to her seat.

Corina sobbed all the way through the service and all the way to the cemetery. She held onto Alberto as her son and husband were laid to rest. She hid her face in his jacket so nobody could see what a mess she looked. Mary cuddled them both and they all cried together. Once everyone had thrown a handful of earth onto the coffins, they made their way one by one to speak to Corina to say how sorry they were. She could not speak, but nodded at each and every one of them that approached her. She was introduced to David, the telephone operator that had taken Joseph's 911 call. He had never had someone kill themselves whilst on the telephone to him before and it had stuck in his mind. In fact, he was going to engage in a course of counselling to help him come to terms with it, but he was desperate to pay his respects to Corina. Corina tried to thank him for coming, but she could not get the words out. She shook his hand and hoped he would be okay. She knew it must have been terrible for him to get such a call and she was grateful that he had made the effort to come to the funeral to see her.

Alberto made an announcement that there was going to be a get together back at The Four Seasons Hotel and hoped they could all join the family for a celebration of Joseph's life, when he suddenly noticed a man that watched them from behind a tree that was close by. He looked at Corina to see if she had noticed that they were being watched. She had noticed and she also recognised him, as did Alberto. They both froze, not knowing what to do. He was the mystery man in the photographs.

…..

Back at the Four Seasons, Corina tried very hard to be polite to everyone that approached her to give her their condolences, but she was totally drained and felt she could no longer speak to these people that she didn't know, when she suddenly realised that James hadn't attended the funeral. She made her excuses to get away from an old lady that talked to her about how Joseph had cured her and went to find Alberto. He was in deep conversation with his brother Giuseppe and glared at her when she interrupted their conversation.

"Have you seen James? I wanted to tell him we saw the man at the cemetery" she whispered into his ear.

Yet again, he forcibly pulled her to one side and growled angrily at her "I told you this morning, we are not going to mention anything to do with those photographs again. Just leave it, Corina. My son was not gay and you are not to ask James for any more help with trying to find out who that man is!"

"But aren't you just a little bit curious? I just want to know what has been going on and for how long! Now, have you seen James or not?"

"Corina, you will stop this now. It will bring no solace to you if you dig deeper than you have to. It was obvious it was a one off. And, I have told James not to show his face today, he is not welcome!"

"How is it obvious? And, James was Jo's best friend, people will think it's strange that he never came…. I'm going to call him to see if he will come over"

Alberto started to lose his patience again, he began to take deep breaths to try and calm himself down. It didn't work, and he snapped at Corina again.

"You will not call James; I have told you he is not welcome here and this conversation is ending now. I am the head of this family and what I say goes. You will respect my wishes and you will not talk about the photographs again. Do you understand me? Now, please go and speak to Mary, she is looking like she needs rescuing from that old lady"

Corina looked over and spotted the same old lady that had chewed her ear off with conversation previously. She had got Mary backed up into a corner and Mary looked desperate to get away. Corina was curious to know why Alberto had suddenly pulled out the 'I am the head of this family' card; he had never said that before. He was always such an easy going loving man, just like Joseph, but everyone's lives had changed since Joseph's death and their emotions had continually caused them to say, and do things, that were out of character…. apart from Mary. She was still Mary, pottering around, being maternal and keeping secrets…. she was good at keeping secrets. Alberto glared at Corina again and motioned his head in Mary's direction. She knew she had to go and rescue her and quick, before Alberto got cross again and lost it with her.

"I'm so sorry to interrupt" Corina sidled up next to Mary "But, could I please have a word with my Mom?"

She smiled sweetly at the old lady and then led Mary away to her bedroom.

"Thank you, Corina. She was wearing me out!" they sat down on the end of the bed, both of them looked pale and tired "And, it's lovely to hear you call me Mom again, I have missed that, you know"

Corina ignored the Mom comment as she hadn't meant to call her that at all, it had just come out without her realising. She grabbed Mary's hand and held it tight "Do you have anything else to tell me? Like something you think I should know about?"

"What do you mean, Corina?" Mary looked baffled as she placed her other hand on top of Corina's.

"I mean, have you told me everything you know about Joseph and why he killed himself? There's nothing more that's going to pop up in another family argument when I least expect it, is there?" Corina waited for Mary's reaction, she studied her every move. She could normally tell when someone was lying, her psychiatric training and her work in the prison had taught her many things about people. The training had taught her about body language and how to tell whether people were lying to her or not.

"Joseph loved you so much Corina, he ended his life to put a stop to the cancer that was eating away at his brain. There wasn't anything any doctor could do to cure him and he didn't want you to see him suffer. You just got home from work too early and I'm sure, in fact I know, he didn't want you to find him like that" she looked at Corina and straight into her eyes "I know you think I am a bad mother for not warning you and I know I probably should have told someone, but it all happened so quick. And, as his mother, I understand totally why he did it. I just wish you had not found him like that, but I will do anything to help you, my dear, you know that don't you?"

Corina knew she was telling the truth; she wasn't hiding anything else from her. Corina was glad she didn't know about the photos and she would keep it to herself and not ever tell Mary. She didn't need to know about what Joseph had done behind their backs.

"Can I persuade you to stay here in Boston, honey?" Mary looked at her with tears in her eyes "I don't want you to go back to England; I'm worried I'll never see you again"

"I'm all set to go back, Mary.... of course you will see me again. You can come over whenever you like and I'll show you all the sights. I'll even show you where Joseph proposed to me and all the places we used to go. You will love it over there!"

Mary looked sad, she knew once Corina was back in England there would be no contact from her. She could tell that Corina was never going to forgive her for keeping her sons' suicide secret to herself. But, she would make the most of Corina while she was still in Boston and she would show her as much love as possible. She knew Corina still had nightmares. She could hear her night after night when she screamed out Joseph's name. She could not begin to imagine what it must have been like to find the man you so desperately loved, in such a horrific way. Mary hugged Corina and stroked the back of her hair, she had always wanted a daughter and even if Corina didn't realise how much she loved her, she would never stop loving her for the rest of her life. She would always be her daughter, where ever she was.

"Come on, let's go back and face the music" Corina gently pushed Mary away; she couldn't help but feel betrayed by her and hoped the feelings of hurt would eventually go away.

"I do love you, Corina" said Mary softly, as she got up off of the bed.

"I know" Corina replied flippantly "Come on, people will start to wonder where we are"

Chapter Nineteen

The next morning, Corina knew she had to go and see James and tell him that she had seen the man at the cemetery. Mary had gone off shopping to stock up on supplies and Alberto was sat in the kitchen while he looked at The Boston Globe newspaper, he didn't bother to look up when she entered the room. He just let out a sigh and shook the paper to straighten the pages up.

"Not speaking to me again?" she sat down opposite Alberto and poured herself some orange juice from the jug that was still on the table from breakfast.

"You are late for breakfast again, Corina. Mary wanted to take you shopping with her this morning" he didn't even look up from his paper again; he continued to look as if he was engrossed in whatever article he was reading.

"Oh, I'm sorry. I didn't realise I had to be at breakfast at a certain time, or go shopping. I'm not a psychic, you know, and I'm getting slightly pissed at your attitude towards me lately. But, don't worry DAD, I shall be out of your hair soon"

"Yes, running away again, leaving Mary and I to pick up the pieces!" he slammed the paper down onto the table so hard that it startled Corina, which in turn made her spill her juice onto her skirt.

"So, I am still being punished for sleeping with James, right?" she wiped her skirt with a napkin "And, what's with this, I'm the head of the family, shit yesterday. Have you suddenly become part of the Mafia or what?"

"Don't be silly, Corina. I have explained everything to Giuseppe and he thinks I should take control of the situation before it gets out of hand"

"Before it gets out of hand?" Corina couldn't believe what she had just heard "Right...so being an asshole is taking control of the situation is it? And, where does that idiot get off telling you what to do.... was he here when Joseph died? No! Did he visit every day? No! Did he come and see me in the hospital? No! Did he even come and say he was sorry to me yesterday? No! He didn't! So don't let him tell you how to handle things. This is not you, this is not how you behave, you are normally a lovely, placid, thoughtful man. The Alberto I know would never bruise a woman's arms like that.... and what do you mean, you've explained everything to Giuseppe?" Corina didn't stop to take a breath "You better not have told him about me and James; you know how sorry I am about that. It was a mistake; I just wanted to feel loved! What's wrong with that?" Corina started to cry; she held her head in her hands and tried to cover her face so Alberto could not see the tears that poured down her face.

Alberto didn't know how to react and deep down he knew he shouldn't be so hard on her, but he was so disappointed in her and James, he couldn't help it. If it was anybody else, he would have understood, but James, Joseph's best friend.... He could not get the thought of them together out of his mind.

"Please don't cry, Corina. I don't mean to upset you, really I don't. I just didn't know what to do. It has been a very hard for all of us to see you in such pain and I don't want you getting involved with James anymore. Will you promise me you won't go and see him again?"

"No, I can't promise you that. I was going to go to the hospital to see him today; I need to find out who the man is that was watching us yesterday at the cemetery. I can't brush it under the carpet like you; I have to know what's going on. I wish you would just accept that!"

Alberto thought for a minute. He knew he couldn't keep the hard man act up for much longer and it would only push Corina away even further. He desperately wanted her to stay in Boston too, just like Mary did. She was still their daughter, even if Joseph wasn't around and she would always be their special girl.

"Okay, Corina. I will support you in this as long as I am there every time you see James; I do not want you to be alone with him. Is that a deal?" he got up from his chair and went around the table to Corina. He opened up his arms and encouraged her to give him a hug. She nuzzled into his chest and wrapped her arms around him, she was thankful that they had both come to an amicable solution at last. She loved Alberto more than she loved her own Father and she hated being in his bad books. She was happy to respect his wishes and see James with him. She knew she couldn't trust herself anyway, she didn't want to be put into a position where she would end up sleeping with James again.

"Dry your eyes, sweetheart, we can go to the hospital now before Mary gets back" he kissed the top of her head and squeezed her tight, which left her feeling secure and loved.

....

They both decided to walk to the hospital, so they could get some fresh air and exercise. It was another dry, warm, sunny day and downtown Boston was busy. Lots of people rushed around them to get to work and they noticed the holiday makers that ambled down the street slowly as they took in all the sights.

"You used to be like that when you first arrived, Corina, do you remember?" he laughed at her, he remembered her face when she saw Boston for the very first time. He had picked up Joseph and Corina from the airport when they had arrived from England. Everything had seemed so huge to her then, it was a far cry from the small Cornish fishing village she had been brought up in before she had moved to Cumbria to be a nurse.

"Yes, I took photos of everything. Now, I can't wait to leave!" she realised she had said the wrong thing, when she noticed Alberto's smile had disappeared from his face "I'm not happy about leaving you though, Dad" she tried to reassure him and linked his arm with hers and they carried on walking down the street.

As they approached the hospital, they both paused simultaneously and looked at each other.

"When we see James, shall we play good cop, bad cop?" Corina asked, then gave him a cheeky smile.

"Behave.... but, I'll be bad cop" he winked at her and then they headed for the oncology department, still arm in arm.

Rachael looked up from her desk to see Corina and Alberto as they walked towards her. She sighed to herself and expected that there might be trouble from Corina, so stood up to greet them with "I must warn you that I am not averse to calling security up here, I don't care whose wife you used to be!"

"There's no need for that Rachael, so if you don't mind, please could you tell Doctor Patton that Doctor Alberto Barsetti and Mrs Corina Barsetti are here to see him?" Alberto grinned at her with the biggest smile that he could muster up.

Rachael took one look at him and melted back into her seat. He was very handsome for an ageing man and she could see where Joseph had got his good looks and charm from.

"We didn't see you at the funeral yesterday, Rachael. I would have thought that working with Joseph for a few years, you would have liked to have paid your respects" Corina glared at her which made her feel uncomfortable again.

"I couldn't get time off. Now, if you would like to take a seat, Doctor Patton will be with you shortly. He is just with a patient. He won't be long" she said snootily to Corina, as she pointed to the seats in the waiting room.

"Joseph always said she was a bitch anyway!" said Corina to Alberto, as they found themselves a seat; she made sure Rachael had heard what she'd said.

"Corina, please don't get stressy. You always get like this when you're stressy. Let's try and remain calm" he placed his hand on hers and stroked the top of it lightly, hoping she would calm down. He knew she didn't like being where Joseph worked at the best of times and it was even worse for her now Joseph was gone. Alberto looked over at the office that used to be Joseph's; he thought to himself that he would like to have Joseph's name plate and wondered where it was. He went back up to the desk and asked Rachael politely if he could have it. She rummaged through a couple of boxes that James had put by her desk and then pulled out a very bent name plate from one of them.

"You mean this one?" she held it out to him and pointed at Corina with her other hand "I'm afraid SHE bent it, when she threw it on the floor in front of a patient the last time she was here!"

Alberto turned and looked at Corina, who in turn shrugged her shoulders and tried not to look guilty.

"Thank you Rachael, I'll take it like that, I will soon have it straightened again" he went back over to Corina, shook his head at her and said "Really?"

She felt like a two-year-old being told off, but she couldn't help the rage she was in that day.

"You should have seen the dirty look she gave me, and anyway she's lucky she didn't have it shoved up her……"

"Ahh, James. Good to see you again" Alberto stopped Corina in her tracks, as he stood up to shake James' hand. Corina thought Alberto was being very calm and gentlemanly like today, she was glad the angry Alberto had disappeared.

"Corina" James went to kiss Corina on the cheek, but Alberto pushed her gently towards James' office, so there would be no bodily contact between them.

They all sat in James' office and looked at each other in anticipation as they waited for someone to speak first. James looked very uncomfortable again. Corina thought he had the same guilty look on his face that she saw the last time she came to his office.

"Why the uncomfortable look, James?" Corina questioned him "Have you found out who was in the photographs with Joseph?"

"No, I just wasn't expecting you and I have a patient arriving shortly. You really should have phoned and made an appointment"

"Actually, James.... those that betray me and sleep with my son's wife, don't get the choice of when I turn up!" angry Alberto was back again.

"Uh oh" Corina mumbled to herself.

Alberto turned and looked at Corina "Let me handle this please, Corina" he then faced James and looked deep into his eyes "So, you are telling us, James, that you don't know who the person is in the photographs?"

"No, I'm afraid I don't, now if you don't mind, I really need to get ready for my next patient" James stood up, Corina noticed that he looked remarkably shaken.

"Well, that sure is funny, James, because when I confided in my brother Giuseppe about what you and Corina did, I also mentioned that Joseph was being blackmailed. I then showed one of the photographs to him to see if he recognised the man, but guess what he did after I left him?" Alberto paused whilst he stared at James with an evil look "Without my knowledge, he decided to go around to your house to talk to you about it and offer his help to you to find out who the blackmailer was"

Alberto stood up and towered over James. Corina's heart started to race, as the look on Alberto's face told her he was not being so calm and gentlemanly like anymore.

"Now, imagine Giuseppe's surprise when he pulls up outside of your house and who should be leaving.... Yes, the man in the pictures.... the same man that turned up to the cemetery yesterday and tried to hide behind a tree!"

He grabbed James by the throat and forced him up against the wall. Corina turned white; she had never seen Alberto act like this before.

"Oh my god, James, what have you done?" Corina stood up and tried to prise the two men apart, but she didn't have the strength to pull Alberto away.

"I want you to tell me what the hell is going on and I want to know who that man is" Alberto squeezed so hard on James' throat that he had started to turn blue.

"Jesus Christ, Dad, let him go. You're killing him!" Corina started to scream, she tried with all her might to pull Alberto away, but he continued to squeeze James' throat. She ran and opened the office door to alert Rachael. "Now would be a good time to call security, Rachael!" she yelled at Rachael, then went back into the office to try and stop Alberto from strangling James to death.

"Dad, please let him go. Security is on their way and you don't want to be arrested for this piece of shit!" she tugged at Alberto's arm to try to get him to release his fingers from around James' throat.

Alberto suddenly snapped out of his rage and released his grip on James' throat. James fell into his chair; he coughed and spluttered as he tried to get his breath back.

"You will tell me what you know now and when security gets here, you will get rid of them, or I swear to God I WILL kill you!" Alberto held James' head up by his hair and shouted into his face.

Corina didn't know what to do with herself, she was so frightened that Alberto would do something silly.

"I don't think I want to know anymore, now let's get out of here, Please Dad, you're scaring me!" She begged him. She was so desperate to leave, that she didn't care what explanation James had to give them. Corina wished she had dropped the subject when Alberto had asked her to. Why was she so stubborn? She thought to herself. He must have known yesterday, that's why he was so angry. He had just tried to protect her. He obviously knew James was up to no good, that's why he had wanted to come with her and make sure she was never alone with James.

"Well James? I'm waiting!" Alberto scowled at James as he waited for his response. James looked terrified and tried to speak, his voice cracked up and he started to cough again. Security had turned up, so Corina went outside of the office to meet them. She tried to explain that everything was alright, but they were adamant that they checked the office to see if Doctor Patton was okay. When they entered the office, Alberto gave James a warning look and James confirmed to security that he was okay. Alberto watched them leave and then went over to James again. Corina didn't want Alberto to hurt James again, so she was ready to call out to security for help.

"James, just tell him, please!" Corina pleaded with him.

"I set the whole thing up" James told her quietly. She could hardly hear him.

"What?" Corina couldn't understand what he had just said.

"I set the whole thing up, I got an intern to approach Joseph and sleep with him and I took the photographs" James hung his head in shame "I was going to blackmail him"

"But, why James? Joseph was your best friend" Corina was stunned at what James had just said.

"Yes, come on James, let's hear why!" Alberto had started to lose his patience again, so Corina held his hand tight to make sure he didn't make another move on James.

"I was jealous and I wanted to hurt Joseph…. he always took everything from me, everything!" James put his head in his hands and realised how stupid he must have sounded "I'm sorry Corina, I just wanted you and I wanted Joseph to see us together. But, you were both so in love, there was no way I could get near you. So, when he found out he was dying, he told me about his bucket list wish and what you had talked about"

Corina looked at Alberto with a puzzled expression on her face; they were both confused as to why James was so jealous of Joseph.

"So, you thought you would make the last few months of your best friend's life hell by blackmailing him?" Alberto was so mad "You are a sad excuse of a Doctor and if my son wasn't involved in this, I would make sure you never practised medicine again!"

"Joseph never saw the photos, Corina. I promise. He never knew anything; as far as he was concerned he had done everything he felt he needed to do on his list and he died still loving you"

James started to cry and hoped for some forgiveness. He realised what a complete idiot he was and regretted that he had let his jealousy for Joseph take over his life, but he just couldn't help it. He had a jealous personality and he only became a doctor because that's what Joseph had wanted to be. He wanted to be a somebody and being a doctor got him noticed, people respected him and he could get away with most things.

"I don't know what sort of mess you have gotten yourself into, James, but you tell that intern never to come near me or my family again. And, that goes for you too, do you hear me?" Alberto stood over him again, which made James cower back into his seat.

James nodded, he looked at Alberto in complete fear and said "I hear you"

Corina didn't know what to make of any of it, but she thought James had got off quite lightly when she considered how angry Alberto was. She got up and walked out of the office, she couldn't bear to look at James, so didn't bother to say goodbye. She waited by Rachael's desk for Alberto to appear. Rachael didn't know what was going on, but she daren't ask Corina, so they just ignored each other. Alberto came out of the office in tears, he held out his hand to Corina and they both left the oncology department for the last time. They both felt extremely deflated and confused. When they got outside, Alberto stopped and hugged Corina.

"Life is so precious, Corina. You need to go and do what Joseph wanted you to do, you need to try to live life to the full. You must live every day as if it was your last. And, if that means you have to do that in England because you don't want to be here in this place surrounded by bad memories, I will understand, and you have my blessing…. as long as you promise never to lose contact with me and your mom" he held her tight and cried into her long brunette hair, whilst hid his face from the outside world.

"I promise, Dad. You will always be a big part of my life. And, don't forget, I had mostly good memories here, thanks to you and your family, and of course Joseph…. It's just that the bad ones seem to have taken over my mind and I know I could never settle here again. Don't cry, Dad, I'll only ever be a plane ride away" she wiped his tears away with her hankie and kissed his cheek.

Arm in arm, they slowly walked back to the apartment, they enjoyed the sunshine and reminisced about the good times in Boston. Their new lives were just starting over, but they both could not imagine a new start without Joseph.

Chapter Twenty

For the past week, Corina had been very busy as she finalised plans for her move back to England. Her flight was booked for the next day and she dreaded the fact she would have to say goodbye to Alberto and Mary. She had been in touch with Harriet, who had found her a flat to rent close to Harriet's house and Harriet had kindly sorted out payment for the deposit, so Corina could move straight in when she got there.

"Mary....umm, I mean mom...if you could keep on at the realtors for me about selling the house quickly, that would be great. I don't want them dragging their feet, as I will need the money to live on until I get another job" Corina had tried to make an effort to start to call Mary mom again, but it was still hard for her to accept that Mary knew about Joseph's cancer before she did.

It was seven in the morning and Mary and Corina ate their breakfast at the kitchen table. Corina felt stressed and anxious about getting everything done in time and wondered where Alberto was. Alberto was still in the shower though; they could hear him as he sang his favourite Pavarotti song.... badly. They both looked at each other and giggled. They had a busy day ahead of them before their final dinner together that night. They had decided to go to The Boston Harbor Hotel to make the most of their last evening together. It seemed only fitting that they should have dinner there, as it was the hotel that Corina had first met all of Joseph's family at their wedding party all those years ago.

"What about all the furniture, honey, and all of your personal things?" Mary didn't think Corina had thought everything through or organised everything properly. She thought she was in too much of a rush to get back to England.

"The furniture can be included in the sale, I'm going there today to box up my personal stuff and I'll put it in storage for the time being. I'll let you have a key, so when I'm ready for it all, do you think you could send it over, do you mind doing that for me?" Corina watched Mary's facial reaction and she could see Mary was getting upset about her leaving.

"That's fine, Corina" she tried hard to hold back her tears "Oh, I nearly forgot to tell you, I bumped into James yesterday and I told him you were leaving tomorrow. He seemed sad to hear you were leaving so soon. I told him you would probably be at the house today sorting things out, so why don't you give him a call, dear, maybe you could meet him to say goodbye?"

The thought of James made Corina cringe, but she pretended to Mary that she would call him later. Poor Mary was none the wiser about James; she had no idea of what he had tried to do to Joseph and she had no idea that Alberto had tried to throttle him at the hospital.

"I bet he misses his friend though, Corina. I asked him why he didn't come to the funeral too, as I was surprised he wasn't there"

"So, why didn't he come then?" Corina was interested to hear what excuse he had come up with.

"Apparently, he had to do an emergency operation at the hospital, dear. How unfortunate for him that it should be when his best friends' funeral was on" Mary poured herself another coffee "He said he would visit the grave though and pay his respects"

"That'll be nice" Corina said fleetingly "Would you be able to sell our cars too please, Mom? I totally forgot about the cars!"

"I'll get your Dad onto that, if you don't mind. Cars are not my thing, dear" she stirred a little milk into her coffee "I wish you didn't have to go, I shall miss you dreadfully"

"I know, but as I said to Dad, I'm only a plane ride away and I'll call and write, I promise"

"Did someone mention my name?" Alberto was out of the shower and was dressed and ready for action "If I drop you off at the house,

Corina, I'll go grab some boxes from Giuseppe. He said he had some you could have"

"Okay, great. I'll just grab my jacket and we can go" Corina kissed Mary on the top of her head as she passed, then disappeared into her bedroom to get her jacket.

....

Alberto pulled up outside of the house in Marilyn Road to drop Corina off. Corina looked at the house and let out a huge sigh, she turned to face Alberto as if to say something, but nothing came out. She didn't need to say a word. Alberto knew she wasn't happy about going into the house again and either was he. He hadn't been there since the day Joseph had died and he didn't know how he was going to react being back inside the house again.

"I'll try not to be too long Corina, but you know what he's like when he starts yakking!" he kissed Corina on the cheek before she got out of the car and he watched her go up the drive and into the house. Giuseppe lived in Canton Avenue, so it wasn't too far away, but he knew Giuseppe's constant talking would be the thing that held up his return with the boxes. He thought Corina had lots to do to keep her occupied while she waited for him anyway, so he hoped she didn't mind the wait on her own.

The door was still shut to the lounge when Corina got inside the house. She didn't think she would ever return to that place again and the atmosphere felt strange and eerie. She also felt a little scared to be there by herself and wished she had gone with Alberto in the car to Giuseppe's. So, she decided she wouldn't sort the lounge out until Alberto had come back and went into the kitchen to grab some bin liners. She then headed upstairs to her bedroom to sort out her and Joseph's clothes. She took all of her clothes that she couldn't take with her to England and put them in the bin liners, so she could donate them to the needy. She did the same with Joseph's clothes, but kept his stethoscope and his old University of Massachusetts Medical School sweater that he used to wear when he had trained as a doctor. She sat down on the bed and burrowed her face into it so she could cry. She felt very emotional again and she didn't really want to be sorting his clothes out alone. She wondered if Mary and

Alberto would like something, when she heard the front door open and bang shut again downstairs.

"That was quick, Dad" she peered down over the spiral bannister to see where Alberto had gone "I'm upstairs, can you bring a few of the boxes up here with you, please?"

"With pleasure!" James sneered up at her, as he appeared at the bottom of the staircase.

"James, what the hell are you doing here? Alberto will be back soon; he will go mad if he sees you here!"

"I've come to say goodbye to you, Corina" James started to make his way upstairs. Corina could see the look of hatred in his eyes and she wasn't sure whether to stand her ground, or run and lock herself in her bedroom until Alberto had come back. But, her body had made the decision for her and she found she couldn't move.

James approached her and shouted in her face "Get in the bedroom!"

"James, you're scaring me, why are you behaving like this?" she didn't move, so James pushed her with such force that she landed on her bottom in the doorway of the bedroom. He then made his way behind her and pulled her forcibly by her hair, so she was out of the way of the doorway. He slammed the door shut and then locked them both inside. Corina was extremely scared and started to scream out for help.

"Nobody can hear you Corina" snarled James at her "Nobody comes near the death house anymore; that's what people call this place you know…. THE DEATH HOUSE…. even the kids cross the street to get past it. I wish you the very best of luck selling this place!"

Corina struggled to get up. Her coccyx throbbed and the pain shot up through her back and into her neck. She tried to grab hold of her bedroom chair to try and balance herself, so she could get up, but James kicked her feet out from underneath her and she fell back onto the floor again in excruciating pain.

"I didn't say you could get up, bitch!" James shouted at her, he then watched her as she cowered away from him. She began to try and hold her ankle still with both hands to help ease the pain of his kick.

"James, why are you doing this?" she cried at him in agony. Her ankle had snapped with the force of his kick.

"It's payback time for you using me, you can also be punished for Joseph's wrong doings towards me too" he bent over her and held her chin up so their noses touched each other's. She could smell bourbon on his breath and the pain from her ankle made her yell out in agony.

"You are fricken nuts, James!" she screamed "I don't ever remember Joseph being horrible to you. Please, let me go. I need to get my ankle seen to, it really hurts, James please!"

He didn't let go of her face, but banged her head hard against the wall to shut her up. Her head began to spin, so she couldn't focus and the pain from her ankle had begun to make her feel nauseous.

"Did you know there's a very fine line between love and hate, Corina?" he continued to push his nose hard up against hers "I've been thinking about you a lot lately and I have decided that if I can't have you, then nobody can. Because, I don't actually love you anymore, Corina……I fucking hate you!" he slammed her head hard against the wall again "I've decided you can be with Joseph again, as you both deserve each other!"

Corina still couldn't focus on his face; in fact, she couldn't focus on anything and James didn't seem to make any sense to her. She could feel a small trickle of blood, that ran out of her nose and then dripped off of her chin and down onto her blouse. She found it difficult to hold her head up and resigned herself to the fact that James was going to kill her. James picked her up and threw her over his shoulder, he unlocked the bedroom door and then carried her downstairs to the lounge. Corina noticed a gun stuffed in the back pocket of his trousers, but she couldn't move her arms to reach it. Her head felt strange, and she had to close her eyes to try and stop her head from spinning. The blood that continued to drip from her nose made a trail on the carpet from the bedroom, right down the stairs and into the lounge, and as he threw her onto the couch her ankle banged against the coffee table, which made her scream out in agony again.

"Shut your mouth, whore!" he squeezed her jaw and forced her head back onto the back of the couch.

Corina had started to hallucinate; she was sure she could see Joseph stood behind James. She so wanted it to be him and she thought he had come to get her, so they could be together again.

"Joseph" she mumbled to the blurred figure of him. She tried to hold out her hand to touch him, but she still couldn't lift her arms and in reality, there was nobody there anyway.

It was only James, but he was determined to end her life. He didn't seem to care about the consequences; he didn't seem to care about anything at that moment in time. He was a sociopath and had planned her death since Alberto had tried to strangle him in his office. He was determined that Alberto wouldn't get away with what he had done to him and he would use Corina to hurt him. Corina was quite a handy tool for getting back at the Barsetti family, so when Mary had told him that Corina would be at the house today, he knew it would be the perfect time to kill her. He had waited patiently in his car a block away, for Corina to drive past him to get to the house. He decided he would make it look like suicide, as he would make sure he shot her in the lounge, so the authorities would think she had done it to be with Joseph. She had already tried to kill herself once in the house, so they would think that she was the desperate widow losing her mind. They would definitely think she had wanted to be with her beloved husband again. He pulled the gun out from behind him and teased her with it. It made him feel very much in control.

"Which way would you like to die, Corina? Would you like to be shot in the temple or have me put the gun in your mouth and shoot you that way? Just like your cowardly husband…. how 'bout it?" He forced the gun into her mouth and banged the back of her throat with it, he laughed at her when she started to gag, as he could see she was petrified. He loved the control he had over her now. She would do anything for him and it was very gratifying for him to watch her squirm as she tried to move her head away from the gun.

"Not so happy to die today, huh Corina?" he slid the gun back out of her throat and mouth and placed it hard up against her temple, then moved it slowly down over the side of her face and down her neck and into her cleavage. James moved the gun from side to side, so it ripped the buttons of her blouse off and he began to peer at her breasts through her lace bra. He started to feel aroused, so placed the gun on the coffee table so that he could touch her.

"Maybe we should have one last fuck for old time's sake, do you fancy that Corina?" he leant over and nestled his face into her neck and kissed her gently, whilst he moved down slowly towards her breasts.

"WHAT DID I TELL YOU ABOUT COMING NEAR MY FAMILY AGAIN, JAMES?" shouted Alberto, armed with the gun that he had always kept in the glove box of his car to protect himself.

Alberto had noticed James' car parked a block away when he was on the way to his brother's house. He had felt uneasy about it, so he'd decided to come back to the house to check on Corina. He was thankful that he did, as Corina didn't look very good at all. He thought she looked dead. The startled James tried to grab the gun off of the coffee table, but in haste knocked it flying onto the floor.

"Don't do it James, or I will shoot you!" Alberto was all set to shoot him if he moved, James froze as he knew that Alberto meant was he said.

Corina hadn't moved an inch as she was unconscious. The blood ran from her nose and ear, also her ankle looked so badly broken that it was not in the correct position. Alberto knew she needed medical attention quickly, so picked up the phone and called the police for help. He still had his gun pointed at James and he warned the police that he was prepared to shoot James if need be. Alberto begged the police operator to please send someone quickly, as he thought Corina was either dead, or dying.

"Why don't you just shoot me, Alberto? Go on, do it for your son!" James goaded Alberto, but Alberto remained calm. He would only shoot James if he felt threatened or if he hurt Corina again. James knew his life as a doctor was over and he would probably spend a long time in state penitentiary for what he had done to Corina. James decided in an instant that he wanted Alberto to shoot him to end his miserable life, so he threw himself to the floor to try and get the gun.

Alberto shot James in the top of the thigh to try and stop him from reaching for the gun. Then, in total disbelief and horror, he witnessed James pick the gun up off of the floor and shoot himself in the side of the head with it. James had killed himself instantly. James' body lay motionless in a pool of blood that gushed from his gunshot wound. Alberto stood still for a minute in complete shock.

There was a sudden realisation to Alberto that James could easily have shot him instead, as Alberto wasn't quick enough to move out of the line of fire. Alberto's mind suddenly sped back to reality and he rushed over to Corina, who has been plastered in blood from James' bullet to his head. He was relieved to find that she was still alive and breathing. He could hear the sirens from the ambulance and police, as they approached the house and he felt thankful that help was on the way so quickly. Corina needed to be in hospital and he was grateful that she hadn't been able to see James shoot himself. He knew she wouldn't have been able to handle that after all that had happened to her recently. He cradled her in his arms and waited for the medics to come into the house. He stroked her hair gently and cried for her and his son. He could not believe that even before his son had made the decision to end his life, something had triggered a spiral of hatred and deceit in James. James obviously had a past with Joseph that wasn't all fun, good times and laughter. But, they had both seemed such good friends and Alberto had no idea that James had it in for Joseph so badly. He tried hard to think of the times the boys had fallen out with each other whilst growing up, but nothing major sprang to mind. They'd had the usual tiffs that boys had, but they soon made up. James had always been in awe of Joseph and followed him where ever he went. Alberto had thought it was strange though, that James hadn't gone to England with Joseph to work in an English hospital, but there was now no way of ever knowing what had gone on between them.

Alberto felt very gullible for falling for James' charms and his offer of help with Corina, he knew it would take him a while to sort out and put straight in his mind what had just happened.

Chapter Twenty-One

Corina lay sedated in the hospital after she'd had an operation to relieve the swelling and bleeding inside of her head. Her skull had been fractured with the force of her head being smashed hard up against the wall by James. She had also needed another operation to pin her ankle back into place, but Mary and Alberto sat patiently by Corina's bed and hoped there would be no lasting damage from her injuries. Mary didn't want Corina to go back to England and wished the circumstances why she was still in Boston, were different. She would rather Corina had made her own mind up to stay and not be forced to stay because James had hurt her. Finding out from Alberto that James had killed himself too and what he had done to her family, was a big shock to Mary. She could not register it in her mind that James was capable of doing the bad things he had done. She knew full well that her son was no angel, as he had always been a bit of a handful growing up, but he had always had a kind and caring nature. She was thrilled when Joseph announced he was going to be a doctor and Alberto was so proud too as his son was following in his footsteps, he would have liked him to go into orthopaedics, but he was still just as proud.

She thought of Alberto and what he was going through. Her poor husband was having a hard time sleeping, and he was still having visits from the police to go over and over what had happened that day. Her family had made the headlines in all the papers, she also remembered watching the news that morning after coming home from shopping and seeing Corina's house on the television. This was before she even knew what was going on. They had shown someone being taken out of the house in a body bag and there were reports from neighbours that they had heard gunshots. The wait to hear from police, that it wasn't Alberto or Corina in the body bag, was a long agonising one for her.

Alberto put his arm around Mary; he could see she was finding it hard seeing Corina like that and coming to terms with everything that had happened to their family recently. She looked tired and upset and he knew she was worried about Corina's injuries. Corina looked so fragile lying there, she was hooked up to monitors and a machine was breathing for her. They were waiting for the doctors to come in and wake her up so they could see what brain damage there was, if any. They so wanted Corina to wake up and have no lasting effects, but Doctors could not give them a definite clean bill of health until after she was awake and able to pass certain neurological tests.

"Mary, when Corina is better we will take her back to England to settle her in and have a holiday there with her"

Alberto had to get out of Boston and soon. He needed to get his head straight, to come to terms with what had happened since his son had taken his own life. His head felt fuzzy, as he had so much to think about and sort out in his own mind. He had to admit to himself that he finally understood why Corina had run away from Boston to get away from everything. Boston seemed a very hard place to be in at that moment, he felt full of sadness and heartache for his family and he had to leave it all behind for a while. He just hoped Corina would be fit enough to fly back to England and he hoped she would wake up and be the Corina everybody knew and loved before Joseph committed suicide. Deep down, he knew that wouldn't happen, and deep down he knew Corina would be scarred for life with what she found that day. It would take her a long time to feel normal again and an even longer time to feel truly happy.

"That's a good idea Alberto, Dear" she hugged him and felt thankful that he was still with her. She would cherish every moment with him, because she loved him with all of her heart. She would cherish every moment with Corina too, as Mary loved Corina as if she was her own daughter.

"Do you think we should let her parents know what's happened to her, Alberto?"

Mary thought if it was her daughter she would want to know, but then they hadn't made any effort to contact Corina for the last ten years. Corina had never even mentioned them, so Mary knew she certainly didn't miss them. Mary could not understand Corina's parents; she would give anything to have her son here with her, along with Alberto and Corina, all alive and well and enjoying life. Some people do not deserve the precious gift of children, she thought to herself.

Alberto looked Mary straight in the eye and said "We are her parents dear, and we will love her and look after her until the day we die"

Chapter Twenty-Two

Corina was thankful that her flat was on the ground floor, as her ankle was still painful to walk around on. She was supposed to be using her crutches still, but it was awkward moving around with them in her flat as she kept bumping into things. There were boxes everywhere, so she mainly held on to the furniture to help her walk. It had been a couple of months since James had attacked her and she was happy to be back in Cumbria close to Harriet. Thankfully, she didn't have any serious brain damage from her head being smashed up against her bedroom wall in Milton, but she still suffered from dizzy spells and nausea.

She had only been back in Cumbria for two weeks and Alberto and Mary were staying with her so they could have a holiday. They needed a well-earned break away from Boston, but were happy to help her unpack everything and help settle her in. They really liked Cumbria and they were amazed at the size of the mountains and the wonderful scenery. The Lake District was the most beautiful place they had ever seen, they had taken lots of different photographs and taken in all the fabulous sights. They understood straight away why Corina had loved the place so much and wanted to come back. Even the air smelt clean and refreshing and the little villages were all so different to the towns in America, everywhere was so quiet and tranquil. They loved it, and were not really looking forward to going home without Corina.

"You know you can stay as long as you like, don't you?" Corina told Mary and Alberto, when they started to discuss going back to Boston "And, I'm not ready for you to go back home yet, I'm still feeling a bit wobbly in myself"

"Are you still feeling sickly, honey?" Mary asked her, whilst she felt Corina's forehead to see if she had a temperature "You do look a little bit pale; do you think we should take you to see a doctor?"

"Yes, I think we should take you to see a doctor, Corina and don't worry we won't be leaving you just yet!" said Alberto.

"I'm happy you are staying, and do you know what....I'm not even going to fight with you about going to the doctors, as I really don't feel right" Corina did feel pretty awful, the nausea and dizziness seemed a lot worse since she was back in England "I'll see if I can get an appointment with my old GP tomorrow"

"Good girl" Alberto kissed her on her forehead "Shall we have a wander into town and see if we can find a decent coffee shop? I haven't found the coffee machine yet and I don't think I can face any more of your English instant coffee!"

Corina knew where there was a nice little coffee shop, so they made their way slowly into town and down along to Bank Street. Alberto and Mary had to hold themselves back, so not to overtake Corina as she hobbled along on her crutches. James had done a good job of breaking her ankle and it was taking a while for it to heal completely. It was very painful to walk on and she still didn't have full movement in it where it had to be pinned. She couldn't believe James had killed himself too and she felt a bit responsible as she had pushed him away. She did really fancy him, but when she found out about the photos and his plan to bring Joseph down, she went off him pretty quickly. She had also heard all sorts about James from hospital staff that had worked with him and Joseph, apparently he had made a lot of mistakes and Joseph had to cover them up on many occasion. There were discrepancies found with drug prescriptions that were signed by James for patients that didn't even exist. The hospital was also investigating a whole host of complaints from patients. Obviously, James was not the person she thought he was, and even though she was sad that he was dead, she was relieved that he was no longer able to hurt her.

They all sat down at a little table in the window and ordered their coffee. All of a sudden, Corina felt a wave of nausea come over her and her head started to spin. She put her head between her knees in the hope that her dizziness would pass.

"Corina, we passed a doctor's surgery on the way here, maybe we should pop in there on the way back and get you an appointment? You don't look very well at all" Mary looked concerned and kicked Alberto under the table for him to back her up.

"Maybe I should nip down there now and see if I can get you an appointment?" Alberto jumped up out of his chair to grab Corina as she fell to the floor. She had fainted, but once she was sat back in her chair again she came back around quite quickly.

"Did you hear what we said, dear?" Mary rubbed Corina's cheek to wake her up a bit more "Dad is going to go down to the doctors and get you an appointment"

Corina nodded in appreciation, she was thankful to Alberto for going to the surgery for her; she felt terrible and wasn't going to pass up the opportunity to make herself feel better again. Mary had ordered some Victoria Sponge Cake for them all to go with the coffee, so when their order arrived they both tucked in and asked for Alberto's coffee to be served when he got back. The waitress was very attentive and offered her help to Corina, she could see Corina wasn't feeling too great and hoped she didn't faint again.

It didn't take Alberto long to get back from the doctors and when the waitress served him his coffee, he beamed a huge smile at her when he tasted it. He was happy to come back to the coffee shop again, they had excellent coffee and good service, what more could he ask for? He was in coffee heaven! Alberto drank all of his coffee and then motioned to the waitress to bring him another one. Corina grimaced at him, she was feeling sickly again and wondered how he could drink so much coffee.

"They were really nice at that surgery, Corina" said Alberto "I don't know why you don't like going to the doctors...but, I have explained everything that has happened and they said I could take you straight down there after we've finished our coffee. We may have to wait a little while when we get there, but a nice lady doctor said she would fit you in. So, that's great, isn't it, Honey?"

"Yes, that's great, Dad. Thank you so much" Corina had started to go green, as the coffee and cake hadn't gone down too well, so she got up to go to the bathroom. She knew she was going to throw up and hoped she could get there in time. She managed to get to the bathroom with the help of Mary and Mary gently rubbed her back as she vomited down the toilet.

"Oh, my poor baby, this sickness really is taking its toll on you" Mary continued to rub Corina's back until she had finished "Do you feel any better now?"

"A little bit, thanks Mom. I think we should go to the doctors now, I would rather wait there in case I faint again" Corina grabbed some hand towels and wiped her mouth clean. She felt terrible and really wanted to lie down and rest.

"Come on, let's go get your Dad and we'll head off" Mary helped her back to Alberto and after he paid the bill they all made their way slowly down the road to the doctor's surgery.

....

They all sat and waited patiently in the surgery, but they only had to wait about half an hour before Corina was called in by Doctor Alison Lightfoot. Corina followed the doctor down the corridor until she reached the doctors room. Corina thought she looked very young to be a GP, so thought maybe she had only just qualified. She looked very fashionable anyway.... not like her old GP that she used to have, he had appalling dress sense....and bad breath....it was enough to put her off going to the doctors for life. Alison held the door open for her, while she struggled in on her crutches and waited for her to sit down, she then sat down at her desk once Corina was comfortably seated.

"I hear you have been through a lot, Corina" the doctor swivelled around in her chair to face Corina "What can I do for you today?"

Corina didn't know where to start and burst into tears "I'm sorry, I didn't want to cry, but I feel terrible" she took a tissue that was being offered to her by the doctor "It's been a couple of months since I was attacked, so I was hoping my nausea and dizziness would have gone by now and my ankle is so painful still, I can hardly walk without crutches"

"I'm going to give you a thorough check over, Corina, as I obviously don't have any medical records for you here. Hopefully, we can get to the bottom of why you are still feeling poorly. Your ankle will take a while to heal, as from what your Dad said, it was a nasty break and had to be pinned. I will have a good look at it though…are you able to get up onto the examination table for me?"

Corina nodded and got up and lay on the table. The doctor examined her ankle thoroughly.

"Everything looks good there, Corina. I'm afraid you will just have to be patient with it; ankles can be very difficult things to heal. I will refer you to an orthopaedic surgeon, so he can review you and keep an eye on it"

"It's okay, my Dad is a retired orthopaedic surgeon, so he will keep an eye on it" Corina didn't want to make any fuss and she really hated going to hospitals for her own ailments. She would rather work in one, not be a patient.

"From what I gather, he will not be staying in Cumbria forever, so I will refer you anyway. I'm going to check your head now, Corina. Then, look in your eyes. Is that okay?"

"Yes, but I am feeling a bit sick again actually" Corina was worried she was going to throw up again.

"I have a bowl here, so don't worry" Alison started her checks and thought everything looked fine with Corina's head. Also, Corina's eyes were reacting to the light from her examination torch as they should be. Everything looked normal to her "Can I feel your stomach, Corina?"

The doctor carried on her examination and felt Corina's stomach, she also felt the area around her caesarean scar "Is there any chance you could be pregnant, Corina?"

"What?" Corina looked shocked "I don't think so"

"It's just that I can feel that your uterus is larger than normal, I can just about feel it above your pubic bone. That would certainly explain your sickness. If you could go to the toilet and do a sample of urine for me, I can do a pregnancy test straight away" the doctor watched Corina squirm in her seat when she mentioned the pregnancy test "Are you okay, Corina? I'll take some bloods too, when you get back from the toilet"

"Pregnant?" she thought of James and when she made love to him in the hotel, and then again on the plane" Oh my God, my Dad is going to go crazy!"

"You are a grown woman, Corina. Why would your Dad go crazy?" Alison didn't know the whole story; she knew Corina's husband had killed himself and that she had lost her baby. She also knew she had been attacked, but didn't know by whom. She didn't really have enough time to go through everything with Corina's Dad when he had come in earlier to try and get an appointment. It was just by chance that she was in reception, so she had chosen to speak to him after she had overheard him talking to her receptionist about Corina.

"It's a long story, but it obviously isn't my husband's baby. The father would be the man that attacked me; I had a sex with him after Joseph died. Oh no, this is awful" Corina started to cry again.

"Let's not jump to conclusions; we need to do the test first. You may not be pregnant at all" Alison tried to reassure her, but she was pretty sure she was pregnant "When was your last period?"

Corina had completely forgotten all about her periods. She was so used to not having one, because to her it seemed like she was pregnant forever and then when she stopped bleeding after having her son, she didn't have any more. So much had gone on between then and now, that her periods were the last thing on her mind.

"Ummm.... nearly 3 months" Corina felt stupid, she didn't think she could get pregnant so soon after giving birth. And, worst of all, she didn't even think about contraception and neither did James. They were so intent on making love to each other that they both must have totally forgotten.

Corina hobbled to the toilet, did a urine sample in the pot that the doctor gave her and then hobbled back with it…. trying not to spill it on the way. She closed her eyes whilst the doctor dipped in the stick, and then waited for a few minutes until the test brewed its result.

The doctor looked at the two blue lines that showed a positive result and took it over to Corina to show her.

"You are pregnant, Corina. There are two blue lines, so it's a positive result"

Corina didn't know what to say, she was so shocked that she had been stupid enough to get pregnant. She was silent through all of the rest of the checks that the doctor performed and while she had the blood test too.

"Come back and see me in a week, Corina. Also, if you could make an appointment at reception to see the midwife as soon as possible too…that would be great" said the doctor, she reached over and placed her hand on Corina's shoulder "Try not to worry, Corina. I'm sure everything will be fine"

Corina still didn't say anything and left the room, she was horrified at the thought of carrying James' baby. She limped over to Alberto and Mary and burst into tears again.

"What on earth's the matter, Corina, dear" Mary got up and cuddled her "Tell me what's wrong"

"I have to make an appointment to see a midwife" Corina sobbed onto Mary's shoulder.

"A Midwife?" Alberto repeated back at her "A Midwife, did you say?"

"Yes, Dad, I'm pregnant… I'm so sorry" she noticed the look of disgust on his face; she hadn't seen that look since the day of Joseph's funeral, and when Alberto had let her know how upset he was with her and James for sleeping together.

"Let's just go home and have a chat about it, Alberto" said Mary. She didn't want Alberto and Corina to make a scene in the waiting room, so tried to get them to leave straight away.

"Pregnant?" Alberto was stunned, he hadn't expected her to come out and say that. He had put the thought of Corina and James sleeping with each other to the back of his mind. He was far too busy trying to get the vision of James shooting himself out of his mind, rather than thinking about what they had got up to.

Mary and Corina were already at the desk making an appointment to see the midwife, so they hadn't seen Alberto leave the waiting room to go outside. He needed some fresh air to take in the news of Corina's pregnancy, he was not impressed at all.

"I don't think your father has taken the news too well, dear" said Mary to Corina, on their way out of the surgery. They looked around for Alberto, but couldn't see him anywhere.

Corina was still crying.... she hadn't taken the news of her pregnancy very well either.

Chapter Twenty-Three

Mary and Corina decided to go straight back to the flat in the hope that Alberto would be there waiting for them. But, when they got back Alberto was nowhere to be seen. The car that they had hired was gone from Corina's parking space, so they assumed he had already been back to the flat and taken it.

"He will be back soon, I'm sure. He's probably gone to Keswick to go and sit by the lake and have a think. He loves it there" Mary tried to reassure Corina, but she honestly didn't have a clue where he might have gone.

Corina knew he wouldn't be happy about her being pregnant, but she wasn't over the moon about it either. She didn't want James' baby. In fact, she didn't want anybody's baby at that moment in time. She just wanted to get her ankle fixed and then get back to work. She had already made enquiries to HMP Haverigg in Millom to see if they had any positions available for a psychiatric nurse. They were more than happy to wait until she was able to walk properly again. Her calibre of nurse was highly sort after, especially as she had worked in such a notorious American prison. She had shown that she could cope with the most dangerous of criminals, so a category C prison in England would be a walk in the park for her. Corina had no intention of working for the NHS so would also enquire to other prisons too, but this baby had completely ruined her chances of being offered a job.

"What am I going to do? I don't want a baby!" Corina looked desperately at Mary "Especially James' baby"

"Let's wait for your Dad to come back, then we can have a talk about it" Mary didn't know what she was going to do either and hoped Alberto would be able to think of something "Why don't you go and have a lie down, dear, you look exhausted"

Corina made her way to her bedroom to have a lie down. Hopefully, she would feel better after a nap and Alberto would have returned home.

....

Alberto had gone to Keswick. He parked the car in a supermarket carpark and walked down to the jetty to catch the ferry across to Portinscale. He sat on the marina in Portinscale and watched the boats go up and down. Some ducks swam past, along with a pair of magnificent swans. They looked majestic and were most certainly in love, he wondered if they would have a baby. He then shuddered at the thought of Corina carrying James' child. She would have to get rid of it. He would go back and insist she got an abortion. He would pay for it if need be. She needed to get on with her life, not bogged down with a psychopath's child. He got up and walked up the lane and along the road, thoughts of James ran through his mind and how sneaky he had been. He was a bit lost, so cut through the grounds of The Derwent Bank Hotel and bumped into the gardener who gave him directions on how to get back to Keswick on foot. He started to walk and after he passed The Derwent Water Hotel he found the footpath back to Keswick that the gardener had suggested he take. It was about a mile long, but he didn't mind, as he could practise in his head what he was going to say to Corina. He managed to find the supermarket where the car was parked and then began his drive back to Carlisle.

Mary looked out of the window and hoped Alberto would come back soon. She hated it when he went off without telling her, but he was doing a lot of that lately, especially back in Boston after James had died. Mary knew Alberto was having a hard time dealing with the aftermath of the recent events and she also knew he would be very cross that Corina was pregnant. Mary didn't know how to react about the pregnancy and she wasn't really sure how she felt about it. She always believed that everything happened for a reason and hopefully it would all make sense in the end. But, nothing really made sense to her anymore. She had lost her only son and James' parents had lost their son. She wanted to know why it had all happened and why it had happened to them. Surely there were evil people out there that deserved what her family had gone through?

They had tried to be good, kind people all of their lives, but still had to cope with the heartache. Life just wasn't fair.

Corina was awoken from her nap by the noise of her front door being slammed shut. The bang made her jolt upright. She had been in the middle of a dream about Joseph and she thought she had heard a gunshot. Her head started to spin again, so she lay down again to get her bearings and to stop herself from being sick.

"Corina, I want you to come out here please. We need to talk about this pregnancy business" shouted Alberto from the lounge.

"Alberto, she is having a nap. There's plenty of time to talk about that later" Mary was shocked by Alberto's insistence that they talked about it straight away.

"Mary, there is no time; she must be nearly three months pregnant by now. We have to arrange an abortion straight away!" Alberto was insistent and started to look in the yellow pages for abortion clinics.

"You can't make her have an abortion, Alberto. It's her body; we have to let her decide!" Mary didn't believe in abortion and was horrified that Alberto had even suggested it.

"It's okay, Dad is right. I need to have an abortion and quickly. It's probably for the best" Corina had appeared from her bedroom and she knew Alberto had her best interests at heart.

"No, Corina! You know how precious life is, how can you think of having an abortion when you haven't long lost your son to stillbirth. Please, think about this carefully…. please!" begged Mary.

Mary was upset; she didn't want Corina to get rid of the baby. It just didn't feel right to her. Mary glared at Alberto, who stared straight through her. He didn't care about this baby; it wasn't his grandchild, his grandchild was dead, dead and buried alongside his only son. He continued to try and find a clinic in the phone book and ignored Mary. Mary sat down on the settee and started to cry. Corina limped over to her and sat beside her. She put her arms around her and cuddled her to try and make her feel better.

"Please don't cry…. how will I ever explain to this child that's its father tried to kill me and then shot himself? I just can't cope with it and I need to go back to work. I can't afford to bring a child into the world. The house in Milton has not sold yet, so what am I supposed to live on?" Corina tried to explain to Mary, but Mary had an answer for all of her worries.

"Corina, you don't have to tell the child anything and we will help you with money...."

"No we won't, Mary...." Alberto interrupted "I am not financing a psychopath's child and neither will you!!" Alberto looked fired up; his Italian temper had started to show and Mary knew she had to back down, there was no use in arguing with him while he was in that frame of mind.

"I'll phone Doctor Lightfoot, I'm sure she can arrange an abortion for me" Corina went back into her bedroom to phone the doctors surgery and left Mary and Alberto to their disagreement.

Mary was determined Corina was not going to get rid of the baby, but Alberto was determined an abortion was the only way forward.

It was going to be a fraught and uncomfortable evening ahead.... for all of them.

Chapter Twenty-Four

It was two-thirty in the morning and Mary couldn't sleep. She lay awake with thoughts of Corina and the baby she was carrying. She thought to herself, maybe it was for the best that Corina had an abortion, as what else could she do? But, Mary hated abortion and would never dream of having one herself as she had so much trouble getting pregnant with Joseph. She had also had miscarriage after miscarriage when she tried for another baby after him. She would have loved a little brother or sister for him, but it was not to be. She then thought about James' parents and the fact that they should really know about Corina being pregnant, as she was sure they would like to have a say in what happened to the baby. But, whatever happened she knew she would stand by Corina with whatever she decision she came to and in the morning she would let her know that she had her full support.

....

"Did you manage to speak to Doctor Lightfoot about an appointment, Corina?" asked Alberto at breakfast.

"Yes, I did. But, unfortunately she won't refer me as she doesn't refer women for abortions, so I either have to go to another GP in her practice, or go to a private clinic" Corina was trying to eat her cornflakes, but began to feel very sick again "The sooner this baby is gone the better!"

"Well, I'll phone one of the clinics in the yellow pages and get you an appointment.... jeez, you look terrible, Corina!" exclaimed Alberto as he looked at Corina, she had literally turned green.

"Why, thank you.... will you please excuse me while I go and puke!" Corina excused herself, then limped slowly to the bathroom and muttered to herself about making it in time. She passed Mary in the hallway, so Mary waited outside of the bathroom until Corina came out again.

When Corina came out, Mary helped her back to her chair and then sat down to eat breakfast with her and Alberto.

"I just wanted to say, Corina, that whatever you decide to do, I will support you. I don't agree with abortion, but it's your body so the choice is yours. I am here for you, whatever you decide to do"

Mary looked at Corina with tears in her eyes; she noticed Alberto was smiling at her and he winked at her when he caught her eye. Mary did not smile back, she was not happy with the way Alberto had been so forceful yesterday and she was going to make sure he understood how unhappy she was about it all.

"Thanks, Mom. I really appreciate that. I know how difficult it is for you and I'm really grateful for your support" Corina could see how upset Mary was, so she reached over and squeezed her hand to let her know she cared.

"Right, where's that phone book? I'm going to phone a clinic" Alberto wandered through to the lounge to get the yellow pages and picked up the phone to call the clinic nearest to where Corina lived. The nearest private clinic that performed abortions was in Blackpool.

"Is Blackpool okay? I have no idea where that is!" Alberto shouted through to the kitchen from the lounge.

"Yes…If that's the closest!" Corina didn't care how far away it was, as long as she got an appointment soon. She could hear Alberto making an appointment for late that afternoon, so it would give them enough time to get to Blackpool.

....

On the way to Blackpool Mary seemed a bit quiet, Corina knew she wasn't happy about her having an abortion, even though she had offered her unconditional support. Alberto had completely brushed off Mary's feelings and point of view, so this had left Mary feeling very upset about the whole thing. Mary fidgeted in her seat and then went to say something to Alberto, but he interrupted her "What's wrong with you.... have you got worms or something?" he laughed at her and thought he would maybe cheer her up if he joked around.

She was not impressed at all and replied "I'm glad you think my uncomfortableness is caused by worms....is that your professional opinion as a doctor?" she glared at him and Corina knew an argument was about to erupt.

"Mary, I'm just trying to make you smile.... I don't really think you have worms!" laughed Alberto again.

Mary ran her fingers through her bobbed shoulder length hair, which was lovely and thick and completely white. Corina looked at Mary and hoped she would have such beautiful hair when she reached Mary's age. Corina could hear Mary let out a huge sigh before she gave Alberto a piece of her mind.

"Well, I don't feel much like smiling" she wriggled around in her seat again. Corina could tell she was about to tell Alberto something that he didn't want to hear "You know how everybody hated me for keeping Joseph's secret to myself.... well, I'm not going to do that again...I have learnt a hard lesson that it's wrong to keep secrets to try and protect other people.... so that's why I have called James' parents and told them that Corina is expecting James' child"

Mary looked at Alberto defiantly, it wasn't very often she stuck up for herself against him, but she knew she had done the right thing. She felt strongly that James' parents should know that they have a grandchild on the way. Their son was dead too, so she thought they should have a say in whether Corina got rid of the baby or not.

"Mary!" Alberto shouted at her "I think this is a bit different, don't you? For a start, James hurt Corina, he tried to kill her for goodness sake!"

Corina remained silent; she didn't really know what to say. She just sat in the back of the car quietly and watched them both, as she felt sick again. She needed to concentrate on not throwing up over the back of Mary's seat and all over her lovely white hair.

"It doesn't matter, Alberto. What matters is that they know now and that they would like to speak to Corina about it, so they will be phoning her later this evening!"

"You are unbelievable….do you know that, Mary….unbelievable!" Alberto shook his head in disbelief. He made a point of slamming down the indictor which his hand once he saw the signpost to Blackpool, he knew he needed to get off the motorway at the next junction.

"Do you think we could stop somewhere soon for me to be sick? I don't think I can hold it in for much longer" Corina asked Alberto, she was desperate for him to stop soon as she felt awful.

Alberto pulled into the nearest layby and waited for Corina to get out and go and do what she had to do behind a hedge. He didn't speak to Mary; he ignored her whilst he fiddled around with the radio. He changed the stations over, he would choose one, listen for a couple of seconds, then change it again, until it annoyed Mary so much that she shouted at him to stop. Then, they both sat in silence until Corina came back and got in the car.

"Nice atmosphere" joked Corina, as she made herself comfortable in the back "Right, we can go now"

….

They all approached the reception desk very cautiously once they had arrived at the private clinic, and when asked Corina gave the receptionist her name. Corina thought the receptionist was much nicer than Rachael back in Boston. For a start, this receptionist didn't have a face on her like a smacked bottom; she also smiled and made her feel at ease.

She was called in to see the doctor very quickly and the doctor didn't seem judgemental of her at all. Corina had expected medical staff to look down on her for wanting to get rid her baby, so she was pleasantly surprised at how easy going this doctor seemed to her.

"So, you've had a positive pregnancy test, Corina?" asked Doctor Davidson, he was a middle aged man with fairly good looks and Corina couldn't help notice how tall he was…. he was very tall.

"Yes, yesterday at my GP appointment" confirmed Corina.

"You have made a very quick decision to end your pregnancy, Corina. Did your GP refer you here for an abortion?" Doctor Davidson enquired "By law, we need two doctors' consent before we can go ahead and you will need to see a counsellor too, so we can make sure you are making the right decision"

"No, my GP wouldn't refer me, but she said another GP in her practice would. I want to get rid of this baby because the father tried to kill me….is that a good enough reason, do you think?"

The doctor looked shocked "Tried to kill you?"

"Yes, three months ago my husband killed himself and I lost my baby three days later to stillbirth. My life is a mess and I just want to go back to work and earn some money, so I can get on and make a new life for myself….and that doesn't include having a baby whose father was a psycho!" Corina looked upset and the doctor could see she was about to cry, so he passed her a box of tissues "I really can't have this baby!"

"Okay, Corina. I will contact your GP surgery and ask them to send me the referral for you. If you pop up onto the bed, I will do a quick ultrasound scan to see how far along in the pregnancy you are"

The doctor got up and guided Corina over to the bed and helped her get up onto it. He took her crutches and placed them by the door out of the way. Her bladder was quite full, so she didn't have to drink any more fluids and when the doctor squirted the cold gel onto her pelvic area, she thought she was going to wet herself. The doctor placed the probe onto her skin and instantly he could see the foetus. He made sure the screen faced away from Corina and she was glad because she didn't want to see the baby.

After taking some measurements and having a good look, the doctor said "I would say you are about 10 to 11 weeks pregnant, Corina, does that seem about right to you?"

Corina nodded, she knew exactly when it was conceived. But, she didn't care about it, she wanted it gone.

"I'm afraid you are too far gone to have the abortion pill, so if you chose to go ahead with ending this pregnancy, you would have to have the surgical option. This means the foetus would be taken out by a gentle suction method, either under sedation or general anaesthetic. It's a very simple procedure taking less than five minutes, and once you feel recovered enough, you can go home on the same day" the doctor explained it all carefully to Corina, though Corina looked like she hadn't taken anything in.

"Okay, Corina. You can wipe the gel off of your stomach now, we have finished the scan" he placed her crutches in easy reach for her to get when she had finished cleaning herself up.

"When can I get it done?" asked Corina, she struggled to walk back across the room to sit down again.

"I need to have the referral from your GP first, Corina. You also need to see our counsellor, which I can arrange for you to see her here today before you leave, then if you choose to go ahead we can make another appointment for you to come back in the next week" he watched her carefully this time to make sure she was listening properly.

"Okay, thank you. I understand" Corina got up and shook his hand "Could I please go to the toilet now, I'm busting!"

"Yes, of course!" the doctor laughed "There's a ladies' toilet just outside my door to the left and afterwards if you wait in reception, our counsellor will come and find you"

Corina made her way to the toilet and locked herself into one of the cubicles; it was such a relief to finally empty her bladder. Afterwards, she hobbled back to Mary and Alberto, who were obviously still not talking to each other as Mary was sat four chairs along from Alberto, he had his head down and was ignoring her by pretending to read a magazine. Mary got up to greet her and then helped her to sit down "How did it go, Corina?" she asked quietly, so not to disturb Alberto from his 'reading'.

"Yes, how did it go, Corina, dear?" Alberto did not want to be left out, so got up and sat next to Corina. Mary still didn't acknowledge Alberto and blanked him when he put his hand on her shoulder.

"Well, he said I was about ten to eleven weeks pregnant, so I would have to have a surgical procedure, but that's fine.... I just need to wait here to see a counsellor and then we can go home"

Corina looked pale again to Mary, so she handed her a banana from her hand bag to help keep Corina's strength up. Corina ate it, but she didn't really want it, she didn't have much of an appetite lately. The internal phone rang in reception and after the receptionist finished with the call, she called over to Corina to ask if she could please go to the counsellor's room down the hall on the right.

"Do you want me to come with you, Corina dear?" asked Mary

"No, it's okay Mom, I'll be fine" Corina declined politely, she didn't want Mary listening to the nitty gritty of her conversation with the counsellor. She thought Mary was best left to Alberto and their little tiff.

Corina made her way to the counsellor's room down the hall and on the right. She entered the room awkwardly as she got one of her crutches stuck on the door handle as the door opened.

"No fucking way!!......Corina Green......I thought it might be you when I saw the name Barsetti!"

Rebecca walked up to Corina and put her arms around her and squeezed her tight. She was pleased to see her after ten years and held her close to her body for a while before Corina pulled away and joked "Still a bloody lezzer, I see....and using the F word to a patient is not very professional, you know!"

They both laughed as they sat down on the big comfy chairs that were placed strategically in the room. Corina couldn't believe her eyes. Rebecca Jones working in an abortion clinic, she couldn't really picture her working here, but she did look very relaxed in her job.

"You met the extremely tall Doctor Davidson then?" Rebecca winked at Corina "You wouldn't have to kneel down to give him a blow job, would you, Cor!"

"Becs!" Corina had missed Rebecca's filthy jokes and wished she had kept in touch more often. She made herself comfortable in the chair and then asked "How come you are working here?"

"I just wanted an easy life, you know…and it's pretty easy here. There's no chance of me ever having babies, so I don't really have any preconceived ideas on abortion….and the pay is good, so that helps!"

Rebecca looked Corina up and down "And, what is with your accent, girl? You sound American…. I don't like it…stop it!"

Corina giggled "I can't help it; it's being around the oldies since I got back from Boston. I don't really speak to anyone else apart from Harriet…. who, by the way, is married to a shrink and has two beautiful daughters"

"You mean she has finally lost her virginity…. no way!" Rebecca flicked her shoes off and pulled her legs up underneath her to make herself more comfortable while she spoke "I'm still in touch with Hazel and Jenny. Hazel is up in Scotland with her Scottish lover boy…. very apt seeing as she is still a ginger…. and she's working in a drug rehab. Jenny is down in London working for the NHS, she runs the local mental health community team in her area, so she's done well for herself….so tell me, what's been happening with you? I'm assuming you and Joseph have split up, seeing as you are here for an abortion"

Corina looked upset and tried to hold back the tears, but they came anyway. She didn't know where to start.

"Hey, it's okay, Cor. You can tell me everything…. I'm a counsellor now, you know" Rebecca tried to make Corina laugh again, but it hadn't worked.

"Ugh, where do I start?" Corina gathered her thoughts and then took a deep breath before she started to explain what had happened "I got a job working in a prison and I got promoted to suicide prevention offer, but I didn't even notice my own husband was suicidal…Joseph killed himself three months ago, he thought it would be best for me that he died that way, when he found out he had a brain tumour"

Corina paused to compose herself and Rebecca lent over and held her hand "I found him, Becs, it was awful. He blew his head off with our gun and I can't get that vision out of my head. When I try to sleep it's there and sometimes it appears when I least expect it!"

The tears poured down Corina's cheeks, Rebecca passed her the tissues and let her carry on talking "I was seven months pregnant at the time… and the baby was stillborn three days later"

"Oh God, Corina. I'm so sorry"

"And, then I did something stupid, I tried to kill myself to be with Joseph, but I didn't know what else to do, Becs. My heart was broken, it still is broken and this baby has to go!" Corina banged on her stomach as if to will the baby dead.

"Whoa, whoa, whoa…Calm down, Corina!" Rebecca got up and stopped Corina from hitting her stomach "Can I ask you who you got pregnant by? I mean, it's obvious it's not Joseph's"

"It was James, Joseph's best friend. After I tried to kill myself, I stayed with the oldies and then found out that Mom knew about Joseph wanting to end it all and she didn't tell anyone, so I flew back to England and stayed with Harriet, because I was so bloody angry with them both"

"Okay Corina, take a deep breath and carry on" Rebecca tried to take in all that Corina told her, but she too got emotional for her friend.

"So, Alberto sent James over to get me, so I would go back to Boston for the funeral and we ended up banging each other!" Corina hung her head in shame.

"Well, what's wrong with that? You're only human and we all need a good shag every now and again!"

Corina shrugged and carried on "It turns out James was messed up in the head and tried to blackmail Joseph for sleeping with a man"

"Sleeping with a man?" Rebecca looked confused.

"Yes, it was on his bucket list, apparently!"

"What.... like you sleeping with that consultant...what was she called again? Oh yes, Doctor Marta Jorgenson.... she was hot, I was well jell" Rebecca remembered Marta and her long blonde hair and pretty looks.

"Yes, but the difference is... I told Joseph about that, he didn't bother to tell me he had slept with a man behind my back and James took photos of it all"

"Dirty bastard!"

"And then, Alberto tried to strangle James when he found out that he had tried to blackmail his son, so James took umbrage with that. And, because I told him I was going back to England and I wasn't interested in a relationship with him, he came to my house and tried to kill me. He smashed my head against the wall and snapped my ankle when he kicked me. Then, when Alberto interrupted him, he shot himself!" Corina finally relaxed and drew breath.

"Bloody hell, Corina. It sounds like something that would happen in a horror movie!"

"And, now I'm pregnant with this baby, so I want it gone. Please say that I can have an abortion, please!" Corina begged her.

Rebecca looked at the desperation on Corina's face and knew she was in turmoil "Okay Corina, I understand. I will support you in this, but you will have a few days to change your mind before you come back in for the procedure and I will see you again before you go down to theatre, just to make sure. This isn't something that you should take lightly, or make a rash decision about" explained Rebecca "Now, come here and give me a big hug"

They both got up out of their chairs and hugged each other.

"I've missed you, Corina" said Rebecca as she gave Corina a final squeeze.

"Same here, ya lezzer!" Corina squeezed back twice as hard and then wiped her snotty nose on Rebecca's shirt.

"I see you haven't changed.... still got your playfulness, I see!" said Rebecca as she wiped the snot away with a tissue.

Arm in arm, along with the crutches, they made their way out to reception to see Alberto and Mary. Corina was pleased that they could finally meet Rebecca after she had told them so much about her over the years.

Chapter Twenty-Five

Later that evening, Mary and Corina were in the lounge together. They felt relaxed as they talked about how wonderful it was to see Rebecca again. Alberto was out in the kitchen making his signature pasta dish for their dinner, when the phone rang. Mary knew it would be James' parents, so looked at Corina to prompt her to answer it. Corina made her way to the phone, she felt apprehensive as she had no idea of what their reaction would be when they found out she was going to go ahead with the abortion. She had been given an appointment to have the abortion in three days' time, as her doctor's surgery had faxed her referral through whilst she'd had her counselling session at the clinic with Rebecca.

"Hello, Corina Barsetti speaking"

"Hi there, Corina, this is James' mom, Angela, speaking. How are you?" Angela sounded pleasant enough to Corina and she still recognised her voice, even though she hadn't seen her for about two years.

"Hello Angela, I am fine, thank you…. how about you…and Bryan?" Corina felt uncomfortable, really uncomfortable, as she really did not want to be having a conversation with Angela about her pregnancy.

"We are still grieving for our son, Corina. So, I am sure you can understand what we are going through…. But, enough of the small talk. I have heard from Mary that you are pregnant with James' baby and that you wish to have an abortion" Angela's voice quivered with emotion as she continued to talk to Corina "I am not very happy that you are considering this, so I have spoken to our family lawyer to see if we can stop this abortion from going ahead"

"And, what did your FAMILY lawyer say then?" Corina started to get defensive with Angela as she didn't want lawyers involved. For a start, she couldn't afford one to fight her case and she did not want the inconvenience of it all, as in three days' time she would be back at the abortion clinic.

"Well, we can't stop you apparently...we don't have a leg to stand on...so I'm calling you this evening to ask you to please reconsider" Angela started to cry down the phone, she was desperate for a part of James and was willing to do anything for Corina to keep the baby "If you would please carry this pregnancy to term for us, we can then adopt the baby; you would not have the burden of a child you didn't want. We are willing to pay you whatever you want....name your price, Corina please!"

"You want to buy this baby?" Corina was shocked; she hadn't considered adoption at all, let alone selling the baby.

"If you put it that way, then yes.... we want to buy our grandchild!" Angela was still very upset, but she was also very serious and would pay any price Corina wanted.

"They want to buy your baby?" interrupted Alberto. He looked annoyed. Alberto had entered the lounge; his apron was covered in pasta sauce as it had exploded all over him.... due to him trying to listen to the conversation Corina was having with Angela and he had forgotten to turn the heat down "Tell them to go f......"

"Alberto!" Mary shouted at him "Mind your language and please go and clean yourself up, Corina needs to talk to Angela in peace!"

Mary looked at him and rolled her eyes. She thought he looked ridiculous stood there covered in pasta sauce; he looked like he had just committed a murder and had blood splashed all over him.

"Go on, go and change!" Mary pointed to the door "This has nothing to do with you!"

Alberto moved out of the room quickly and he looked sheepish as he passed Corina. He wasn't used to Mary ordering him about and it was a bit of a shock to him. Corina looked at Mary and thought she had become very women's lib in her old age, she wasn't used to seeing Mary stick up for herself so much, but she liked it. She wasn't very pleased that she had phoned Angela and Bryan to tell them she was pregnant though, but there wasn't a lot she could do about it now. She supposedly had a lot to think about.

"I am all set to have an abortion, Angela, but I will give your proposal some thought. I am not promising anything, but I will have a good think about what you have said" Corina told Angela, she had no intention of thinking about it; she just wanted to get off the phone.

"Thank you, Corina. I will call you again in a couple of days" Angela sounded hopeful that Corina would seriously consider her offer.

"Goodbye, Angela" Corina put the phone down and then noticed how glad Mary looked.

Mary looked pleased with herself as she had two whole days to work on Corina. She had time to make Corina think twice about aborting her baby. Mary thought that letting Angela and Bryan have the baby was a fantastic idea. Little did she know, that Corina wasn't going to think about that option at all…. she was all set to have an abortion in three days' time and in her mind nothing was going to stop her.

"Are you okay, Corina? You look a little cross" Mary rubbed Corina on her back as she sat down beside her.

"Can you believe they want to buy this baby? That's just ridiculous!" Corina blurted out in a raised voice.

"I agree…its bloody ridiculous!" shouted Alberto from the kitchen. He was busy cleaning up pasta sauce off the walls and anywhere else he could find it.

"Are you eavesdropping again, Alberto? For goodness sake, keep your opinions to yourself!" Mary shouted back.

Mary looked at Corina, who still couldn't believe this was the Mary she knew. She was getting feisty and Corina really liked it. It was just a shame Mary wasn't this outspoken when Joseph had confided in her about killing himself, thought Corina, as she might not be in this predicament now.

"Actually Corina, I happen to think it's a really good solution for all of you" said Mary; she still looked pleased with herself.

"How do you figure that one out? I need to go back to work!" exclaimed Corina, who was looking more and more confused by the minute.

"I think we should go out for dinner as I've had a bit of an accident with the pasta sauce" Alberto had ventured back into the lounge and winked at Corina. He was still covered in the sauce. Corina took one look at him and laughed. The laughter did not make Mary very happy at all.

"What is wrong with you two, you are like a couple of children! Now, this is a serious matter. I think it would be best for everyone if Corina had the baby and gave it to the Patton's"

Mary wasn't in the mood for joking around about spilt pasta sauce, there was an unborn child involved and a grieving family back in America that were desperate for their grandchild. Just because Corina didn't want it, she didn't have to get rid of the baby. Mary could not see why Corina didn't think this was a good idea.

"I'm going back to work in a prison, Mom, that's why it's not a good idea. They are waiting for my ankle to get better before I can start…. how can I go back pregnant?"

"What if your ankle takes six months to heal properly…. which is how long your father thinks it will take…you could have had the baby by then!" Mary had certainly given this some thought and had an answer for everything.

"Six months, Dad? Why do you two insist on keeping secrets from me? I've had enough of this; I'm going to bed to think about all this IN PEACE!" Corina got up and hopped along the lounge on one foot to get to her bedroom.

"But, what about your dinner?" asked Alberto "I thought we were going out?"

"You and Mary can go out and spend some time together" shouted Corina from her bedroom "I'm not hungry!" With that, she slammed the bedroom door and lay on her bed. She started to cry as she felt so confused about what to do.

"I wish you were here, Joseph. I miss you so much. Why did you have to go and leave me?" she whispered to herself "I need you to tell me what to do"

Chapter Twenty-Six

"Becs, its Corina"

"Bloody hell, Cor...its four thirty in the morning. Did you wet the bed or something?"

"What? No! I'm sorry, but I couldn't sleep. I need to talk to you"

"Have you decided you want my body after all these years? Sorry, but I'm straight now"

"Yeah, right... And I'm the Queen's Mother.... seriously though; I need to talk to you!"

Rebecca yawned and sat up in her bed; she leant over and put on her bedside lamp. She caught a glimpse of herself in her mirror at the end of her bed and screamed, she didn't like what she saw. She thought she looked like a wild banshee having a nervous breakdown, she had also forgotten to take her make up off, so the black eyeliner had smeared down her cheeks. Ozzy Osborne had nothing on her, she thought to herself.

"Oh my god, what's the matter, Becs?"

"I just look like I should be committed, that's all....do you want to talk on the phone, or shall I come over to you? Luckily for you I have a day off tomorrow!"

"If you could come over, that would be great. I'm at Rickerby House in Carlisle...Flat Number two"

"Oooooh, I say, very posh! I'll be about an hour....and I'll warn you now...I'm coming as I am, so don't be scared!" Rebecca laughed "See you in a bit, sexy!"

Rebecca lived about three miles away from Blackpool in Carleton, so she was about seventy miles away from where Corina lived. She thought she would drive over to Corina's and catch up on her sleep after they'd had a good chat. Rebecca was glad she had got to see Corina again and she thought to herself how strange life was sometimes. She believed in fate, she thought they were meant to meet up again after all these years. It just wasn't in very good circumstances that they had found each other though. She then thought about Joseph and how in love Corina was with him. Corina was absolutely smitten with him from the first time she had seen him and Rebecca remembered how she would talk about him all of the time, so much so it would get on her nerves. Rebecca had always thought Joseph was a pompous prick though, but Corina couldn't see it, she was far too much in love with him to see what a big head he was. Rebecca thought he was one of those doctors that thought he was god and could cure everybody and he had that 'I'm better than you' air about him. Even though she felt sorry for Corina that Joseph was dead, she couldn't help thinking that karma had come up behind him and bitten his backside.

"Better not say that to my little sex kitten!" said Rebecca to herself as she pulled up outside of the magnificent looking Rickerby House, with its sweeping circular gravel drive and its mature well maintained gardens.

After she parked the car and got out, she could see Corina as she waved at her from a downstairs window, and as she got closer Corina pointed at the huge door to the right of her to direct her to the correct entrance. Corina buzzed her in and waited by her front door for Rebecca to appear.

"Jeez, you were right. You do look like you need committing!" Corina giggled at Rebecca as she held out her arms to give her a cuddle.

"Can you please stop talking like a yank…its unnerving!" Rebecca hugged Corina back, then nestled into her neck and kissed it lovingly.

"You're not getting horny are you, Becs? I didn't call you over here for sex you know!"

"Yeah, I know. But, you know me, I never give up....and if you can sleep with Doctor Jorgensen, then I reckon I'm in with a chance one day!"

"It would ruin our friendship, now come in and go and get in my bedroom before my parents hear you"

Corina directed Rebecca to her bedroom with another point of her finger. Rebecca stuck her tongue out at her as she passed.

"You are so forceful......I love it!" Rebecca blew her a kiss from the doorway and then threw herself onto the bed.

Corina hobbled into her bedroom and got in her bed, she then waited for Rebecca to sort herself out. She watched Rebecca as she stripped down to her bra and pants and then slid into the bed next to her.

"I've been waiting years for this moment!" laughed Rebecca "Now... what's up, babe?"

"James' parents want to buy my baby" Corina came straight out and said it "They want me to carry this thing to term and then buy it!"

"Do it!" said Rebecca straight away, she began to take off her bra under the covers.

"What?"

"Do it, its easy money. I'd do it!" said Rebecca again, she then threw her bra over onto the chair in the corner of the room.

"Are you being serious?" Corina stared at her in disbelief.

"Yes, do it, Corina! It's a win, win, situation for everyone. I mean, you don't really think you are going to get back to work any time soon do you? Not with your ankle like that and you need to sort your shit out. You haven't grieved properly for your husband yet, so you need some time to do that before even thinking about going back to work in a prison"

"Has Mary phoned you by any chance?"

"No, Cor, she hasn't. Just think about it logically. You have something that they want and they are willing to pay you for it. You need the money, right?"

"Yes, but...."

"Well then, bloody get on and do it!"

"But, it feels wrong to sell a baby" Corina was still unsure.

"But, it feels right for you to kill it instead?" Rebecca looked at Corina and waited for her reaction.

"No, I mean, I don't know! Oh, I am so confused. Why is this happening to me?" Corina started to cry again.

"Because you fucked your husband's best friend and now you have to deal with the consequences. Sounds harsh, I know. But, shit happens girl and I'm not going to pussy foot around you while you feel sorry for yourself, because you are old enough to know about contraception and how babies are made. That baby has got the chance of a good life, but you're still thinking about flushing it!" Rebecca pointed at Corina's stomach "It's not as bad as you think, honestly Corina, what have you got to lose?"

"Well...nothing really, seeing as you put it like that!" Corina looked thoughtful; she knew Rebecca would tell it to her straight once she was outside of the clinic. She wasn't allowed to force her views on women that were considering abortion when at work.

"It's six months out of your life. Six months! That's nothing, and I honestly think you need time to recover from everything. What Joseph did has fucked with your mind, and you can't go back to work like that, seriously Cor....and another thing, we have to sort that accent out.... now say after me.... HOW NOW BROWN COW!"

They both laughed hysterically, then Corina slid down into the bed to lie beside the topless Rebecca.

"How can I take you seriously when you have your tits out like that?" Corina giggled at Rebecca.

"I just need you to see what you're missing, I bet Doctor Jorgensen didn't have tits like these" said Rebecca, she lifted them up with both hands and then let them flop down on top of the covers.

"No, you're right she didn't" Corina giggled again, she was never going to live that experience down, Rebecca wasn't going to let her forget that one night of drunken lesbian passion.... ever.

"It's nearly six fifteen, if we are not going to have sex, we better get some beauty sleep.... boo hoo!" said Rebecca, she began to snuggle down under the covers "I certainly need it!"

Corina felt so much better for having Rebecca there. She felt at ease with her, even though she knew Rebecca would love to sleep with her. She turned the bedside lamp off, turned on her side and got herself comfortable under the covers, when she felt Rebecca pinch her bottom.

"Goodnight Becs" said Corina quietly.

"Good morning, more like" said Rebecca, then she farted out loud.

They both giggled again.

It was just like being back at The Cumberland Infirmary, Rebecca hadn't changed one bit.

Chapter Twenty-Seven

"Corina's not come for breakfast yet, Alberto. Do you think I should go and check on her? She was a bit upset last night and it's nearly ten-thirty…. it's not like her to sleep in" said Mary to Alberto, who was still looking for pasta sauce stains left on the walls from the previous evening's sudden explosion.

"I think I've wiped them all off now…. Yes, do that Mary. Good idea, Honey" he replied, as he carried on and inspected the wall behind the cooker.

Mary made her way to Corina's bedroom and put her ear to the door, she could not hear Corina at all, so she gently tapped on the door and quietly opened it, she then peered her head around to see if Corina was awake. Much to her surprise, she saw that Rebecca was in bed with Corina and by the looks of it, Rebecca was naked. She didn't want Corina to see that she knew Rebecca was there, so she reversed quietly out and closed the door. She headed straight back to the kitchen again to tell Alberto.

"You'll never guess what I've just seen!" she exclaimed to Alberto.

"A unicorn?" Alberto had his head in the fridge and didn't bother to take it out to look at her.

"Don't be silly, Alberto! Rebecca is naked in Corina's bed with her……do you think they…you know…. did it?"

"Did what?" Alberto finally took his head out of the fridge, armed with eggs and butter "I wonder if Corina has any flour…."

"You know…did it" Mary said quietly, she then looked around as if to see if anybody else had heard her.

"Oh my God, Mary…Did what…. just spit it out!" Alberto raised his voice at her "I'm trying to make pasta here!"

"Had sex!" she was embarrassed to say it, as she didn't really understand what lesbians did. She had never looked at another woman in a sexual way, she just loved Alberto and he was enough for her.

"What? Don't be so stupid, Mary!" Alberto had found some flour and he was excited that he could finally make his own pasta. He thought the shop bought stuff he had cooked last night was terrible, so he was determined he was going to make his own.

Mary continued to witter on "I'm not being silly; they looked pretty close in the bed together, and how did she get there? Corina must have sneaked her in last night…sounds dodgy to me!"

Alberto sighed and shook his head. He had heard everything last night when Rebecca had come to the flat, because he couldn't sleep. He'd had a nightmare about James and the baby. He had dreamt the baby was born with a gun in its hand and had shot him as it appeared out of the womb. He giggled to himself about the dream and thought it was ridiculous. Mary glared at him as she thought he was laughing at her.

"It's not funny, Alberto. She's done it before you know!" Mary looked worried.

"Well, I can categorically state that Corina and Rebecca…. did not have sexual relations last night. Now, if you don't mind, I'm trying to cook here!" Alberto shimmied her out of the kitchen so he could cook pasta in peace. He hated interruptions when he was cooking and he was going to make sure she understood not to disturb him again this morning by slamming the door after her as she left.

As Mary walked down the hall to go to the lounge, Rebecca appeared from out of Corina's bedroom. She was still topless whilst she rushed to get to the main bathroom as Corina was throwing up in her en-suite bathroom.

"Oh shit, sorry Mary!" Rebecca didn't feel embarrassed at all though "Ummm, where's the bathroom please?"

Mary looked stunned as she pointed to the main bathroom. Rebecca winked at her as she passed and made no effort to cover her breasts. Mary blushed, then went into Corina's bathroom to find Corina.

"Corina, are you okay, dear?" Mary approached Corina, who by this time was brushing her teeth to get rid of the awful taste in her mouth "I didn't realise Rebecca was here, I just had an encounter with her rather large breasts!" Mary blushed again.

Corina laughed, she wiped her mouth with a towel that had a picture of the wedding chapel in Vegas on it. There was a love heart embroidered on it too, with Corina and Joseph written inside. When Mary noticed it, she felt sad that her son was no longer there with them.

"You'll get used to her, Mom. She's not ashamed of her body, so no need to be embarrassed. And anyway, you'll be pleased she came, as I have some good news for you. Just let me have a bath and I'll tell you all about it" Corina started to run the water and added some bubble bath to it "You can stay if you want, I don't mind"

Mary decided to stay, she really didn't want another encounter with Rebecca's breasts. She turned her back as Corina undressed to try and be polite.

"Mom, you don't have to turn away. We all have the same bits you know" Corina giggled at Mary's obvious embarrassment "And, you better get used to seeing more than that if you're going to be my birth partner!"

"Birth partner?" exclaimed Mary, her heart started to race with excitement "You mean you're going to have this baby?"

Corina stepped into the warm water and sat down, she leant back slowly to lie in the water and covered herself with the luxurious bubbles so her head was still visible above the sea of white fluffiness. Her long brunette hair was scraped up off of her face to the top of her head and secured with a bright pink hair band. Mary thought she looked beautiful and that her son was very lucky to have known her.

"Yes, I'm going to let Angela and Bryan have the baby, but I'm not sure about taking money for doing it though…it doesn't seem right somehow" Corina sat up again and handed Mary a sponge so she could wash her back for her.

"I'm so pleased, Corina. You have definitely made the right decision and I will help you in any way I can" Mary rubbed Corina's back gently with the sponge in a circular motion as she spoke "I am sure everything will be fine and I am very proud to call you my daughter. We have all been through a lot, so it can only get better from now on, dear"

"The only thing I'm dreading now is telling Dad" Corina began to shave her legs as she spoke "Jeez, I am so hairy since I got pregnant again!"

"You always were a bit of a baboon with your dark hairiness" laughed Rebecca as she came into the bathroom. Her breasts were still out for all to see "Mind if I jump in?"

Mary thought to herself she must get used to all the nakedness if she was going to be Corina's birth partner. It wasn't that she was embarrassed by naked bodies, as she had been a nurse for most of her life and had seen most things, she just wasn't used to women being so open in front of her. But, the girls were a different generation to her, so they did things differently and they weren't ashamed of what they had. Mary passed the sponge back to Corina and went over and sat on top of the closed toilet seat, so she could speak to them without looking like a spare part whilst she just stood there. Rebecca had thrown her pants into the wash basket and joined Corina in the bath; when she noticed Mary was watching her as she got in.

"It's called a Brazilian, Mazza, you should get one…. it's very hygienic you know. Alberto would love it… as he wouldn't get your hair stuck in his teeth!"

"Rebecca, please! That's my Mom; she doesn't need to know about Brazilians…. jeez!" Corina felt embarrassed for Mary and hoped Mary wouldn't be offended. But, Mary laughed out loud and gave Rebecca a taste of her own medicine.

"Rebecca dear, my generation invented the Brazilian, so there was never any fear of Alberto getting hair stuck in his teeth" she winked at Rebecca flirtatiously.

"Ewww...Mom, please!" Corina winced at the thought of Alberto performing cunnilingus on Mary.

"Go, Mazza!" yelled Rebecca, as she flicked bubbles up into Corina's face.

"Where do you think my son got his insatiable sexual appetite from, Corina?" Mary started to feel young again and she felt like she might get used to be being around Rebecca, with her openness about sex and her body. She also thought it was funny to see Corina cringe for a change.

"Ugh, I don't want to know, Mom.... come on, stop it now, you two!"

Rebecca and Mary laughed at Corina and the look of disgust on her face. They heard Alberto come into the bedroom to see what all the commotion was about, so Mary quickly got up and shut the bathroom door so he couldn't see the girl's naked bodies. They all giggled together as they heard Alberto ask what was going on.

"Nothing, dear!" shouted Mary "We will be out in a bit, could you please put some coffee on? We all need to sit and have a talk together"

"I'll put the coffee pot on, but we don't need to bother about having a talk" he shouted back "I heard the conversation last night, so you can count me out, as I'm not interested!"

The giggling in the bathroom stopped abruptly. Corina knew Alberto wouldn't take her news very well. Mary held up a towel and prompted Corina to get out of the bath.

"Hurry up, Rebecca dear, we are going to need you as well. He can be a bit of a hot head at times!"

"Alright, Mazza.... I've just got to rinse this baboon hair off me and I'll be there" Rebecca pulled the plug out of the bath and then showered herself off.

"Oh, and Rebecca" said Mary "Remember to put some clothes on!"

They all giggled again, but quietly this time, so Alberto couldn't hear them.

....

In the kitchen, Alberto got the cups ready for coffee, but he made Corina a cup of tea as he knew if she had coffee for her first drink of the day, she would throw up again. Mary came into the kitchen and got the milk out of the fridge for Alberto.

"You want hot milk with your coffee, dear?" Alberto asked Mary "You want me to froth it up?"

"That would be nice, honey" she approached him from behind and gave him a hug. She nuzzled her nose into the back of his shoulders "I love you, Alberto"

"Enough of that" said Rebecca, as she came into the kitchen "I've had enough yukkiness for one day…. I've just had to bathe in a bath load of Corina's hair!"

"Not nice" said Alberto, he was not really sure if he understood Rebecca or not, he would need a bit more time to try and figure her sense of humour out.

"Mmmm, I heard you're not into hair" whispered Rebecca to herself, as she winked at Mary.

Mary lifted her index finger up to her mouth to tell Rebecca to shush, as she noticed Corina was on her way to the kitchen.

"I have made you a cup of tea, Corina" said Alberto, he pulled a chair out from under the table for her to sit on.

"Thanks, Dad" she kissed him on the cheek before she sat down.

"Okay everyone" said Alberto, as they all got themselves seated "I heard the conversation between Rebecca and Corina last night, so I'm assuming it's been decided that Corina is going to have the psycho's baby, right?"

"Yes, I am" said Corina. She looked flushed, she had suddenly come over all hot and bothered "As Rebecca said, it's only six months out of my life, and if you….as a retired orthopaedic surgeon…. think my ankle will take that long to heal properly so I can't work, then why not have the baby and give it to the Patton's?"

"Well. If Rebecca says so, we better do it!" Alberto said sarcastically.

"Alberto, don't be like that. It is for the best and I think Corina would regret having an abortion. She's had enough to cope with, so six months of relaxing while she waits for the baby to come will do her good" Mary held his hand under the table to try to make him feel better.

"Mary, you should have seen the look of hatred in his eyes when he was all over Corina. I don't think any child needs bringing into the world from a father like that!"

"Alberto, you can't blame the baby for having a father like him… just like you can't force Corina into having an abortion" Rebecca had her serious counselling head on again as she spoke to Alberto.

"Rebecca, I really don't think this has anything to do with you!" Alberto got up and went to walk out.

"Oh Dad, please don't leave. I don't want any more arguments. Please!"

"Yes, come on, dear. Come back and have coffee with us. You will get used to the idea. You know deep down it's for the best" Mary patted his chair and willed him to sit down. Alberto looked at her with tears in his eyes. Mary knew it was difficult for him after he had seen James shoot himself and what he had done to Corina, but it wasn't the unborn child's fault and she hoped Alberto would come to realise that in the six months left of the pregnancy.

Alberto paused for a few seconds and then decided to sit back down with them all. Corina looked at him and smiled. He winked back at her and started to drink his coffee. Mary put her arm around him and pulled him close to her, then kissed the side of his head.

"Ahh, how sweet!" said Rebecca "Right, who fancies a walk into town? I want to go and see Harriet. I'm going to get her to give you lot a few elocution lessons.... I'm so sick of that Boston accent you've all got going on!"

"Mary and I will stay here, you two go and have some fun" said Alberto. He was still not sure which way to take Rebecca. Her sense of humour was weirder than Corina's. It must be an English thing, he thought.

"Can we drive though, Becs? My ankle won't like all that walking"

"Of course, my little sex kitten! One shall drive you to Harriet's in style" Rebecca pointed out of the window at her brand new silver Porsche Boxster.

"What the hell is that?" asked Alberto "That's not a car, that's a go-kart!" Alberto was only used to big cars and his entire family drove SUV's back in America.

"Alberto, Darling!" joked Rebecca "That GO-KART is a status symbol here in the UK….and I pull all the gorgeous ladies when I drive it"

"Really…. could I borrow it then one day?" Alberto laughed as Mary hit him on the top of the arm.

Corina loved seeing her family messing around like this; she loved to see them laugh, even though they were all hurting and coping with grief in their own different way.

"I'll cancel your appointment for the abortion then, shall I?" asked Alberto, forlornly.

"Yes please, Dad. And, thank you for everything" Corina hobbled over to hug him before she headed off to Harriet's with Rebecca in her 'Go-Kart'.

She was proud of her Dad and loved him with all of her heart.

Chapter Twenty-Eight

Corina had travelled back to Boston with Rebecca for the last two months of her pregnancy, so the Patton's didn't have to come to England to annoy her, and also the baby would be born as an American citizen. The Patton's had paid for her to have counselling, so she would not have any doubts when it was time to give her baby away to them. Corina and Rebecca were staying with Alberto and Mary at The Four Seasons and Rebecca was absolutely thrilled to be able to take some time off from her job to be with Corina in Boston. Corina still had some pain in her ankle, but she was now able to walk without the aid of her crutches. She still had a slight limp, but it was improving slowly. The extra weight from being pregnant didn't seem to help though, so she hoped it would improve after she had given birth. She couldn't wait to get back to work; she just wanted her life to have some sort of routine and normality and she wanted to be earning her own money, not relying on Alberto and Mary or The Patton's. She had told them that she didn't want a large sum of money for the baby, she only wanted looking after while she was pregnant, then once she had given birth, they would pay for her flight home.

"This birthing tour leaflet says we have to go to the east campus, Corina" said Rebecca...she didn't realise they were already stood in front of the east campus building at The Beth Israel Deaconess Medical Centre.

"I know, Becs, we are stood right outside it.... we just have to wait for Mom, she'll be here soon"

Rebecca didn't have a clue where she was and wasn't used to all the Americanisms like Corina was. She thought Corina looked nervous, so thought she would try and relax her with one of her jokes.

"Do you think the doctor's will think we are a lesbian couple?" asked Rebecca, she winked at Corina, then stuck her tongue out at her.

"No, because they know I was married to Joseph. Also, Alberto and Mary worked in this hospital for many years, so they know our family!"

"Are you stressed?"

"No!"

"Sure, you are!" Rebecca did a fake American accent.

"Well, if I wasn't...I am now!"

Rebecca looked at Corina and made a funny face "What's up, Corina? I can tell you aren't yourself"

Corina looked thoughtful for a minute and then she confided in Rebecca "I'm just a bit scared about the birth...what if something goes wrong and what if the baby dies like last time?"

"I'm sure everything will be fine, Corina. They have been checking your placenta regularly by scanning you and they've said every time that everything looks good" Rebecca tried to reassure her, but Corina just shrugged and started to pace up and down.

"Why is my Mom always late for everything?"

"Corina, calm down, we have plenty of time....and here comes Mazza now" Rebecca could see Mary as she rushed down the street towards them. Mary started to wave at them when she got closer.

"Hi....is everything okay?" puffed Mary, she could see the disgruntled look on Corina's face as she went to give her a hug.

"I wanted you here on time so I could get myself settled inside!" snapped Corina whilst she tapped the face of her watch.

"I'm not late, honey. It's fine, we have plenty of time. Come on, let's go inside" Mary went to link arms with Corina, but she huffed and walked off by herself towards the entrance.

"Hormones..." Rebecca whispered into Mary's ear, they then followed Corina into the medical centre.

When they got inside the building, they went to the reception desk and were told to carry on up to the tenth floor where a member of the obstetrics team would be there to meet them on the delivery unit. There was silence in the elevator whilst they travelled up to the tenth floor, apart from Corina's huffing and puffing, she felt extremely hot and flustered. As the elevator doors opened Corina crashed to the floor. She had fainted again.

"Could I please get some help over here?" shouted Mary to one of the nurses.

The nurse rushed over with a wheel chair and they managed between themselves to lift Corina into it, then wheel her into a room. She managed to get up on the bed by herself, but was feeling pretty awful. As she put her legs out in front of her on the bed she noticed her ankles were swollen. She instantly panicked and started to cry as she feared the worst.

"This is what happened last time...the baby is dead, I know it!" Corina cried at Mary "I want them to take it out now!"

"Corina, calm down" said Rebecca "Let the nurse check you over, the baby is not dead.... look...I can see it moving!"

They all watched as Corina's stomach moved about vigorously. The baby was pushing out with its feet and they could see the shape of a tiny foot through Corina's skin. Corina put her hand on the foot to try and feel it, but it quickly moved away.

"Ahh, the baby is ticklish!" laughed Mary "You see, Honey. Everything is fine"

Corina suddenly felt quite maternal towards the baby. She had never felt that feeling before, she had never looked at the scans or got excited when the baby moved around inside of her, she had always looked at it as being an affliction. She suddenly felt very confused, but decided to keep her feelings to herself for the time being.

The nurse took Corina's blood pressure and then she hooked Corina up to a baby monitor to check the baby's heartbeat "Your blood pressure is a bit high, Mrs Barsetti, but that might be because you got yourself worked up a bit after fainting" explained the nurse "I'll come back and check it in ten minutes, just to give you a chance to relax"

Everyone sat and listened intently to the quickness of the baby's heartbeat. Mary smiled at Corina, who smiled back at her, whilst she relaxed her head down onto a big fluffy pillow.

"Sounds like a horse galloping!" said Rebecca, she pretended to ride a horse like a jockey on her turned around chair.

"Trust you!" said Corina, who rolled her eyes and giggled out loud "Do you think I'll still be able to get a tour of the delivery unit, Mom?"

"I'm pretty sure you can, dear. Wait and see what the nurse says when she comes back" replied Mary, she began to wipe away the remainder of Corina's tears with a tissue.

There was a knock on the door and Doctor Shapiro, Corina's obstetrician, entered the room. She was a petite lady in her fifties and had a very motherly and understanding nature about her.

"Hi Corina, how are you feeling? I heard you fainted in the elevator…you sure do like to make an entrance, huh?" Doctor Shapiro laughed whilst she gave Corina a hug.

Corina still hadn't got used to American doctors hugging her when they saw her, as it was very different back in England. She could not imagine being hugged by NHS hospital doctors; it just wasn't the done thing. She started to think about the first time she went to see a gynaecologist with Joseph at The General in Boston. Her doctor obviously knew of Joseph and that he was a fellow doctor at the hospital, as he had hugged her tight when Joseph told him that they had got married. Corina had found this a bit unnerving and she was even more embarrassed when during her pap smear he had invited them to dinner at his house. She felt the invitation was very inappropriate whilst opening up her vagina with a speculum to take a smear from her cervix. He then told her she had the most amazing vagina, with perfectly symmetrical labia and could he possibly take a photograph for an article he was writing for a medical journal on surgical correction of overly large labia in women. He wanted to use the picture of her vagina as an after surgery success picture. She remembered looking at Joseph in horror whilst he agreed with her gynaecologist that her vagina was definitely a good looking one. He thought she should most definitely consider getting the photograph done, as this would mean he wouldn't have to pay the doctors fee. Corina wondered to herself about the journal with the picture of her vagina in it, and whether or not it was still in circulation, whilst Doctor Shapiro checked the readings on the baby monitor.

"It all looks good to me, Corina. I'll just get the nurse to check your blood pressure again while I'm here"

The nurse had come back into the room to check Corina's blood pressure again and when she got the thumbs up from Doctor Shapiro, she left the room, leaving the doctor to it.

"That is looking much better, Corina. Everything seems normal…. I know you are anxious because of what happened before, but you really must try to relax and not work yourself up so much" said Doctor Shapiro, she gently patted Corina's stomach.

Rebecca started to point her finger at Corina as if to tell her off and Mary nodded her head in agreement with the doctor.

"You are thirty-six weeks pregnant now, so it won't be long until the baby comes, as I can feel the baby's head is engaged" the doctor felt around Corina's big baby bump "This baby is in the right position for birth, so all we have to do now is wait patiently"

"There's nothing patient about Corina!" laughed Rebecca "She is the most impulsive and impatient person I know!"

"Well, I'm afraid baby will come when baby wants to come, so I would try and make the rest of the pregnancy a calm one, if I were you, Corina" said Doctor Shapiro, she was very aware that Corina was giving her baby to the father's parents, but she just wanted her to relax and not get herself worked up.

"Shall I take you on a tour of the unit now, so you are prepared for the birth?" asked the doctor, as she removed all the wiring from

Corina's belly that was attached to the baby monitor. Corina nodded and felt relieved that the baby was okay.

Once Corina had made herself look presentable, they all followed Doctor Shapiro out of the room and into the corridor for a look around, so they could make themselves familiar with the unit in preparation for the birth.

"It all looks a bit clinical though, doesn't it Mom?" whispered Corina into Mary's ear, so Doctor Shapiro wouldn't overhear.

"It is a hospital, dear" Mary whispered back to Corina and gave a confused look to Rebecca.

"Everything okay, ladies?" asked Doctor Shapiro, as she sensed Corina was a little uncomfortable.

"Yes thanks, Doc" said Rebecca, she had noticed a pretty nurse walk past that she thought was very hot "The view from where I'm standing doesn't look too clinical at all!"

Corina shook her head at Rebecca as she watched her looking at the nurse. Rebecca's eyes followed the nurse all the way to the end of the corridor until the nurse stopped and turned to look at them, as she must of sensed she was being stared at. She gave a flirty smile to Rebecca, who in turn, smiled back and made a telephone sign with her hand. The nurse smiled again and then disappeared into a room at the end of the corridor.

"Really, Becs, we are on a birthing tour!" sighed Corina, she then saw that the nurse was headed back towards them again and as she passed Corina noticed her slip a piece of paper into Rebecca's pocket. Rebecca looked at the piece of paper, which had the nurse's name and number on it.... she was starting to like Boston even more now.

Doctor Shapiro had carried on into the birthing pool room with Mary in the hope that Corina would follow them.

"How did you know she was like you?" Corina asked Rebecca inquisitively, whilst they made their way to find Mary and the doctor.

169

"It's the same as when you fancy a man, Corina, you just know there's something there. It's no different for me just because I'm gay…. and if she wasn't the same she wouldn't have given me this" said Rebecca, she held up the piece of paper that the nurse had just given her. "Looks like me and Deborah here, are going to have a spot of fun!"

"That's not very professional though, is it? I mean, she's on duty!"

"Are you fucking kidding me?" laughed Rebecca "What about you banging that junior doctor in the on call room whilst you were both supposed to be on duty? Pot, kettle, black, springs to mind!"

"Oh yeah, I forgot about that!"

"And…. what about when you sneaked into the hospital to be with Joseph after you had qualified? He was on duty and you weren't even supposed to be there!"

"Yes, okay, Becs! I get it…. those on call rooms did come in handy, though" sniggered Corina "Those were the days!"

"Slut!" said Rebecca, as they entered the birthing pool room "Ahh, now this doesn't look so clinical, does it Corina?"

"Wow, it looks great" said Corina whilst she looked around the room "This looks more relaxing"

The room was tastefully decorated with calming blues, greens and purples. There was a stereo to play music on and comfortable chairs for birthing partners. And, as well as the huge pool, there was a bed for the mother and a cot for baby, along with all the necessary equipment should anything go wrong.

"Well, I am assuming you are quite taken with this room, Corina. Does a water birth sound like something you would like to do?" asked Doctor Shapiro.

Corina suddenly realised she was far too excited about the idea of giving birth in the birthing pool room, she thought the feeling was unfitting seeing as she was giving her baby away. She started to back out of the room and into the corridor.

"Maybe I should just book an elective caesarean under general anaesthetic?" said Corina to Mary, she looked scared and worried again, she just wanted to run as fast as she could out of the hospital.

"Why would you want to do that, dear?" asked Mary.

"That way they could just take the baby and I won't know anything about it" replied Corina. She felt confused again and another surge of emotion came over her "I need to go now, Mom"

Corina headed off down the corridor towards the elevator, everyone followed her quickly so she would not go off without them, as they all sensed she was upset. As she reached the elevator, Doctor Shapiro stopped her from getting inside by putting her arm across to block the door.

"Corina, please could I have a word? Why don't you two go on down and I'll send Corina downstairs in a little while? I won't keep her long" said Doctor Shapiro to Mary and Rebecca. They both nodded and left the doctor with Corina.

"Corina, I think you should have another counselling session before you give birth, just so it's clear in your mind about giving this baby up" Doctor Shapiro was concerned that Corina was having second thoughts.

"Yes, I will do. Thank you" Corina rushed into the elevator and closed the door before Doctor Shapiro could say anything else. Corina hated having to face up to her problems.

She would rather just run away from it all.

Chapter Twenty-Nine

"Knock, knock!" shouted Rebecca as she entered Corina's bedroom. Corina was now thirty-eight weeks pregnant and was the size of a small house in Rebecca's eyes "You okay, Fatty?"

"Where have you been? I was expecting you for breakfast" Corina looked tired whilst she rubbed baby oil into her huge stomach and breasts, to help try and alleviate the stretch marks.

"I've been with Debs…. I really like her, Cor…. like REALLY like her!" Rebecca flopped onto the bed "Wow, look at your tits, they are huge!"

"Yes, funnily enough I've been carrying them around for months…does this Debs feel the same about you?" asked Corina, she felt a pang of jealousy, but didn't really understand why as she would love to see Rebecca settled and happy.

"I think so; she is definitely hot for me…if you know what I mean?" Rebecca winked as she got off the bed and then wiggled her tongue around in Corina's face.

Corina ignored Rebecca's tongue movements in her face and asked "Do you fancy going for a walk over to the gardens? I can't seem to get comfortable, so I thought some fresh air might do me some good and help me sleep tonight"

"…If I must" huffed Rebecca. She hated going to the public gardens. She would rather be propped up in a bar somewhere drinking Jack Daniels and Coke and hanging out with Debs. Flowers, swans and duck statues just weren't her thing.

"Well, don't strain yourself. I bet if DEBS asked, you would be flying out the door armed with a strap on!" Corina struggled to get her trousers on as her bump was stopping her from bending over properly to pull them up.

"Do you want me to help you with that, stroppy tits?" laughed Rebecca "You are not getting jealous are you?"

"Yes…no…oh, I don't know. My hormones are making me feel crazy and I'm really missing Joseph" Corina covered her face with both of her hands to try and hide the fact that she had started to cry.

Rebecca moved closer to Corina and hugged her "It's okay to cry, Cor. You don't have to hide it from me. I know you are missing Joseph and it's good to cry…just let it all out"

Rebecca helped Corina to get dressed whilst she continued to cry. The tears poured down over Corina's puffy cheeks and down onto her blue patterned maternity blouse that Rebecca had just pulled down over Corina's head…. and was now forcing her arms into. She hadn't cried for about a week and that was when she was alone in the lounge whilst she watched 'The Young and The Restless' on television, she had remembered how Joseph had hated that programme with a passion. She missed him so much that her heart felt like it was about to break into tiny pieces, her heart was most definitely broken. She then thought of her son, and how precious he had looked as he lay in her arms on the day that he had died. He was perfect in every way and just looked like he was fast asleep. She wondered if he was with his daddy somewhere, though she didn't know where as she didn't believe in God and heaven…not since her life had been turned upside down by suicide and death. God hadn't done anything for her; she'd only had ten years of happiness out of the whole of her life. Her childhood was rubbish, also her life now was a struggle and every day she fought to keep her own emotions in check. She tried hard, very hard, each and every day, to try and figure out why all of the heartache had happened. She must have been a real bitch in her past life; she must have done something really bad to deserve all that had happened to her.

"Are you thinking about Joseph?" asked Rebecca quietly, as she wiped away Corina's tears.

Corina nodded and hugged Rebecca tightly "I'm glad you are here, Becs. I love you so much"

"I love you too, fatty. Now come on, let's go for that walk" Rebecca kissed her on the cheek then grabbed her hand and headed out of the apartment and across the road to the public gardens.

....

"Shall we go and sit on your bench?" asked Rebecca as they entered the gardens.

"Yes, okay. I can blubber some more then, eh?" Corina smiled at Rebecca and they linked arms and made their way to Corina's special bench by the lagoon.

It was the fifth of March so there was still a bit of a nip of coldness in the air. Rebecca felt a bit chilly so snuggled up to Corina for warmth. Corina felt like she was a walking radiator as she felt hot most of the time. Rebecca wasn't really prepared for the Boston winter that they had just had, it had been much colder than England. They'd had lots of snow too, but spring was approaching. It was a time for new life and new beginnings for both of them.

"So tell me about Debs then" said Corina, they huddled up closely together on the bench.

"Well, she's a nurse as you know, and she's got a gorgeous apartment on Avery Street with fab views of the Harbour.... it's like twenty-seven floors up!" replied Rebecca excitedly.

Corina giggled at Rebecca's excitement about the apartment block. She remembered she used to be just like that... in complete awe of all the Boston sights.

"She just feels comfortable; you know? And, I understand now"

"Understand what Becs?" asked Corina, intrigued by what Rebecca was about to tell her.

"I totally understand why you married Joseph so quickly and I'm really sorry I didn't support you at the time, because I know now what that feeling is like...when you really love somebody and just want to be with them where ever they are"

Corina looked at Rebecca and saw happiness in her eyes. It was the same look she and Joseph had in their eyes on their wedding day and she understood the feeling Rebecca had for Debs, even though she had only known her for a couple of weeks.

"Becs, that is so lovely. I am really pleased for you"

"And, do you know what, Cor? She feels the same for me. She knew it on the day we first saw each other.... just like you and Joseph. She really, really likes me. No, she said she loves me.... she told me this morning!" Rebecca burst into tears of happiness "Oh shit, sorry for crying, Cor, but I can't help it. I'm so happy!"

"That's so cute, Becs. I don't think I've ever seen you this emotional and in love.... does that mean you don't want to sleep with me anymore?" Corina winked and elbowed Rebecca gently in the ribs.

"I'll always have eyes for you, my little sex kitten!" laughed Rebecca.

Suddenly Corina's face changed from a pleased look for Rebecca to a screwed up, agonised and in pain look "Jeez, that hurt" said Corina as she rubbed her stomach "Oh no, here it comes again!"

"Oh shit, is the baby coming?" yelled Rebecca.

Corina screamed out in agony "Oh, why does it hurt so bad?" she stood up to try and make herself feel better, she rubbed the small of her back and moved her hips from side to side "Surely, you're supposed to get some warning, not just BAM, I'm coming?"

"That's probably why you were so uncomfortable last night.... umm, Cor, I think you've just pee'd your pants!" said Rebecca, she pointed to the puddle of water on the ground and she could see there was more fluid running down Corina's trouser leg.

"That's my waters gone, oh shit, I don't like this pain. Here it comes again. Ohhhhhhhhhh!" she grabbed hold of Rebecca's hand and squeezed it so tight that Rebecca winced in pain.

"Let's go back to Mary, she'll know what to do" said Rebecca in a complete panic.

"I can't walk, Becs. It's coming. I want to push!"

"No, Corina…hold it in. We need to get back to Mary"

"I can't fucking hold it in… it's coming!" screamed Corina, she felt an intense urge to push and started to fumble with her trouser clip to try and undo it so she could take her trousers off.

"What the hell are you doing? You can't take your trousers off here; we are in a park for god's sake!" Rebecca didn't know what to do and she wished she had listened to what was being said in the birthing classes…instead of dreaming about Debs and her lovely boobs.

A lady passer by stopped and asked if everything was okay when she noticed Corina was doubled up in agony.

"Could you please stay with her while I run and get Mazza?" asked Rebecca, still in a panic.

"Mazza?" enquired the lady; she looked confused, but she tried to help Corina to remain upright.

"That's my Mom" squealed Corina in agony, she tried to push again with the painful tightening of her contraction "I have to get these trousers off!"

The lady, who was in her mid-forties, helped Corina to take her trousers off and then wrapped her coat around Corina's waist so other passers-by couldn't see Corina's private parts, then Corina knelt on the grass and held onto the bench for balance. The lady rubbed the small of her back when another contraction started up again.

"That's feels good" said Corina "What's your name? I'm Corina by the way!"

"Hi Corina, I'm called Catherine and you're lucky that I was passing, as I'm a Doctor" said Catherine, she put her hand on Corina's tummy to feel for another contraction.

"A doctor of what?" screamed Corina, the pain had come again and the urge to push got stronger.

"Well, funnily enough I'm an Obstetrician" laughed Catherine.

"No way!" Corina looked at her in disbelief, she couldn't believe her luck.

"Is this your first baby, Corina?" enquired Catherine.

"Do you know Doctor Susan Shapiro from the B I D?"

"Corina, concentrate now honey. Is this your first baby?" Catherine ignored the small talk as Corina was getting close to giving birth.

"No, it's my second.... oh shit, it's coming!" Corina growled through the pain, she could feel the baby's head pushing onto her perineum. It stung like crazy and she had an urge to bite the wooden bench with her teeth, but refrained and screamed out loud instead.

Mary and Rebecca arrived with blankets to wrap the baby in and Alberto was going to bring the car to take them straight to hospital. Mary went around to the other side of the bench, so she faced Corina to give her some encouragement.

"You okay, baby?" asked Mary, when she knelt down in front of Corina.

"It hurts like hell, Mom. Make it stop, please!" shouted Corina, another strong, painful contraction took over her body.

"It'll stop when the baby is born, honey. You need to do as the lady says, okay? It'll soon be over" Mary reassured Corina and felt excited that she was soon going to be a grandma.

Rebecca paced up and down whilst she waited for Alberto to arrive with the car. There was a small crowd of people that had gathered and they quietly waited for the baby to arrive.

Catherine whispered in Corina's ear to see if she minded her having a look to see where the baby's head was. Corina nodded ferociously in agreement.... at that point she didn't care who looked at her vagina, she just wanted the baby to come out.

"Okay, Corina. One big push and you should deliver your baby's head" urged Catherine "Push, push, push, keep it coming, good girl, that's it, keep going.... Okay, stop and pant for me now"

Catherine pulled the umbilical cord over the baby's head, as it was wrapped around the baby's neck. Corina started to scream with the pain as it got worse again, then with one big push the baby slid out quickly into the hands of Catherine. Catherine passed the baby up through Corina's legs towards Mary, who was armed with blankets to wrap the baby in. Corina instantly looked at the baby's face. The baby looked like her son and had the same thick brown hair. She grabbed the baby from Mary so she could see what sex the baby was….it was a little girl. She wrapped her back up again and nestled the baby tight into her body to keep her warm.

Suddenly Corina heard a round of applause from the crowd that had gathered to watch her and there were shouts of "Well done" and "Congratulations" being called to her. She felt very protective towards the little bundle in her arms and realised there and then she wasn't going to give her up to the Patton's. She was overcome with a maternal feeling of love when the baby yelled out her first cry. Her loud cry made Corina's breasts tingle and she had an overwhelming urge to breast feed her. Rebecca came over and had a look at the baby, both she and Mary cried when they looked at Corina holding her so close.

"I just can't believe you gave birth in the public gardens" laughed Mary as the tears ran down her face "Your favourite place in Boston!"

"I know…trust me! Thank you so much, Catherine" said Corina, who by this time felt exhausted.

"I've got someone to call an ambulance, Corina, as you still need to deliver the placenta after we've cut the cord and I'll have the correct supplies to do it in the ambulance" replied Catherine "And, you are most welcome…. it's not every day I deliver a baby in the public gardens on the way to work!"

"I'll go back with Rebecca and tell your Dad honey, then we will meet you at the hospital" Mary leant over and kissed both Corina and the baby on the head. Corina watched Mary and Rebecca as they made their way up past the lagoon until they were out of sight, she felt thankful that she had their support. It would have been so easy to have walked away from Mary when she found out she had kept

Joseph's secret, but she was glad she had forgiven her and let the anger towards her go. She cuddled her baby closer to her body and kissed her on her tiny forehead, she could see the baby trying to focus on her face, so Corina moved closer, so she could speak to her.

"Hello little one, I'm your Mommy" Corina smiled at the baby and the baby let out a tiny whimper.

The love she felt for her daughter, at that moment in time, was overwhelming.

Chapter Thirty

Later that afternoon at the medical centre, Corina was in her private room and she was sat up in bed as she breastfed her baby. She stroked the baby's thick brown hair whilst the baby suckled on her breast.

"Does that feel like.... sexual?" asked Rebecca inquisitively whilst she watched Corina breast feed the baby.

"No, of course not!" laughed Corina "But, I know why you have asked...I was worried about what it would feel like...but it's totally a different feeling"

"She is cute though, Cor. You sure you want to keep her?" Rebecca leant over and touched the baby's hand.

"Yes, of course I'm sure, there is no way they are going to have her...I was having second thoughts a few weeks ago, that's why I didn't go to that counselling session Doctor Shapiro set up for me"

"I thought you were having second thoughts, but I wanted you to figure it out for yourself, that's why I didn't say anything. Have you thought of any names yet?" asked Rebecca.

There was a gentle tap on the door and Mary entered with Alberto and Catherine.

"Look who I found in reception!" said Mary. She felt proud that Corina had made her a grandmother and even though it wasn't her son's baby, she wouldn't treat the baby as anything less than her granddaughter. She was over the moon that Corina had decided to keep her.... Alberto, on the other hand, didn't look too enthralled as he took his first look at the 'Psycho's' baby.

"Nice to see you breast feeding, Corina" said Catherine as she appeared from behind Alberto, she was armed with flowers and a pink congratulations balloon with baby girl written on it.

"What does it weigh?" asked Alberto whilst he continued to check out the baby.

"SHE weighed in at seven pounds, fifteen and a quarter ounce!" snapped Corina.

Rebecca winced at the thought of passing a baby out through her vagina and was thankful she didn't ever have to do it. She didn't want to have a baby; she would rather have a dog.

"Oh, well......well done.... has someone told The Patton's of your plans to keep their baby?"

"Alberto!" Mary looked at him with anger in her eyes "The baby belongs to Corina, not them......and no...I haven't got round to telling them yet!"

"Rather you than me!" retorted Alberto "I don't have a good feeling about this"

"Well, I don't care what you think, Dad. She is my baby and I'm keeping her...end of!" stated Corina.

Catherine stood back, she looked very embarrassed that she had witnessed what she thought should have been a private conversation, she had only wanted to bring Corina a gift and say hello to the baby while she was on her break. Corina noticed Catherine's awkwardness and patted the space on her bed, to encourage Catherine to sit down on it next to her.

"Anyway" said Corina, she gave Alberto a dirty look "I am glad you are here, Catherine, as I wanted to thank you again for helping me this morning. In fact, I have decided to name the baby after you and my Mom.... Catherine Mary" Corina looked proudly at her daughter "Catherine Mary Barsetti....it has a nice ring to it, don't you think?"

"Well, I am honoured, Corina. It's a wonderful name.... even if I say so myself!" laughed Catherine.

"Huh?" grumbled Rebecca "Nice of you to include your best friend's name!"

Corina laughed "Actually, those are only her middle names...her full name is Rebecca Catherine Mary Barsetti.... of course I didn't leave you out!"

"Rebecca Barsetti?" said Rebecca at she looked at Corina with tears in her eyes "I'm going to cry again, that's really cool of you...I'm so proud!"

They all laughed at Rebecca as she tried to cope with her outburst of emotion...apart from Alberto, he stood at the end of the bed and frowned.

"Rebecca Barsetti.... Doctor Rebecca Barsetti.... now that has a nice ring to it!" said Rebecca thoughtfully.

"Becs, she's just been born...she might not want to be a doctor!" laughed Mary.

"Well, as long as she doesn't turn out like her father" said Alberto nastily, he then left the room and slammed the door behind him.

"Oooooooooh.... he's a bit pissy!" said Rebecca, she wiped her tears away with the sleeve of her cardigan.

"You can't blame him though, Becs, he has been through a lot. He will come round though.... he always does" Corina passed the baby to Catherine, who put her over her shoulder to gently wind her.

"I'm going to go out and find him" said Mary "Nice to see you again, Catherine, and thank you so much for your help delivering my granddaughter"

Catherine smiled as Mary left the room and then turned to Corina "I know you don't know me very well.... but you wanna fill me in on what's going on? I'm a bit intrigued"

Corina looked at Rebecca and grimaced.

"Well, where do we start?" laughed Rebecca.

"Oh, you don't have to tell me if you don't want to.... but I have a feeling I'm going to be seeing a lot more of you and the baby, so I would like to know the story so far" Catherine then looked a bit embarrassed "…sorry, I shouldn't be so nosy…and I shouldn't assume that you would want to see me again!"

"No, it's okay, Catherine…. I had a feeling we will be seeing a lot more of you too…we sort of just clicked didn't we?" Corina looked at Catherine, who nodded back at her in agreement "Becs, do you want to take Catherine to the family room for a coffee and tell her all the sordid details? I'm feeling really tired, so I'm going to take a quick nap while Rebecca is asleep"

"Ahh, Rebecca" Rebecca felt so humbled that the baby was named after her "Come on, Doc…. I hope you have your good listening ears on…. this may take some time!"

Catherine put the baby into the crib next to Corina's bed and tucked her in. She left with Rebecca, leaving Corina to have a little nap.

…..

Mary looked for Alberto, but she couldn't find him anywhere. She knew he was upset and was worried about his wellbeing. She had got as far as the main entrance, but didn't have a clue which direction he had gone in. She decided to ask at reception to see if they had seen him. The staff on reception knew of Alberto, as he had worked at The Beth Israel Deaconess for many years as an orthopaedic surgeon. He was a very well respected surgeon, and because of his fun and easy going nature, he had many friends at the hospital. He was still being invited back to the hospital for staff parties and had received many wedding and christening invitations from staff over the years.

"I don't suppose you have seen Doctor Barsetti pass through this way, have you?" asked Mary to Brianna, who was manning the reception desk today with Julia.

Mary thought they were like chalk and cheese. Brianna was a larger lady in her mid-thirty's, who was always very happy and approachable and then there was Julia…a pale, skinny, frail looking woman in her late fifties. She was extremely quiet and didn't seem as approachable as Brianna. Alberto had told Mary once that if Julia ate a fraction of what Brianna ate, she would put on weight in no time.

"Oh, Hi Mrs Barsetti!" boomed Brianna "How are you?"

"I'm good thanks…. have you seen him or not?"

"Yes, he went that way" Brianna pointed towards the direction of the chapel.

"Thanks, honey" said Mary, she headed off quickly to the chapel to see if Alberto was there.

"You're welcome… oh …and congratulations!" shouted Brianna at Mary, but she had already rushed out of sight.

Mary quietly opened the door to the chapel and took a look around to see if Alberto was inside. She spotted him right at the back, he was sat down with his head in his hands. She thought he was praying at first, but then quickly realised he was crying. She approached him quietly, so she did not disturb him and sat down slowly beside him. She gently put her hand on his knee to let him know she was there to support him. Alberto sobbed even louder when he realised she was there; he couldn't stop himself. It was like she had given him permission to release all of his pent up emotion from the past events.

"Alberto, my darling, everything is going to be alright…you'll see" Mary whispered to him lovingly in her kind and gentle voice.

Alberto couldn't speak. He thought that when the baby was born; Corina would give it to The Patton's and that would be the end of it. Then, he could try and forget James and what he had seen him do. He wanted to grieve for his son properly and not have his grief overshadowed by the visions he still had every day of James shooting himself. He wanted Corina to get on with her life too; he didn't want her bogged down with a child that wasn't Joseph's and he wondered how he could possibly accept the child as his granddaughter. He was confused and he didn't know how he was going to move forward with everything.

"Alberto, I feel Corina is doing the right thing by keeping the baby. I know you are upset with her over it, but she's the one that has to live with her decisions. I am going to call James' parents in a while and explain everything to them.... Alberto, are you listening?"

Alberto continued to cry and kept his head in his hands. Mary put her arms around him and rested her chin on the top of his head. She had never seen her husband like this before; he had always been so strong in the past. It was normally her that ended up a blubbing wreck of emotion.

"Alberto, what are you concerned about the most?"

She passed him a tissue from her handbag and watched him wipe away his tears, then blow his nose.

"I'm worried that I won't be able to love that baby as my own grandchild.... I don't think I can accept her into my family" Alberto's tears poured down his face again, he then looked at Mary with sorrow in his eyes.

"But, you love Corina like she was your own daughter...what's the difference? She was your son's wife, she's not a blood relation...but you can't imagine life without her, can you?"

"That's different, Mary. She didn't try and kill anyone or shoot herself in front of me!"

"And neither did that baby, Alberto! That baby is innocent in all of this and she doesn't deserve to be treated any differently. Corina shouldn't be shunned because she loves her baby and wants to keep her!"

"Just leave me alone, Mary. I can't help how I feel and I need to sort this all out in my own mind. I'll see you at home later"

"Okay, but are you sure you are going to be alright here by yourself?"

"Yes, I'll be fine. I just need to get my mind straight. You go ahead and I'll see you later" Alberto took hold of her hand and kissed it. He wished he could be as forgiving as her, but then she hadn't seen what James was like. Maybe if she had seen James' hate towards Corina, she would feel the same way he did right now.

"Okay dear, see you in a bit" Mary kissed him on the lips and got up from her chair. She got to the chapel door and then turned to him to wave him goodbye. He lifted his hand to wave and then blew her a kiss. She then left him alone and headed back up to Corina's room.

Mary got back to Corina's room and found that Corina and the baby were both asleep. Rebecca had noticed Mary was back, so called for Mary to join her and Catherine in the family room.

"Everything alright, Mazza?" asked Rebecca, when Mary sat down in one of the big comfy chairs that engulfed her tiny frame.

"Alberto is very upset and he's not happy about the baby"

"Rebecca has explained everything to me, Mary, so if there is anything I can do to help, please ask" said Catherine.

"Thank you, but he needs to get things straight in his own mind. He will come around; it'll just take a while"

"I am so sorry for the loss of your son too, Mary. I know it's not the exactly the same, but my younger sister killed herself five years ago, so I know how suicide can affect families" Catherine looked at Mary and fought hard to hold back her own tears. She really missed her sister and her family were still devastated by what her sister had done, as it was out of the blue with no warning of any intention to kill herself at all.

"This is mind blowing" said Rebecca "Talk about fate…. how bizarre that you come along just in time to deliver Cor's baby and now you say you've had a suicide in your family, so you know exactly why this family is so fucked up and can understand it!"

"I wouldn't say you were all fucked up, Rebecca" laughed Catherine "You are all just grieving and trying to cope with everything that has happened"

"I'm sorry about your sister too, Catherine. It is strange how things happen, Rebecca…. some things are fated…. looks like what happened today is one of those fated moments" Mary looked stressed and tired "I'm going to have to call James' parents soon…I'm not looking forward to it at all!"

"Don't call them yet, Mazza. Wait until tomorrow, there's no rush" Rebecca looked in her compact mirror at her short, spikey, black hair "Do you think I should get a couple of low lights put in, Mazza?" she played with her hair and messed it up with her fingers.

Mary loved how Rebecca could lighten the mood instantly by changing the subject "If you want, honey. It looks nice anyway" Mary didn't know what a low light was anyway. She had let her hair go grey naturally and had never dyed it; she had always had a simple blonde bob, which was now a simple silver grey bob. It was very easy to maintain and she liked her hair like that.

"Right ladies, I'm going to go back to work now" said Catherine "Tell Corina, I will be in to see her tomorrow"

"Yep, I'm off too" replied Rebecca "I have a date with the hottest nurse in Boston"

"I take it you're not talking about me, then?" laughed Mary.

"Sorry Mazza, but you're not my type" Rebecca stood up and kissed Mary on the cheek "Try not to worry, sweet cheeks. I'll see you later"

"Bye dear, have fun"

Mary stood up while Catherine and Rebecca left the room and then sat back down to gather her thoughts before going back in to see Corina. She looked forward to having a cuddle with baby Rebecca, but she had decided to wait until tomorrow to call The Patton's. She knew they would take it badly, so she needed a good night's sleep to be able to cope with their reaction.

Chapter Thirty-One

"Mom, is that you? You sound different"

Mary answered the phone to Corina. It was ten-thirty in the morning, but she was in bed and still half asleep. She'd had an awful night's sleep, as she had been awake for most of the night worrying about how The Patton's would take the news about Corina keeping the baby. Then, just as she nodded off, Alberto had woken her up with one of his nightmares and had screamed out loud about James. Her voice didn't seem to work properly and she found it hard to talk to Corina.

"Yes, it's me dear. I'm just a bit tired, that's all" Mary forced her words out, but her voice still didn't sound like her.

"You sound awful.... anyway; they said I could come home with Rebecca today, so could you please come and get me?" asked Corina "I want to get the baby registered before I leave the hospital though, they said I could do it here"

"Okay, honey. Just give me an hour or so and I'll be there"

"Thanks, Mom.... love you"

Mary tried to say 'I love you' back, but it didn't come out. She put the phone down and got out of the bed to look for Alberto. She wrapped her dressing gown around her and headed for the lounge. She found Alberto reading the paper in his recliner chair. He still had his pyjamas on and looked unshaven.

"Alberto, that was Corina on the phone"

"I didn't want to answer it in case it was The Patton's" said Alberto, he continued to read the obituaries in the paper.

"It's okay, honey. I'm going to pick Corina up in an hour; they said she could come home. Do you want to come with me?"

"No thanks.... I see Doctor Krieger died...Do you remember him, Mary? He worked in oncology with Joseph and James.... they sure are dropping like flies in that department!" laughed Alberto.

"It's not funny, Alberto. Why don't you want to come with me to pick Corina up?" asked Mary impatiently.

"Because, I am sat here in my pyjamas looking at the obituaries....and do you know what? I'm glad that some other poor asshole is going through what I'm going through at the moment!" shouted Alberto at Mary, who in return looked at him with contempt.

"Well, I wouldn't wish the loss of a son on anyone!" shouted Mary back at him "It's okay, DEAR, you stay here and wallow in your own self-pity, while I go and pick up our daughter and grandchild from the hospital" Mary felt tired and irritable and wasn't in the mood for Alberto's feisty Italian temper tantrums.

"DAMN IT WOMAN, THAT BABY IS NOT MY GRANDCHILD....SO DON'T EVEN THINK ABOUT BRINGING IT BACK HERE...YOU HEAR ME?"

Alberto got up off of his chair and threw the paper across the room; it hit the top of the fireplace and knocked over an ornament. It was a special ornament that Joseph and Corina had bought them for their fortieth wedding anniversary. It smashed on the hearth, the tiny pieces of white and blue porcelain flew across the room and landed on the wool rug next to Mary's bare feet.

Rebecca, who was stood in the lounge doorway after she had heard Alberto raise his voice, had come to see what all the commotion was about.

"What's going on?" asked Rebecca, she looked at Mary, who was crying as she knelt next to the broken ornament.

"AND, GET THIS BLOODY LESBIAN OUT OF MY APARTMENT TOO!" shouted Alberto, he shoved past Rebecca in the doorway and knocked her out of the way to get out of the lounge.

"Jesus Christ, Alberto!" said Rebecca, she rubbed her shoulder to ease the pain of the knock "There was no need for that!"

"Just leave him, Rebecca. There's no use talking to him when he's like that" Mary looked extremely upset, so Rebecca went over to her and gave her a hug.

"What was all that about?"

"I just told him I was going to pick up Corina, but he doesn't want the baby here" Mary wept as she started to pick up the pieces of the broken ornament. She wrapped them in one of Alberto's newspapers and put them on the hearth to sort later, in the hope that she could possibly glue them back together.

"Ahh, so he has still not taken it well then!" said Rebecca, she helped Mary to her feet. She thought Mary looked tired and felt a big desire to help out as much as she could. She was a guest in her home, so didn't want to over step the mark if Alberto wasn't happy.

"Obviously not" Mary sat on the couch and tried to think of what to do next. She didn't want to bring Corina back to the apartment with little Rebecca if Alberto was going to get upset again. And, she also had to call The Patton's, but wanted Corina there with her when she did it.

"What about if Corina and I went to stay at her house in Milton with the baby, seeing as it hasn't sold…just until things settle down?"

Mary let out a big sigh "Well, let's go and see what Corina wants to do. She might not want to go back there. I'll just go and get dressed and then we can go to the medical centre"

….

As Mary and Rebecca walked into the main entrance of the medical centre, they were greeted by Brianna's loud "Good Morning, Mrs Barsetti, what a beautiful day to be bringing your grandchild home…. isn't it Julia!"

Julia shrugged and looked uninterested "We've just seen Corina and the baby" continued Brianna excitedly "She's so fricken cute!"

"Yes, she is rather cute" replied Rebecca "Though, what do you expect...she is my name sake!"

"Oh, is she.... really?" Brianna looked Rebecca up and down and then gave Julia a confused look, who in turn shrugged her shoulders again and remained to look uninterested.

"See you later, Brianna" said Mary, she pulled Rebecca away to get to the elevator quickly, as Rebecca looked like she was ready to punch Brianna.

"Corina must be feeling pretty good if she has been down to see Tweedle Dum and Tweedle Dee this morning" said Rebecca sarcastically, she ruffled up her hair whilst she looked at herself in the elevator mirror.

"Yes, I just hope we aren't about to ruin her day with the news that Alberto doesn't want the baby in the apartment!"

"I'll suggest we go to the house in Milton before you tell her about Alberto...okay Mazza?"

They both took deep breaths as they left the elevator and approached Corina's room. Doctor Shapiro waved at them from her office as they passed; they both smiled and waved back. Mary knocked on Corina's door and they both went in. Corina was already packed and ready to go.

"Where's the car seat? They won't let me take her out of here without looking at her car seat and checking it!" asked Corina impatiently.

"You didn't ask me to bring the car seat, Corina, but luckily it's in the car...don't worry, I can go back and get it. Have you registered the baby already then?" Mary noticed an envelope on the bed with 'Birth Certificate' printed on it. Mary then sat down on the bed and pulled Rebecca's cot towards her so she could gently stroke the baby's face with her finger, as the baby had started to wriggle about and whimper quietly.

"Yes, I put Joseph down as the father seeing as I'm married.... the registrar doesn't know he is dead"

"Corina!" gasped Mary "Isn't that against the law?"

"Dunno, she didn't question it, so I put it down. I didn't want to leave it blank. If I wanted to put James' name down, he would have to have been present at the birth registration because we aren't married...so as that is pretty impossible, I just put Joseph's name...she asked me his occupation and everything"

"But, Joseph isn't her father!" said Mary, who by now had picked up little Rebecca and began to cuddle her close to stop her from crying.

"Who cares!" replied Corina "Rebecca won't know.... I'll tell her that her daddy is dead, anyway"

"You will have to tell her the truth one day, Cor. It's not really a good idea to lie to her about who her father is.... I can't believe you have put Joseph's name on it!" said Rebecca.

"Hey, guess what, Becs....my baby, my decision.... now butt out!" snapped Corina.

"Bloody hell, Corina, there's no need for that!" said Rebecca "I'm only trying to help!"

"Well, don't!"

"Now, now, girls" interrupted Mary "We still need to tell James' parents too, as I haven't told them yet"

"That's okay, I will do it later when I get home" said Corina. She looked nervous at the thought of telling them, but she knew she had to get it over and done with...and soon.

Mary flashed a concerned look at Rebecca to prompt her to talk to Corina about going back to the house in Milton.

"Cor, how do you and the baby fancy staying at the house in Milton with me?" asked Rebecca.

"Are you mad?"

"Don't think so, why?"

"Do you honestly think I'm EVER going to go back there again? No way, I'm going to stay with Mom and Dad until I go back to

England" Corina looked confused, why would Rebecca would suggest such a stupid idea?

"It's just that...." Rebecca paused "It's just that.... Alberto is having a bit of difficulty coming to terms with the fact you are keeping the baby and he doesn't want me in the apartment anymore, so I thought you may like to keep me company at the house" she avoided the fact that Alberto had also banned the baby from the apartment.

"Can't you stay with Deborah?"

"Probably, but I want to stay with you"

"Corina dear, I'm afraid your father is very upset and doesn't want the baby in the apartment either" Mary tried to explain, but immediately Corina lost her temper. Her hormones were all over the place again.

"What?" shouted Corina "Where am I supposed to go? I can't go back to the house, I can't!"

Corina started to pace up and down, Mary knew that once Corina had started to pace it was not good, as this was a sign that she had started to get herself worked up.

"I don't bloody believe this!" continued Corina "What am I going to do?"

"Why don't you try going back to the house with me, Cor?" asked Rebecca gently "We can close off the lounge and just use the spare bedrooms…it's only for a few weeks until you go back to England"

"Until we go back to England"

"Huh?"

"Until WE go back to England, you mean!" Corina raised her voice again "WE are going back to England TOGETHER!"

"Oh, yeah…. I meant to talk to you about that" said Rebecca, who felt embarrassed when she noticed that Corina was glaring straight at her whilst she waited for an explanation.

"Talk to me about what?" Corina continued to glare at Rebecca; though she had an idea of what Rebecca was going to say next.

"Debs has asked me to stay in Boston with her… and I'm seriously considering it"

"But, you've only known her for two weeks!"

"Corina, you of all people should NOT be judgemental about how long I have known her for…. really?"

Rebecca went to stand up so she could face up to Corina, when Mary intervened.

"Come on, Corina. It's time for some calm now. The baby is getting restless….and it's only until Alberto comes round. I will stay there with you too, if you like…yes? Now, come here" Mary held her arms out to Corina and gestured for her to come and have a hug.

Corina avoided the hug and went past Mary to get to Rebecca "I actually waited three months before I came to Boston with Joseph…not two weeks!"

"Wow, three whole months!" the sarcasm in Rebecca's voice was apparent as she faced up to Corina "I recall you married him after only knowing him for just under nine weeks…and you only waited three months to come to Boston because he hadn't finished his year in England…you are such a fucking hypocrite, Corina!"

"Well, that's longer than two weeks…. you don't know her like I knew Joseph!"

"And you, my friend, obviously didn't know your husband very well either, DID YOU!"

"What the hell is that supposed to mean?"

"Corina, come on this isn't helping" Mary could see the argument wasn't going to end well and tried to get Corina to come away from Rebecca.

Corina ignored her again "So, come on Rebecca, spit it out…. what do you mean by that?"

"Your husband was a selfish prick…that's what I mean…I never liked him from the beginning. I always knew he was going to break your heart and he eventually did it good and proper, didn't he?"

"He was ill; he didn't know what he was doing!"

"He fucking knew, alright…he knew exactly what he was doing…he even confided in his mother…he was a conniving selfish prick…if he loved you so much, he would have given you the option of looking after him, but he didn't. He was just plain selfish…. that is all!"

"You Bitch!"

"Yep, well, what is good enough for the goose, is good enough for the gander!" Rebecca sneered at Corina.

"And to think I named my baby after you!" Corina started to cry, she never realised Rebecca hated Joseph so much.

"You got yourself into this mess, Corina. Did you really think Alberto was just going to let you take the baby back into his home? Do you not realise how difficult it's been for him too? He witnessed James shoot himself, he saw what he did to you…. you may be awake night after night seeing what Joseph did, but Alberto is trying to cope with the same…it's not all about you, other people have had to cope with their shit too, but they pussy foot around you all the time…you're a big girl now, not some brat who stamps her feet to get her own way!"

"Don't hold back, Rebecca, just say it like it is!"

"I told you before; you got yourself in this shit, so it's no big surprise!"

"Yes, pregnancy wise…I understand that, but slagging off my dead husband is out of order!"

They were both so intent on arguing that they hadn't noticed Mary had left the room with the baby to get away from the shouting.

"Oh…I could tell you so much more about your husband and what he used to get up to at The Infirmary…. you were so blind to it!" Rebecca began to snigger to herself, when she felt a hard slap across her face from Corina.

"In case you hadn't noticed…my husband is not here to defend himself. I don't care what he did. He was with me for ten years and he loved me. He did love me…. HE LOVED ME. Do you hear me Rebecca? HE LOVED ME. And, I loved him, I still love him…and I miss him. I miss him so much…. I don't care what he did…. Please, don't tell me what he did!"

Corina sobbed and covered her ears, she was desperate not to hear any of more of Rebecca's hateful comments about Joseph. She could not fathom out how the argument had escalated from staying at the house in Milton, to Rebecca's display of hatred for her husband.

Rebecca looked at Corina as she sat on the bed and sobbed. She looked helpless. Rebecca started to feel guilty that she had said the things she did to her, but it was the truth…she didn't like Joseph, she never had. She thought she had probably gone a bit too far though, and went over to the bed and put her hand on Corina's shoulder.

"Corina, I'm really sorry, I shouldn't have said those things…. But, I never liked Joseph and now you know it. But, I love you Cor, and I thought you would understand how I feel about Debs and wanting to stay"

"I do understand, and I don't know why I questioned it…I just don't want to go back to England without you. I'm unsure about my future and I didn't expect to want to keep the baby, so I'm feeling a bit lost. I love you too, Becs and I'm sorry I hit you"

"That was a good slap, Cor…Bloody hell, it's not like you to be violent!" laughed Rebecca, she started to rub her face. There was a bright red hand mark on her right cheek "Remind me not to piss you off again!"

Corina really didn't feel like laughing, she felt tearful and hormonal and her breasts had started to leak milk. Suddenly, she realised that Mary and the baby weren't in the room and rushed out of the room to find them.

"Corina, don't panic, they couldn't have gone far" shouted Rebecca after her.

As Corina rushed down the corridor looking for Mary, she bumped into Doctor Shapiro.

"Hi, Corina, how are you feeling?"

"Have you seen my Mom? She's got the baby"

"Yes, she is in the family room with her, she is talking to the baby's other Grandparents. Is there a problem?"

"Other Grandparents?" Corina did an about turn and ran back into her room to get back to Rebecca. Doctor Shapiro followed her, she felt concerned that Corina wasn't coping very well.

"Becs, quick, we have to get to the family room. Mary has the baby and apparently James' parents are there!"

"Oh shit! How did they know about the baby?"

"Corina, calm down" said Doctor Shapiro, she stood in the door way, blocking Corina's exit "I don't think your Mom knew about them coming either, she looked just as shocked as you do now"

"But, what if she gives them the baby or they take the baby away from me? Come on Becs, let's get down there!"

"Corina, she's not going to give them the baby or let them take her. You need to take a deep breath and calm yourself down" said Doctor Shapiro, looking concerned.

"I am calm!" shouted Corina "We have to get down there!" she pushed past Doctor Shapiro and sprinted to the family room. Rebecca and Doctor Shapiro were in hot pursuit behind her.

Corina burst open the door and stood in the doorway gasping for breath.

"My goodness me, Corina dear, what have you been up too? You look like you've just run the Boston marathon!" exclaimed Mary. She still had little Rebecca in her arms and rocked her gently from side to side, as she continued to stir and wriggle about because she was hungry.

"Just give me my baby!" Corina held her arms out for Mary to give her the baby "Don't ever take her away like that again…. ever!"

"Hello Corina, how are you?" interrupted Angela.

"I'm fine, how are you?" Corina actually felt agitated.

"I'm good, thanks. I expect you are wondering what Bryan and I are doing here?"

Doctor Shapiro came in behind Corina and whispered in her ear "Do you want me to stay?"

Corina nodded as she took little Rebecca from Mary. They all sat down, whilst Rebecca stood in the doorway as if she was guarding it. There was no way she would let Angela and Bryan out alive if they tried to take the baby.

Corina discreetly took her left breast out of her maternity bra and gently placed the baby on to suckle. Bryan looked away, he felt embarrassed even though he couldn't see any of her breast. Corina felt a tingle as the milk flowed from her other breast. The relief of her milk coming down was apparent on Corina's face, she felt her breasts were going to explode with the pressure. Mary passed her a breast pad to place in her bra as her top was getting soaked with her milk.

"Blimey, Cor, you could breast feed the whole of Boston!" laughed Rebecca from the doorway.

"It's nice to see that you have given the baby a good start in life, Corina" said Angela as she peered over to look at the baby.

"What are you doing here?" asked Corina. She was very matter of fact in her questioning. She didn't want them here and wanted them to get the message that they were not welcome, sooner rather than later.

"Alberto called us this morning. He said you'd had the baby and that you were ready to leave the hospital today" replied Angela.

"And, did he tell you that I shall be keeping her?"

"Keeping her? No, he said the baby was ready to be picked up!" Angela looked at Bryan in shock. Bryan didn't flinch, he couldn't care less if they had the baby or not.

Mary looked angry, she was going to give Alberto what for when she returned home to get a bag packed. She had decided she would definitely be staying with Corina until she went back to England. He could cope without her for a change; she was going to give him some space to think about what he had done.

"Yes, I shall be keeping her. I changed my mind a few weeks ago and when I saw her, I loved her straight away. So, don't think you will be taking her from me!"

"What about all the money I have paid out for you to have counselling....and your flights, amongst other things?" Angela looked upset and it was obvious that she was fighting back the tears. Bryan looked pretty pleased that Corina had changed her mind. He thought he was too old to be playing Daddy again. He wanted to enjoy his retirement....in peace.

"I shall pay you back, Angela" said Mary, she knew Corina couldn't afford to pay her back, so didn't want her to stress out over money.

"I'm not stopping you from seeing her while I'm here, and when I return back home you can come and visit" said Corina begrudgingly. She really wanted them to go and leave her alone with her baby, she did not want them to interfere with anything.

"I think you've done this on purpose!" stated Angela.

"Done what on purpose?" asked Corina, she could feel her heart start to race as she saw the look of frustration on Angela's face. It was a familiar look, she had seen it on James' face too and they looked very much alike. As she looked at Angela, she thought it was like looking at a female version of James and it had started to make her feel very uneasy.

"You've done this to get back at us for what James did to you.... not only did you force your sexual advances onto my son, just to get yourself pregnant...but you also sent him crazy, so he killed himself...there seems to be a bit of a pattern going on here!"

"You fucking bitch!" sneered Rebecca from the doorway "What a horrible thing to say....my God...you can see who James took after!"

"I think it's time for you to leave, Mrs Patton" said Doctor Shapiro "This isn't getting you anywhere. Corina has decided to keep the baby, so there's not a lot you can do about it at this moment in time"

"She got pregnant on purpose. I know it!" continued Angela "Just because you lost your baby, you thought you could try to trap him to get pregnant and replace your dead son!"

"What? I didn't know I was pregnant until after he died!" Corina didn't like what she saw in Angela, she was definitely just as nasty as her son.

"You flirted with him for years whilst you were still married to your husband, James told me what you used to be like with him. He loved you and you played him!"

"What...the.... actual...fuck!" laughed Rebecca.

"He tried to kill me, Angela! How is that love?" Corina was confused.

"He was obsessed more like!" Rebecca could not believe what Angela was saying "Sooo, quiet Bryan in the corner over there...what do you think about all this?"

Everyone turned to look at Bryan, who shuddered at the thought of going against Angela. He went to speak, but nothing came out. If looks could kill, Angela would have killed him twice over. She was not happy with Corina at all and wasn't going to give up her grandchild without a fight.

"I really think you should leave now, please" asked Doctor Shapiro again "I will call security if I have to!"

"Oh give it a rest, Doc!" said Angela, as she passed her to leave the room. Rebecca moved quickly to one side to let her out. Bryan followed Angela like a loyal dog; he held his head low and refused to look at anyone as he left the room. Just as everyone thought they'd gone, Angela appeared back in the doorway.

"Don't think you've seen the last of me, Corina Barsetti, I will have that baby if it's the last thing I do!" Angela then turned and stomped down the corridor with Bryan, who remained two steps behind her. Everyone could hear Angela's loud stomping footsteps, until they had got into the elevator and disappeared.

Corina looked shocked as she continued to feed the baby, she felt very glad that she hadn't let her daughter be adopted by them.

"It's okay dear, we won't let her take the baby" reassured Mary.

"What a nasty piece of work!" said Rebecca, she shook her head in disbelief.

Corina started to cry, she hoped she had the emotional strength to fight Angela. She felt her life was in a mess once again, but as she looked at her precious baby she knew she would find the strength to fight from somewhere. The baby was her life now and nobody was going to take her precious Rebecca from her.

Chapter Thirty-Two

It had been five days since Corina had left hospital with the baby, she tried to make the best of being back at the house at Milton with Rebecca and Mary. Corina hated being there without Joseph and the memories of finding him, and then being beaten up by James there, were at the forefront of her mind. They had not opened the door to the lounge, or gone into Corina and Joseph's bedroom, as everything was still left as it was from the day Corina was attacked. Mary and Alberto had not sorted out the house for the realtor agents to sell either as they had been in England with Corina. They did not think she would ever come back to Boston, so they had planned to sort it all out when they had returned from England. There were still stains from the drops of Corina's blood that lead from the bedroom and down the stairs to the lounge. Mary had tried with all her might to scrub them away, but they had stained the cream coloured carpet, so this too was a constant reminder for Corina every time she went up and down the stairs.

Catherine had come around to see Corina and the baby after she had finished her shift at work. It was six in the evening and Catherine looked tired after a busy day delivering babies.

"Would you like to stay for dinner, Catherine?" shouted Mary up the stairs to her. Rebecca had made a make shift lounge in one of the bedrooms, so they all had somewhere to sit and chat comfortably.

"That would be great, thanks, Mary…if there's enough to go around?" replied Catherine.

"Oh, there's more than enough…. and you are very welcome to eat here anytime" she called from the bottom of the stairs.

Mary walked back into the kitchen to finish off making her Boston Beans to go with steak and mash potato. Boston Beans were her speciality dish; she had tried to teach Corina how to make them too.... But, Corina would always forget to soak the navy beans overnight before cooking with them, so they were too hard to eat and tasted vile. Mary sniggered to herself at the thought of Corina's hard Boston beans and how Corina had asked her why she didn't just open a tin of baked beans, as it was so much easier. Obviously, Corina did not get the concept of homemade Boston beans and soaking them was far too much effort for her.

Upstairs in the lounge, Rebecca cuddled the baby and admired her pink snazzy pyjamas that had 'Spoilt by Grandma' written across them. She certainly had been spoilt by Grandma as Mary had gone out and bought everything she needed, including a pram...it was top of the range, as little Rebecca was going to have nothing but the best.

"Have you seen Alberto since you got home, Corina?" asked Catherine.

"No, and I don't think Mary has spoken to him either since she went home to pack some things on the day I left hospital" replied Corina.

"Do you think he will come around to the idea of you keeping the baby?"

"I don't know...I hope so, as I really miss him. I couldn't stand the thought of not having him in my life. He just needs to sort his head out, then hopefully he will come around to the idea"

Rebecca passed the baby to Catherine for a cuddle and then flung herself onto the single bed that she had made into a couch. Corina and Catherine were both sat on huge furry bean bags that Mary had brought home with the pram, along with all the other baby things. Her SUV had been packed to the roof with goodies and Rebecca was like a child at Christmas when she unpacked the car.

"So, Catherine, I take it you don't have a husband" enquired Rebecca.

"No, I haven't met the right lady yet"

"I knew it!" exclaimed Rebecca "Corina likes lady consultants...don't you, Cor!"

"Rebecca!" yelled Corina "That was a very long time ago...and I was VERY drunk at the time!"

"Yeah, but you've still got it in you, Cor.... once a lezzer, always a lezzer, they say!" Rebecca laughed and then winked at Catherine, who looked a tad embarrassed.

"I don't think for a minute I STILL have it in me.... I know I definitely fancy men!" Corina threw Rebecca a 'Shut up now' look as she sensed Catherine felt uncomfortable.

"Well, I have been married to a man before, but it just didn't work out. I always knew I was gay, but I never had the courage to come out. It's far more acceptable now, so I'm very comfortable with the person that I am" Catherine smiled at Rebecca "So, you are going out with one of the nurses at The B.I.D.... Deborah, right?"

"Yes, she is amazing!" swooned Rebecca "She's asked me to stay in Boston with her, but I just need to help Corina sort her life out first, then I can make the decision on what to do next"

"You make me sound like some sort of charity case. I can sort my own life out, thanks!" Corina gave Rebecca another stern look.

"I know that, Cor, I just want to make sure you are okay and settled, that's all. I worry about you because, even though you seem happy to have the baby in your life, you still seem sad to me and not your normal self....and I hate seeing you like that. I want you to be happy in all aspects of your life"

"I don't think I'll ever be happy without Joseph, so you'll be waiting a long time!"

"You will be happy, Corina" said Catherine softly "It's early days yet and you have been through so much. Can I ask if you have heard from the Patton's yet? Mary told me that they were very threatening towards you at the hospital"

"I haven't heard a thing from them yet, but I'm sure Angela will be planning something!" Corina suddenly burst into tears, the thought of them taking her baby was too much for her. She got up and took little Rebecca from Catherine and cuddled her baby tight.

"It'll be alright, Cor. We won't let anybody take her from you. I promise" Rebecca got up from her make shift couch and hugged Corina and the baby.

"Hey, Catherine, did you hear Corina slapped me at the hospital? It was a beauty!" Rebecca tried to lighten the mood and she began to giggle at the thought of Corina's hard slap across her face.

"You deserved it!" Corina smiled at the baby and did a baby voice at her "Didn't she…. naughty Auntie Rebecca!"

"DINNER…Come on ladies!" shouted Mary from downstairs.

"At last!" shrieked Rebecca "I'm bloody starving!"

When they had all settled themselves around the dinner table, Mary served out the dinner.

"This looks fantastic, Mary, thank you" said Catherine as she started to tuck into her Boston beans.

"Does anyone mind if I feed the baby at the table? My boobs are about to explode!" said Corina, whilst she fumbled with her bra strap to expose her right breast.

"No, carry on. I love looking at your boobies anyway!" laughed Rebecca.

Catherine and Mary smirked at each other and Corina started to feed the baby, she began to scoop mash potato into her mouth. Mary leant over and cut up Corina's steak for her, so she could eat it with one hand whilst she fed the baby.

"Have you been crying, honey?" asked Mary.

Corina nodded at her, she was too busy spooning slices of steak into her mouth to reply to Mary's question. Breastfeeding had made her feel ravenous a lot of the time and she even found herself snacking in the middle of the night, when Rebecca woke up for her night feed.

Suddenly there was a loud knock on the front door, which startled Mary. She jumped up quickly to answer it.

"Who the hell is that?" said Rebecca. She looked at Catherine, who in turn threw her a concerned look.

"Who is it, Mom?" shouted Corina.

Mary came back into the kitchen followed by Bryan Patton. Corina quickly covered her breast with a tea towel as he came to a halt in the doorway; yet again he looked embarrassed when he noticed she was breast feeding.

"What do you want?" Corina looked worried.

Rebecca stood up and stared at him. This made him feel even more uncomfortable, as she looked like she meant business with her jet black spiky hair and stern look on her face.

"I've brought something for you" he handed a large envelope over to Corina.

"If it's more dirty photographs, you're wasting your time, Patton" said Rebecca sternly, she edged towards him "Corina's already seen them, your sick son made sure of that!"

"It's not photographs, please open it Corina" Bryan looked nervous whilst he waited for Corina to open the envelope.

Corina tried with difficulty to open the envelope with one hand, so Mary took the baby from her. Little Rebecca was not happy about being taken off the breast and screamed out loud in retaliation. Bryan looked repulsed at the noise. Even though it was his grandchild, he really didn't like screaming babies. Corina peered inside the envelope, she then looked at Bryan and waited for him to explain why there were thousands of dollars inside of it.

"What's inside, Corina?" asked Mary.

"Thousands of dollars by the looks of it" mumbled Corina, she looked deflated. He had obviously come to take her baby away and was paying her thousands of dollars for her precious Rebecca.

"Well, you can take your money and fuck off, Patton!" shouted Rebecca, she then grabbed the envelope from Corina and thrust it towards Bryan's chest. He quickly stood back and it fell onto the kitchen floor, sending the money flying across the black and white shiny floor tiles. He made no effort to pick it up and remained still.

Catherine got up from her chair and started to pick the money up. She placed all of it back into the envelope and attempted to give it back to Bryan.

"I don't want it back. I want you to have it, Corina" he felt depressed as he spoke. He noticed she was getting very upset and felt bad for her. He never wanted any of this. He just wanted to get on with his life after losing his son.

"Please, don't take my baby" Corina begged him, the tears poured down her face "Please, I'll let you see her whenever you want.... But, please don't take her away from me"

"I don't want your baby, Corina. I want you to take the money and go back to England with her. Angela is not going to give up, so I need you to go back as soon as possible. The money is for the baby and anything she needs.... But, I just need you to go... and quickly" he stuttered as he came to the end of his sentence.

Corina felt relieved that he wasn't there to take her baby. Also, she couldn't help but feel uneasy at the thought of Angela not giving up. She knew Angela would be on the war path as soon as she found out the baby had gone with her back to England. She also didn't know if she was ready to return to England yet, as she hadn't resolved anything with Alberto, she couldn't possibly go and leave him until she had spoken to him and sorted out their differences.

"I'm going to go now. Angela doesn't know I'm here, so I need to get back. You need to go soon though, Corina, as once she sees the money has gone from our account, my life won't be worth living" he looked gloomy as he turned around to leave.

"Thank you, Bryan" Corina spoke through her tears "Do you want to say goodbye to your granddaughter before you go?"

Bryan looked over at little Rebecca, he didn't have a clue how to respond or how to show any affection towards her.

"Umm...bye, Rebecca" he stuttered again.

"Yeah, bye, Bryan!" said Rebecca sarcastically. She rolled her eyes at Catherine and shook her head, she then sat down to finish her dinner and ignored him.

"I'll see you out, Mr Patton" Mary gave the baby back to Corina and escorted Bryan to the front door, then watched him leave the property. She felt relieved that there hadn't been a huge confrontation. When she returned to the kitchen, she kissed Corina on the top of her head to reassure her that all would be okay.

"Well, I didn't expect that!" said Catherine, she placed her knife and fork together on her empty dinner plate after she finished her food.

"There's fifty thousand dollars here!" said Corina, stunned that Bryan had gone behind Angela's back to give her such a large amount of money for the baby.

"I wouldn't want to be in Bryan's shoes when she finds out all that money is gone... and why!" laughed Rebecca "Poor sad old Bryan, what it must be like to live with Angela....no wonder he's a quivering wreck!"

Corina didn't say anything in return. She looked thoughtful as she put Rebecca back onto her breast. She thought to herself, she would feed her baby and then go to bed to think about what she was going to do next. One of the most important things to do was to go and see Alberto in the morning. She had to make everything alright with him. She missed him and she most certainly missed Joseph. She yearned for Joseph and she hated being in the house without him. She just wanted to feel him again and to talk to him. She wanted to hold him and never let him go. She wished none of the bad things had ever happened. She wanted everything to go back to normal. She wanted it to be just her, Joseph and their baby, living in Milton and enjoying life.

"I'm going to bed now" she told everyone.

"Are you sure, dear...it's very early... and Catherine is here" asked Mary "And, you haven't finished your dinner!"

"I need to go to bed. I need to think"

Corina got up, still with the baby attached to her breast and left the room. She needed to be alone with her baby and she needed some peace and quiet to be able to think properly.

"Night, then!" called Rebecca after her. The sarcasm was yet again evident in her voice.

Corina ignored her and carried on up the stairs to her room. The rest of the women sat in silence, not knowing what to say. They just looked at each other over the big pot of Boston Beans.

Rebecca broke the silence and said "I don't think we should have Boston Beans any more.... Boston Beans are a bad omen"

She then held her stomach and broke wind... loudly.

Chapter Thirty-Three

The next morning Corina left early to avoid the rush hour traffic in Boston, she had decided to take the baby with her to see Alberto to try and sort their differences out. She hoped Alberto wouldn't be too angry with her for bringing the baby, as she didn't want to leave her baby alone with anyone just yet. Corina smiled and nodded in acknowledgement of the concierge as she entered The Four Seasons. The concierge beamed a smile at her as she approached him, he then peered into the pram to take a look at little Rebecca, who was fast asleep and totally oblivious of her surroundings.

"Oh, how sweet!" cooed the concierge "Congratulations, Mrs Barsetti, she is beautiful"

"Thank you, Richard" Corina took the fifty-dollar bill out of her pocket that she had in preparation for meeting the concierge. She handed it to him and as he took it, she said quietly "Could you please let me into our apartment? I have forgotten my keys"

She knew that Alberto probably wouldn't let her in if she had buzzed up, or even knocked on the door, especially if he saw that she had the baby with her.

"It would be an absolute pleasure, Mrs Barsetti" said Richard, he quickly pocketed the money.

She followed him up to the apartment and then waited for Richard to open the door. As she went in, the stench of stale whiskey hit her which made her stomach turn. Richard stuck his nose in the air and looked very unimpressed. He quickly closed the door behind her and left to return to the lobby to go about his business. She didn't know what to do, or what to expect, so stood there motionless while she thought for a moment. Her hands grasped the handle of the pram tight until they had turned blue. Her mind raced as she forced herself to walk towards the lounge. Then, as she stood in the doorway, she feared the worst when she spotted Alberto sat upright in his chair. His head was right back against the head rest and his mouth was wide open. He looked awful, his unshaven face made him look old and the sallowness of his skin made her think he was dead.

The tears poured down her face whilst she whispered to herself "Please don't be dead, please don't be dead"

She left the pram in the doorway and slowly approached Alberto. Her heart pounded in her chest as she reached out to touch him. Suddenly, Alberto flinched and she screamed out loud with fright. He grabbed her wrist whilst she tried to feel for a pulse to see if he was still alive.

"Jesus Christ, Dad, you scared the shit out of me!" shouted Corina at Alberto. When he realised who she was, he let go of his forceful grip from around her wrist.

"Don't creep up on me like that; it's enough to give me a heart attack!" Alberto looked flustered as the colour raced back into his cheeks "What are you doing here?"

"I was worried about you and I wanted to talk to you. I've missed you" Corina looked over at the pram as the baby stirred and let out a loud shriek of hunger.

"Why have you brought that baby here with you? I told you, I don't want that baby in my home...and that lesbian better not be here too!" Alberto shouted at her "Why do you not listen to me?"

"Dad, we need to talk about this. The baby is part of me now. If you want me in your life, you have to accept the baby as well"

"It's a good job I don't want you in my life then, isn't it!" sneered Alberto, he reached for the bottle of whiskey that was on the coffee table in front of him.

"You don't mean that, surely?" Corina looked at him in disbelief "Why are you drinking that at this time of the morning?"

"Shut that thing up!" shouted Alberto. He covered his ears to try and drown out the baby's cries. Corina went over to the baby to try and calm her screams. She picked her up and carried her over to the couch, so she could sit opposite Alberto. The coffee table, which was full of empty beer and whiskey bottles, was the only thing between them.

"Feeling sorry for yourself, are you?" Corina rocked the baby gently whilst she started to breast feed her "Are you trying to find the answers about why this has all happened in the bottom of that bottle of whiskey?"

"I'm not listening to you, Corina…. And, do you have to do that in front of me?"

"Yes, I do, and you will listen to me, because I shall be going back to England within the next couple of days, so I'm going to have my say now, whether you like it or not!" Corina fought hard to fight back her tears of sadness as she spoke. Alberto didn't look like the Alberto she knew and loved, he looked destroyed. It was a shock to see him like that, as he had always been her rock.

"Good riddance!" he took another swig of his whiskey and then relaxed back into his chair "And, take my wife with you!"

"Oh, come on, Dad, you don't mean that!"

"After all I've done for you and that woman…. you both put that baby before me!"

"But, you have forced that on us, Dad. You said you didn't want the baby here and she's my daughter, so I'm afraid she comes first for me now. You would do the same for Joseph. But, that doesn't mean I don't love you, you're still my Dad after all, I'm worried about you and I want to help you. Why don't you come back to England with me… just until you feel better?"

Alberto looked at her in contempt and then continued to drink his whiskey. The atmosphere was awkward and Corina felt uncomfortable. Alberto glared at her and tried to take in what she was saying.

"Dad, how about that idea…you wanna come with me?"

"Isn't it about time you got in contact with your own father? I mean, I'm not your real Dad, so I shouldn't have to worry about you or that baby anymore.... then we can all just get on with our lives"

"...Really, that's what you would like me to do. Is it?" Corina looked miserable, she began to cuddle her baby closer to her breast.

"Yes, really!" Alberto continued to glare at her with the same look of repulsion as before "It's about time you got on with the rest of your life. There's nothing here for you now. Joseph is dead. You need to make peace with your parents and never come back here.... you hear me?"

Corina listened to his voice, it had begun to slur with the amount of alcohol he had already drunk at only seven-thirty in the morning. She didn't want to contact her parents; Alberto was her father as far as she was concerned. She wanted him in her life, not them.

"Dad, please..."

"Now, stop that.... there will be no more calling me Dad!" the tears welled up in Alberto's eyes, his face screwed up with the emotional pain and he tried to stop the tears that had begun to pour down his cheeks. Deep down, he loved her with all his heart; he didn't really want her out of his life. He was just trying to cope with everything that had happened and he didn't know how to make head nor tail of his feelings.

"I'm not going to stop calling you Dad. I can't. Please don't let James ruin our lives...even after his death he is still making our lives a misery. Please, Dad, I love you, please don't push me away......I'm going to call Mom to get her to come over. We can work this out, I know it"

Corina got up, still with the baby attached to her breast and walked over to Alberto. She placed her hand on his head as he leant over to weep into his hands. She gently stroked his hair as he wept and quietly reassured him that everything would be okay.

"I'm going to give Mom a call now, okay, Dad?"

Alberto nodded, but he continued to hold his head down so that he could hide his tears from Corina.

"I'll make you some coffee too, why don't you go and get yourself cleaned up before Mom gets here?"

Alberto struggled to get up and was unsteady on his feet, but he managed to get to his bedroom so he could begin to shower and shave before Mary got there. Corina thought he looked and smelt awful as he passed her, but she felt comforted that he was making an effort to shower before Mary arrived.

Corina went into the kitchen with the baby and picked up the phone to call Mary.

"Hello!" shouted Rebecca abruptly as she slammed the phone to her ear. She was annoyed that someone had called so early in the morning; she was tired and hung over from the night before, as she had met Debs after everyone had gone to bed and spent most of the night talking with her and drinking her favourite tipple.

"Hi Becs, is Mom there, please.... Could I speak to her?"

"Corina.... I was asleep! You better not be calling me from downstairs.... cos if you are, I swear to god, I'm going to come down there and kick your ass!"

"No, I'm with Alberto at The Four Seasons, actually.... someone woke up a bit moody this morning.... what's up, got PMT?" Corina laughed at Becs and her grumpy morning attitude towards her.

"I'm just a tad hung over and was hoping for a lie in.... you're at Alberto's.... what? Oh, Jeez I'm so confused......MAZZA, CORINA IS ON THE PHONE!"

Corina could hear the muffled voices of Rebecca and Mary. Mary was questioning Rebecca about where Corina was and was the baby with her.

"Is the baby with you, Cor? ... hang on, here's Mazza" Rebecca handed the phone to Mary and then collapsed back onto her bed and covered her face with a pillow.

"Hi, Corina, dear. Is everything okay?" Mary sounded apprehensive when she spoke to Corina.

"I'm fine, Mom. I'm here with Dad and the baby.... could you please come over? He is in a bit of a state, but I think it's a good time to talk things over" Corina took a deep breath and continued "He's just having a shower, but you'll need to take a cab as I have used your car to get here"

"Okay, honey. But, what do you mean he's in a bit of a state?"

"He's been drinking and has obviously not been looking after himself....and he thinks we have put the baby first before him. If you could get over here quick, we can talk it over.... while he's still in a talking mood" Corina was desperate to get everything sorted before she went back to England, she wanted to get back there as soon as possible. She did not ever want to come across James' parents again and she definitely didn't want them in her daughter's life.

"I'll just finish getting ready and then I'll be there. Do you want to speak to Rebecca again?" Mary looked over at Rebecca, who still had her face covered with a pillow. The sound of her groaning came from underneath it "I don't think Rebecca wants to talk to you, dear. See you soon"

Corina rushed around and tidied up, to make the apartment look presentable in preparation for Mary's arrival; she sprayed air freshener around the rooms as she tidied. She hoped the smell of alcohol would be covered by the smell of the lavender spray. Alberto appeared out of his bedroom and came into the lounge where Corina was, he had showered and shaved and looked much more like himself. Corina approached him with caution, as she didn't know whether he would reciprocate the hug she was about to give him. He held her tight though, and whispered "I'm sorry" in her ear. Corina sighed with relief as she rested her head on his shoulder. She loved him as if he was her father, so much so, that the thought of him rejecting her and the baby was unbearable. They both moved apart from each other when they heard Mary come through the front door and call out their names.

"We're in the lounge, Mom" shouted Corina.

Alberto looked anxious as he waited for Mary to appear in the doorway. Corina patted his back to let him know that all would be fine. Mary stood for a few seconds in the lounge doorway to look at Alberto; she smiled and started to walk towards him. She opened her arms as she approached him and they both fell into each other's embrace.

"Have you been drinking, Alberto?" Mary questioned him quietly "You know that's not going to make everything go away, don't you dear?"

Alberto couldn't speak. He was overcome with emotion again, but he continued to hold his wife in his arms. The baby started to cry again, so Corina rushed over to the pram to pick her up as she didn't want to upset Alberto again.

"It's okay, little one, Mommy is here" Corina rocked the baby in her arms and she watched Alberto and Mary move to sit together on the couch. Corina then walked over and sat in Alberto's chair with the baby, she hoped that they could now start to talk about what was going to happen next.

"Could I hold the baby, Corina?" asked Mary.

"Sure" replied Corina, she got up to hand the baby to Mary.

As Mary cuddled the baby and talked to her, Alberto peered over to take a look at her.

"She does look like you, Corina" said Alberto "Look at her dark brown hair and eyes…. and the shape of her face" he paused for a minute before he said "I don't see James in her at all"

"That's because the better genes took over, dear" giggled Mary "She is beautiful, isn't she? Just like her Mommy"

"Yes, she is" said Alberto, his eyes filled with tears again "Please can I hold her?"

"Of course, Dad…but, are you sure?" Corina was pleased that he had asked to hold her, but she was a bit worried about the amount of alcohol he had drunk "Just try not to breathe on her…. we don't want her getting tipsy!" Corina gave Alberto a cheeky smile as he took the baby carefully from Mary. She watched him as he gently stroked little Rebecca's face, then she too started to feel a bit emotional as Alberto turned to look at her with yet more tears in his eyes.

"What shall I be known as?" asked Alberto "To the baby, I mean…what will she call me?"

"Well, I'm Grandma, so how about Grandpa?" said Mary. She couldn't believe his change of heart about the baby, but she was pleased that he was making an effort.

"Nonno!" laughed Corina "As you know, that's Italian for Grandpa"

"Nonno suits you, dear" laughed Mary. She stroked the side of Alberto's head as he cooed at the baby.

"Nonno, it is then" laughed Alberto "Benvenuto al mondo piccolo uno … Welcome to the world, little one"

"That's so sweet, Dad. Thank you, for making such a big effort" Corina was overwhelmed with the change in Alberto. She started to cry when she spoke "I love you so much, Dad, I'm so sorry that all this has happened. Even though I have Rebecca now, my heart breaks for my husband and son and I would do anything to have them here with us. My heart goes out to you as you try to come to terms with what happened with James…. I know it's difficult, Dad, but as I said before, we can get through this together and I will always be here for you"

Mary looked at Alberto and spoke gently to him "All our hearts are breaking, Alberto. We have to stick together, so we can get through this as a family. Rebecca is part of our family now and we have to be strong for her"

"I'm going to try my hardest to accept her as my own grandchild, Corina" said Alberto. The pain in his eyes was very much apparent to Corina as he spoke to her "It's been very difficult for me to get over what I saw on that day, just as it's been difficult for you to cope with finding Joseph like you did. I needed that time alone to think… and today when I said those awful things to you, I felt bad and the terrible feeling I had inside me made me realise that I can't live without you, or your Mom. I love you both very much and I think coming back to England with you will do us all good"

He handed the baby back to Corina and then leant over and kissed her softly on her forehead.

"So, I'd better book the flights then" Mary winked at Corina "Oh, what about a passport for the baby?"

"Yes, you'll have to get one before we can fly, Corina" said Alberto "I call the passport agency and find out what we have to do. You better go get some ID photo's done of her"

Corina didn't really want to venture into Boston to go into the Mall to get photographs of the baby done, she was worried she would bump into Angela, but she knew the sooner it was done, the sooner she could fly back home.

"Could I just grab some breakfast before I go into town, I'm a bit hungry... shall we all go and get the photo's done together?" Corina was starving, she hadn't had breakfast before she had left Milton early that morning.

"Yes, let's all go together" said Mary excitedly, she was really pleased that her family were back together again "I'll go put some coffee on"

Mary headed for the kitchen and left Alberto and Corina alone with the baby, they both looked at each other and smiled.

"I am very proud of you for being as strong as you are, Corina" Alberto looked like he was going to cry again "I want you to make a new life for yourself in England with the baby and I have a good feeling that you will be happy again"

"It doesn't feel like I will ever be happy without Joseph, Dad, but I will make sure that I'll do my best for little Rebecca"

Alberto nodded in acknowledgement, he knew exactly how she felt. He missed his only son dreadfully.

Corina paused for a second, then asked Alberto "Dad, I've been thinking lately that I might be ready to see Jo's autopsy and coroner's investigative reports. I noticed they were in your desk when I was tidying up his morning, it was all addressed to me and I would like to know what they say"

"I wasn't trying to hide anything from you, Corina, it all arrived when we were over in England and I just didn't think you were quite ready to read them when we got back"

"I understand that, but I think that when we get back from the Mall, I will sit down and read it all" said Corina.

"Are you two coming through for some breakfast?" called Mary from the kitchen, she had started to make waffles and the smell of them, as they cooked on the waffle grill, wafted through to the lounge.

"On our way" said Alberto quietly, so not to wake the baby, who looked very content as she slept. He thought she must be about ready to burst with the amount of breast milk she had drunk, he then turned to Corina and said "If you are sure you want to read them, Corina, we will go through them together as you will find it all very upsetting"

Corina didn't say anything as she placed Rebecca gently in her pram. She wanted to eat her breakfast in peace without the baby attached to her breast while she ate. She gestured to Alberto to follow her quietly to the kitchen. They both sat down at the table and began to fill their bellies with Mary's waffles.

"These waffles taste almost as good as your Boston beans, Mary" said Alberto, whilst squirting maple syrup all over his third helping of waffles.

"Well, I'm glad you love my Boston beans, dear, as I have a whole pot left over from last night!" laughed Mary "Has Corina told you about our visitor that turned up last night?"

"No... who?"

"Brainless, Bryan" sniggered Corina "He came to give me money to take the baby back to England before Angela can get her hands on her... Fifty thousand dollars!"

"What!" Alberto nearly choked on his waffle and a sticky blob of syrup ran down his chin "Did you take it?"

"Of course she did... and so she should!" said Mary defiantly "She needs the money to bring up Rebecca by herself"

"So, you are telling me that Angela doesn't know he gave you money?" Alberto looked worried, he felt uneasy about the whole situation.

"Yes, Dad, he doesn't want them to bring up the baby, so he gave me the money to go back to England as soon as possible, before Angela finds out" replied Corina.

"Oh my!" responded Alberto "I think the shit will hit the fan when she finds out.... I wouldn't want to be in his shoes when she does!"

"I think we should all move back here, Corina. We are protected here as she won't get past the concierge downstairs... is that okay with you, Alberto, dear?" asked Mary.

"Of course it's okay, this is your home!" Alberto winked at her as she took a gulp of her strong coffee.

Corina felt relieved, she hated being back at the house in Milton "What about the lesbian though, is she welcome to come back?" asked Corina cautiously, she didn't want to push her luck.

"If she wants" Alberto wiped his face with a napkin and picked up his cup of coffee "I'll take this with me to the bedroom, so I can call the passport office to see how long it will take for Rebecca's passport to be sorted"

"Okay, Dad, thank you" Corina smiled at Alberto as he left the room.

Mary watched him leave, then turned to Corina and gave her the thumbs up. Everything was going smoothly so far and Mary was very glad to be back home at The Four Seasons.

....

It didn't take them long to visit the mall to get little Rebecca's passport photographs done. There was no sign of the Patton's and

Corina was pleased with that, as she felt tired and she didn't feel like she had the strength to be confronted by an angry Angela. All she wanted to do was get back to the apartment and finally read the coroner's report about her husband's suicide. She hoped that if she read it she might get some closure and then she could try and get on with her new life as a mother to Rebecca.

"Can I please see the report now, Dad?" said Corina, as soon as they had all settled themselves down in the lounge. The baby was fast asleep, so Corina was keen to get on and read it whilst it was quiet enough to do so.

"Yes, Corina, but there are photographs in there that I wanted to take out before you read it. There is no need for you to be looking at Joseph and the lounge as it was that day. They are very graphic and you will find them too upsetting" Alberto knew that she had already seen it all first hand, but he didn't want to evoke any bad memories by letting her see the suicide scene photographs.

Alberto got up and went to his desk. Corina felt anxious as she watched him take the photographs of the suicide scene out of the envelope, a picture of the gun that Joseph had used to kill himself fell to the floor and Corina got a quick glimpse before Alberto rushed to hide it away from her. He walked over to her and handed over the envelope. As she opened the report, she thought to herself that there was a lot of paperwork to read. They had covered every avenue to make sure that Joseph had in fact, most definitely, taken his own life. She noticed straight away the wording 'Due to or as a consequence of Suicide' that had been stamped on in bold black ink at the end of the autopsy report and at the bottom of the coroner's investigative papers. It upset Corina as the death scene report continued to refer to Joseph as the 'subject'. He was her husband, not a subject. The 'subject' was located in the lounge, which was situated to the right off the entrance hallway…The 'subject' had made a 911 call…. the 'subject' used a Remington 870 12-gauge shotgun…. The prefrontal cortex of the 'subject' was…. she couldn't continue at that point, Alberto was right, she wasn't ready to read the reports fully yet. It had triggered a flash back of Joseph's face from the day she had found him, but she knew she didn't need the photographs to remind her, as she had a permanent photograph of that horrible image stuck in her mind and ready to pop up at any time of the day or night. She dropped the papers onto her lap and looked at Alberto, she hoped he would take them from her, as she felt like she was going to scream out loud with frustration.

"It's okay, Corina, don't look at it anymore" Alberto quickly gathered the papers up "I will take them to England with us and you can look at them when you are ready"

"Why is it taking me so long to get over what Joseph did…why can't I look at the papers without feeling like I'm going to lose it?"

"Corina, it's only been nine months!" said Mary, she tried to reassure her "So much as happened since then and you didn't even carry Rebecca to full term. You can't expect to get over what's happened within nine months, you are putting too much pressure on yourself to heal before you are ready!"

Corina looked deflated "I think I'm going to have a little nap while Rebecca is asleep, Mom" she said to Mary "Will you please let Bec's know what is happening and that she is welcome to come back here now"

"Of course, honey. Do you want a hug?" Mary got up from her chair to hug Corina. She felt very sad about her son too and what he had done to the family, but she had forgiven him. Corina melted into her arms and wept quietly "It's okay, baby, everything will be good again, I promise"

Alberto came over from his desk after he had put the envelope back safely into his desk draw and put his arms around them both "Your Mom is right, honey. Everything will be just fine"

Chapter Thirty-Four

Corina was sat on the floor in her lounge back at Rickerby House, she had started to sort through photographs from boxes that still hadn't been unpacked from when she first moved there. She tried to busy herself as Alberto and Mary had left that morning, they had stayed with her for six months and she now felt a bit lost without them. There was an eerie silence now that they had left, but she had to get used to not having them around. They really didn't want to go back to Boston though, they would have quite happily stayed in England with Corina and Rebecca, but they had to go back and face the music with Angela. She had called them constantly to remind Corina that she too was the grandmother of Rebecca and no way was she going to be forgotten. Angela had come to terms with the fact she could not have Rebecca and agreed to have visiting rights only, but she couldn't wait for Mary and Alberto to return with photographs and updates on how Rebecca had progressed and continued to make sure they remembered to come and see her as soon as they had landed back in Boston. There had been lots of tears between the three of them, but little Rebecca laughed and gurgled at them all. She had no idea what was happening, she was too busy having fun in her baby bouncer and began to throw her toys at the back of Alberto's legs. She thought that it was hilarious when her Nonno pretended to cry out loud in pain. She was such a happy little soul, but was now exhausted and was in her cot for an afternoon nap to recharge her batteries. Corina felt glad she had kept her daughter, she had brought sunshine and smiles to brighten up her days and couldn't imagine not having her in her life. Corina knew that she had to go back to work soon though, as Haverigg Prison was still very keen to have her, but she dreaded the fact she would have to leave Rebecca in child care. She was still breast feeding, so would either have to stop beforehand or express milk for when she was on shift, then just breast feed her when she got home.

After emptying one of the boxes, she came across the picture of her and her friends in her bedroom on the day of their graduation, she giggled to herself when she noticed their lip pouts and remembered how they had all tried to look sexy. She thought of Becs and the fact that she had stayed in Boston to be with Debs, she was happy for her, but missed her too. She remembered that the picture was taken on the day that the romance between her and Joseph had begun and even though she knew Becs hated Joseph, he was the reason why they had all ended up in Boston. If it wasn't for him, Becs wouldn't have met Debs. She wondered what life would be like if Joseph was still alive, would she trade her daughter for a life to be with Joseph again? She quickly pushed that thought out of her mind, there was no way Joseph was ever coming back, so she didn't need to worry about trading her daughter in. She giggled to herself again, at the silly thought of her being worried about making a choice if Joseph ever came back. She ran her thumb over the picture as if to stroke the girls faces, she missed those days and the fun they all had. They were young and carefree and basically thought life was one big shag fest.... all they were worried about was which doctor they would like to sleep with next. But, now she was a widow and a single mum to her dead husbands, dead best friend... how life had changed for her, but she was determined to make the best of it and make a good life for her and her daughter. She thought of Catherine and how she had helped to deliver her daughter in the public gardens, they had a good friendship and she looked forward to seeing her again. Catherine had promised to come over to England for a visit within the next couple of months.

Her thoughts were interrupted by the sudden loudness of her door buzzer. She got up and ran to the hallway to stop it before it woke up Rebecca.

She picked up the door phone and said impatiently "Hello!"

"Hello, Corina"

Corina's heart started to race. She recognised the voice straight away, even though she hadn't heard it for over ten years.

"Daddy?" she replied slowly. She wasn't sure whether to call him that after all this time.

"Yes, darling. Could I please come in and talk to you?" Doctor Henry Green didn't sound so abrupt and overpowering as he did when she had last spoken to him on her wedding day.

Corina buzzed him in and went to the front door to meet him. There was a feeling of awkwardness in the air when they both saw each other; they weren't quite sure whether to hug or not, but gave each other a half-hearted hug anyway. Corina's father was dressed in green cord slacks and a Harris tweed country jacket, over a brown and white checked shirt, complete with matching tie. His hair had started to grey and he had begun to go bald on the top of his head. He had put on weight since she last saw him too, but he still smelled of the same aftershave after all these years. Kouros for men. She thought he smelled nice, but it brought back memories of her childhood and she shuddered at the thought of it.

"Mummy not with you, I see!" said Corina sarcastically "I don't suppose she could be bothered to make the journey up here to see her naughty daughter after all these years!"

"Your mother is dead, Corina. She died five years ago.... of breast cancer" Henry looked sad as he told her.

"Oh" Corina didn't know what to say and felt embarrassed that she didn't feel upset.

"I'm sorry to hear about your husband, Corina. I regret not meeting him, as I understand that he made you very happy.... something that your mother and I were never capable of"

Corina ignored that statement from her father and gestured that he should go to the kitchen and sit down.

"What are you doing here anyway?" enquired Corina, whilst she started to make them both a coffee.

"Harriet called me, she told me that Joseph's parents were leaving this morning and that I should consider reconcilement, as she didn't want you to feel alone and vulnerable"

"Oh" said Corina again.

"How do you feel about that?"

"About what?"

"About us having a father daughter relationship again?" Henry looked uncomfortable, Corina had turned her back on him to finish making the coffee. There was silence. A deafening silence.

"Corina?" she continued to ignore him.

She felt angry that Harriet had gone behind her back and suggested that he came to her house to try and reconcile with her. She felt that he shouldn't have been prompted to make contact now, he should have wanted to do it years ago.

"Corina, say something please!" Henry felt very upset and began to wipe away the one single solitary tear that had started to run down his cheek.

"Are you crying?" sneered Corina "Well, that's a first.... Doctor Henry Green, showing some emotion. Wow, wonders will never cease!"

"I have cried a lot since your mother died" he continued to wipe the tears that now poured down over his cheeks.

"Well, join the club, I have cried a lot too since my husband died.... it's not nice is it... feeling alone?" Corina carried on "I have felt alone and unloved for most of my childhood, because of you and my mother and your attitude towards me, but when I married Joseph I was so happy….and what did you do? Disown me!"

"Corina, I…"

"And, then…. after all these years, you think you can walk back into my life and expect me to welcome you with open arms?"

"Well, I…"

"I bet you wouldn't be here if the bitch was still alive, would you? …. she wouldn't have let you come…the jealous old cow…. well, I'm glad she's dead…. GOOD RIDDANCE!!" Corina shouted loudly at him and then realised the baby had started to cry. The noise of Rebecca's yelling stopped her in her tracks.

"Do you want me to go back home, Corina?" asked Henry quietly. He was incredibly upset at her outburst, but he also felt that he had deserved it.

"No!" snapped Corina automatically, and as she walked to her bedroom to get the baby, she wondered to herself why she didn't say yes.

Corina returned with Rebecca and Henry's eyes lit up when he saw her.

"Corina, she is beautiful!" Henry exclaimed, he quickly stood up to stroke the baby's face.

"Do you want to hold her?" asked Corina sternly. Rebecca stared at Henry for a few seconds and then gave him a huge beaming smile.

Henry nodded, he held out his arms and took the baby from Corina, then sat back down in his chair with her. Rebecca seemed to take an instant liking to her Grandfather and continued to smile and coo at him.

"She obviously likes you" said Corina "Though, I have no idea why!"

"Corina, I want to try and rebuild our relationship, so could we please talk about our past properly, without you making snidely remarks?"

"You don't get to tell me what to do anymore!" Corina was cross, she had so much to say, but didn't want there to be conflict in front of Rebecca.

"I can assure you, I have no intention of telling you what to do anymore, but I want us to be able to put the past behind us and be a family again. I know we were cruel to you when you were growing up and I regret that terribly. I allowed your mother to rule the roost and treat you badly. I can only apologise on her behalf…. and hope we can get over it somehow and carry on"

"But, you knew she hated me, so why apologise for her? …. she was never sorry!" Corina responded with tears present in her eyes.

"She was extremely sorry. In fact, she wanted to see you at the end to try and explain things, but we didn't know how to contact you. Your mothers upbringing was very harsh too, her mother beat her senseless at times.... it was learned behaviour. She cried and cried with guilt because of what she did to you, but she was just so stubborn.... she would never have allowed you to see that she loved you. And, she did love you, she just had a funny way of showing it" Henry tried to explain, but Corina squirmed in her chair at the thought of her mother loving her and never having the guts to show it.

"You didn't try very hard to find me though, Harriet always had my address"

"Harriet only contacted me this week, we never knew what had happened to her after you married Joseph and left England. We didn't even know Josephs last name to make a search, we didn't even know what part of America he came from and by then it was too late. Your mother wrote you a letter though, I will leave it for you to read once I have gone"

Corina burst into tears, then tried to pull herself together to speak, but Henry interrupted.

"I know I should have been a bit more forceful and stopped her from treating you the way she did, but my life was a lot easier when I did as I was told and if I pleased her she would leave you alone"

"So your telling me, you ignored what she did so that you could have a quiet life?" Corina looked at him astounded. Little Rebecca looked over at her and cooed, she still smiled and waved her arms about at the excitement of meeting somebody new.

"I was the local GP, Corina. I had a reputation to keep up. I had to be seen to have the perfect family life, I wasn't willing to admit back then that she was wrong and I was worried she would leave us"

"Are you for real? I cannot even imagine ever treating my daughter like that, or allow anybody else to treat her like that either. You made out you were the perfect parents when your stuck up doctor friends were around, that was the only time I ever got any love from you!"

"Corina, I was scared.... your mother was very volatile"

"What are you saying? God, you sound like one of those beaten wives or something!" Corina looked at him unsympathetically and waited for an answer.

"As I said before, I was the local GP, and I was too embarrassed to come out and say that my wife...." Henry looked very upset "But, I loved her though, and I miss her"

"Too embarrassed to say what?" Corina urged him to continue.

"She never meant to do it, it was just the way she was brought up, I think" Henry stalled, which made Corina feel tense, as she wanted him to just tell her.

"She didn't mean to do what, Daddy? Just tell me!"

"I did love you, Corina, very much, and of course I still do. I wasn't allowed to be a proper father to you. You were right, she was jealous of you, and I'm sorry, I should have been stronger" Henry bounced the baby up and down on his knee as he spoke, she giggled loudly at him and began to try and grab at his tie.

"Why won't you just come out and say what she did?" Corina knew why he was avoiding answering the question. Corina had put the memories of the terribly violent arguments that her parents had out of her mind for years, but she remembered how it was always her mother that started the violence.

"I feel embarrassed, I should have been more of a man and stuck up for you"

"It wasn't your fault that she was a bully and used to hit you. You didn't deserve what she did to you, but you should not have allowed her to treat me like she did, and you should not have backed her up!" stated Corina.

"Don't you think that I know that now... and deep down I've always known that.... but, I will repeat... I should have been more of a man and done something about it. I am sorry" Henry looked Corina straight in the eye as he spoke to her, she knew he was being genuine and she felt sorry for him after all these years.

"I know you're sorry and I accept your apology. I have come to realise recently that life is far too short to hold on to hate, so I forgive you. I am happy to try and rebuild our relationship and have you in our life. You must realise though, that I am very close to Alberto and Mary and I look at them as being my parents, they have been very supportive to me, both emotionally and financially, so I don't want any animosity towards them" explained Corina.

"There will be no animosity from me, I am very grateful that they have looked after you. Now, come here and give your Daddy a proper cuddle"

Henry stood up with Rebecca and moved towards Corina for a hug. They squeezed each other tight, whilst Rebecca made a beeline for Corina's hair and grabbed a handful. She held onto it tight, whilst Corina tried to prise her fingers apart gently to free herself. They all laughed at Rebecca's shrieks of joy as she let go of her mummy's hair.

"I think she's going to be a character!" laughed Henry, he tickled Rebecca under the arm. Rebecca shrieked and giggled some more. Corina was happy that she had accepted her Grandad so quickly, she wasn't normally that excited about meeting people she didn't know. Rebecca had cried and screamed when Harriet first met her and was inconsolable when she picked her up to say hello.

"There's just one more thing though, Daddy... I don't want to read that letter my mother left me. If you say she was sorry, I believe you. I really can't cope with reading a letter from her, I feel I just want to let it go"

"I understand, Corina. I will keep it, so if you ever change your mind you can read it. Now, I really must be getting to the hotel. I haven't checked in yet; they will think I'm not coming!"

"I'll phone them and cancel your reservation, you must stay here. What hotel was it?" enquired Corina.

"That's very kind of you, but only if you're sure.... it's called The Warwick"

"The Warwick?" Corina repeated back at him. She looked a bit perturbed and quickly headed to the lounge to phone the hotel.

Henry listened to her cancel his room on the telephone, he wondered to himself why she had looked so uneasy when he told her what hotel he had booked. When she came back to the kitchen, he asked her about it.

"Is everything okay, darling? You looked a bit uneasy when I told you the name of the hotel"

"Oh, I'm fine. It's just that Rebecca was conceived there and I couldn't believe you were going to stay in the same place…. bizarre really!"

"Is that a bad thing that she was conceived there? I'm a bit confused"

"It's a long story…. I'll tell you another day, if that's okay"

"That's perfectly fine, Corina. Whenever you are ready. I'm still trying to get used to your American accent, we really must do something about that, darling!" laughed Henry. He spoke the Queens English and had made sure Corina had spoken correctly when she was growing up, so hearing her speak in an American accent was very strange for him, even though his mother was an American and he'd had to listen to her accent when she was alive, it was still very disconcerting.

"I'm sure it will diminish once I settle back into English ways" laughed Corina "Do you want to go and get your bag from your car and get yourself settled, while I feed the baby?"

"Okay, darling" Henry handed Rebecca back to Corina and then went to get his bag from the car.

"Just leave the door on the latch, so I don't have to buzz you back in" called Corina after him.

She looked at Rebecca and made a funny face at her. Rebecca chuckled back at her mum and beamed another smile at her. Corina loved how Rebecca was such a happy baby and filled her life with laughter and love. She took Rebecca into her bedroom and sat in the chair to breastfeed her. As she began to feed her, she could hear Henry come back into the flat and take the door off the latch. He whistled happily as he made his way down the hallway to the kitchen and sat back down to finish his coffee whilst Corina fed his grandchild. He felt relieved that Corina had wanted him back in her life again and he was genuinely sorry that he had failed her as a parent. He would try and make it up to her and be the best father that he could possibly be. He was a grandfather now and that excited him, he would make sure Rebecca had a happy and stable life. He missed his wife, but knew Corina wouldn't contemplate a reunion if her mother was still alive. He knew Corina would not let her daughter anywhere near his wife and he knew Corina would have made the right decision, as even though Penelope had apologised profusely for her behaviour towards him and their daughter, he knew she would never change. She was a spiteful, selfish, violent woman and although he loved her, he was relieved that she was gone. He could get on with his life now and not worry about whether he was saying or doing the right thing, he could relax and enjoy his family. His thoughts were interrupted by Corina as she called to him from her bedroom.

"Do you want to put your things in the spare room, Daddy? It's next to the lounge, I won't be long"

Henry took his bag to the spare room. As he entered, he noticed Corina's wedding day picture that hung on the wall above the bed. The photograph was taken next to the Gretna Green sign and Corina and Joseph looked so in love as they smiled at the camera. Henry felt a pang of guilt and he wished he hadn't gone along with Penelope and disowned Corina for getting married to the man she so obviously loved. He thought his daughter looked beautiful in her cream satin dress, it was simple, yet pretty, and she held a small bouquet of flowers tied with a burgundy ribbon. Joseph had a grey suit on with a matching burgundy cravat, he looked handsome, and he regretted that he had not made the effort to get to know him. Joseph had made his daughter very happy for ten years and he was pleased by that. He wasn't enthralled with his suicide and the way it came out of the blue as far as Corina was concerned and he wished that Corina didn't have to go through what she did. But, he would support her and be there for her from now on, he felt he owed that much to her. He placed his bag on the bed and noticed the bedroom had an en-suite bathroom, he thought to himself that Corina lived in a nice flat, he thought the décor was very tasteful and there was a luxurious feel about the whole house and grounds. The house had a nice relaxing feel about it and he was sure he was going to enjoy his stay very much.

Chapter Thirty-Five

Corina had enjoyed her father's stay with her so much, that she had decided to travel back to Cornwall with him and stay there for a few weeks' holiday. As they drove towards Penzance, the magnificent St Michael's Mount could be seen on the horizon and Corina felt nostalgic, she always knew she was close to home when she spotted the mount. They travelled along the sea front to Newlyn and back to her childhood home. As they pulled into the driveway, the side of their huge family home came into view. There was ivy climbing up the walls and it looked like it could do with some tender loving care. The house had been in the family for generations, but it now looked like her father was struggling to upkeep it. The garden looked like it had been well kept though, and the lawn was perfectly mown with pretty flower beds all around.

"The house looks a bit run down, Daddy" said Corina to her father.

"Yes, it has gone downhill a bit since your mother died. I really must get on top of it now. I wouldn't want to leave you a fallen down shell!"

"The garden looks nice though" said Corina, as she got out of the car and took in a breath of fresh sea air. The smell of the beach wafted towards her and it made her want to go straight to the beach with Rebecca. Rebecca had never seen a proper beach before and Corina felt excited at the prospect of taking her there.

"We still have the same old gardener"

"What, Bill?" exclaimed Corina "No way, he must be ancient by now!"

"Yes, dear old Bill. He's still alive!" laughed Henry.

"Do you fancy walking to the beach with us, Daddy?"

"But, you've not been inside yet. We've had a long journey; don't you want to have a cup of tea first?" replied Henry.

"We can have one at the fisherman's mission on the way back. I just want to take the baby and show her the beach. Come on, we can stretch our legs for a bit"

Corina was adamant she wanted to go to the beach first, she wanted to put off going inside the house for as long as possible. The weather was sunny and warm and she had a feeling the house would be dark and damp.

"Okay then, Corina" Henry gave in.

He gave in, because he knew she would just go anyway, so he might as well go with her rather than stay in the house by himself. He went around to the back of the car and opened the boot to get Rebecca's pram out.

"I'm afraid you will have to put this contraption together, me and prams just don't get on. It's like doing a puzzle on the Krypton Factor!" Henry laughed and put the pram on the ground for Corina to sort out.

With a flick of the handle on the side of the pram, Corina effortlessly put the pram up and placed Rebecca's car seat on top with Rebecca still in it. There was a loud click, as the car seat firmly attached itself to the frame. Rebecca stirred from her slumber, she had slept most of the way down from Cumbria to Cornwall, so Corina hoped that a walk to the beach would make her feel sleepy tonight.

As Corina and Henry walked towards the beach, there was a pungent smell of rotting seaweed coming from the sea's edge. Corina's memories of being on the beach as a child came flooding back to her. She remembered how she and her friends would cover themselves in fresh seaweed from the sea and pretend to be monsters. She smirked to herself as they approached the beachside play area.

"Do you think Rebecca would like to go on a baby swing, Corina?" asked Henry excitedly.

"She's never been on a swing before" replied Corina, she too felt a little bit excited at the thought of her daughters first swing experience.

Henry peered over the baby's car seat hood and spoke in a funny voice to Rebecca "Does little miss cheeky want to come with Papa and have a go on the swing?"

Rebecca smiled and gurgled back at him whilst he began to take her out of the car seat in preparation for the epic swing ride, as he lifted her up she squealed with excitement that she was finally being freed from her car seat prison. Corina looked at her father in admiration, she was happy that he was so full of enthusiasm for his granddaughter. She was also thrilled that he had made a big effort to show Rebecca love and understanding, as Corina was determined that her child would be brought up surrounded with as much love as possible. There would never be a chance that her daughter would feel unloved or unwanted at any time in her life, whilst Corina was still around. Corina continued to watch her father gently place his grandchild in the baby swing and make sure she was sufficiently supported. He then began to gently push her to and fro and started to play peek-a-boo with her. Rebecca giggled and waved her arms around in delight. Henry and Corina both laughed at her, which made her laugh even more. She was definitely enjoying her first swing experience very much and Corina decided there and then to bring her down to the park every day whilst she was still in Cornwall. She also had a spot of paddling in the sea planned with the baby too, and even though Rebecca couldn't walk yet, she would make sure her daughter would experience all the fun that the beach had to offer, as when they went back to Carlisle there would not be easy access to a beach. Her mother had never taken the time out to take her to the beach.... ever. Even though the beach was literally a stone's throw away from their house, Corina had to rely on her friend's mum to take her. She had spent more time on the beach with her friend's mum than she ever did with her mother.

"Do you think she's had enough now?" asked Henry, he had noticed Corina was in deep thought "You don't look very happy"

Corina snapped out of her day dream and replied "No, she looks happy. Sorry, I was just thinking about my mother"

"In Boston? I'm sure she's fine, darling"

"No, my real mother!"

Corina giggled to herself at the thought of her father acknowledging the fact that Mary had been more of a mother to her than his own wife.

"Corina, I will make it up to you, you know. Please don't let the awful memories of your mother spoil our new relationship"

"Oh, daddy, don't worry I won't!" Corina sounded encouraging when she replied "I was also thinking about how much of an effort you have made with Rebecca and how proud I am of that. I know we will be okay"

Corina moved closer to her father and gave him a heartfelt hug.

"I am trying hard and I love being with you both. Shall we make our way back home now? We can have tea at the house instead of the mission, it's just that I'm feeling a bit tired after all that travelling and the sea air is making me feel like I want to go to sleep" Henry gave her a final squeeze.

"Yes, of course" Corina smiled at him and then took Rebecca out of the swing.

She carried her back to the house, cuddling her close whilst Henry pushed the pram back. Once inside, Corina was very surprised at how bright and airy the house looked and how much it had changed, as she remembered it being very dark and dreary. Henry noticed the surprised look on her face as she continued to look around the house.

"I've had the place totally redecorated since your mother died. Its' much better, isn't it?"

"It's lovely, daddy" replied Corina "The atmosphere feels nice too…. I think Rebecca and I are going to have a lovely holiday here!" She held Rebecca up high above her head, and as she began to lower her down, she blew a raspberry on her stomach. Rebecca laughed hysterically and wriggled in her mother's arms to get away from the ticklish feeling on her stomach.

"Let's go to the conservatory and have some tea, so we can relax.... I must warn you though...I may fall asleep and snore!" laughed Henry.

"Say no problem, Papa!" said Corina to Rebecca. Rebecca burst out laughing again.

"Does she ever stop laughing?" asked Henry, he too began to laugh "It's so infectious...I think she's the happiest baby I've ever met!"

"She pretty much laughs all the time, she most definitely knows how to cheer me up"

Corina began to giggle too and the more she giggled the more Rebecca laughed back. Henry laughed uncontrollably at them both. It was like a continual circle of laughter and that was the first time, in what seemed like forever to Henry, that the house was filled with joy and laughter.

He felt happy for the first time in years and he was going to relish having his family there with him... even if it was only for a few weeks.

Chapter Thirty-Six

The two weeks of Corina's holiday in Cornwall had flown by, and it was time for her and her daughter to return to Carlisle. Her father had bought her a car so she could drive herself back to Cumbria, he also thought it would be useful for her to have the car to get to and from work when she started at Haverigg Prison. It was a little mini cooper, so would be cheap on fuel and insurance. Henry didn't like the thought of her struggling financially, so asked her if she would like a monthly allowance to help her out.

"Daddy, thank you very much for the offer, but seriously, I have thousands in the bank. Alberto made sure that I invested the money from Rebecca's other grandparents wisely, so I'm okay for the time being. And, I'll be back at work and earning soon, so don't worry" explained Corina.

"I don't like the thought of you struggling, Corina, so if you ever need any money, do not be afraid to ask"

Henry was a little bit apprehensive at the thought of his daughter leaving, but at least she was in England now and not thousands of miles away in Boston. He could go up and see her regularly and continue with their new found father daughter relationship. He held Rebecca in his arms, whilst Corina filled the boot of car. She just about managed to get the pram in the boot, so she had to strap in her luggage on the back seat with one of the seat belts. Rebecca would go in her car seat in the front with Corina, so she would be in easy reach, should she need any attention on the drive up to Cumbria. Corina had planned to make lots of stops at service stations on the way up, so she could feed and change the baby. She thought it would also break up the long journey for them both.

"Right, I think that's all of my stuff" Corina then hesitated for a moment, before she said "I think it's time to go now"

Henry looked saddened as he passed over Rebecca to her, then he watched her as she meticulously checked all of Rebecca's fastenings to make sure her daughter was strapped in correctly.

"I'm so proud of you, Corina. You are a wonderful mother to Rebecca and she is very lucky to have you" said Henry. He was beginning to feel emotional and held out his arms to give his daughter a final hug before she left.

"Thank you, I really must go now, daddy" replied Corina and hugged him tight.

"I love you, Corina"

The words flowed naturally out of Henry's mouth, the look of delight on Corina's face was enough for him to make sure he would continue to tell her that he loved her every day from now on. He was pleased that he had finally made her feel secure and loved after all these years.

"I love you too, Daddy" replied Corina.

She kissed his cheek and then got in the car. Henry watched as she drove down the drive and out onto the main road, he waved until she was out of sight and then went back into the house and sat down on his favourite chair in the conservatory. He could not stop the tears of sadness that had come because Corina had left, but they were also tears of happiness, because he now had a good relationship with his daughter and he would start to count the days until he saw her again.

…..

Corina had made it out of Cornwall and onto the motorway in Devon. Rebecca started to yell out in frustration, as she was bored and hungry.

"It's okay, little one, we will stop at the next services and I'll feed you" said Corina to the baby "Not long now, sweetie"

Rebecca began to scream and scream and was inconsolable. Corina began to feel stressed at the amount of noise that was coming from such a tiny person.

"Rebecca, please, we are nearly there. Just a few more miles to go"

Rebecca yelled even louder and was going bright red with temper. Corina remembered she had put Rebecca's teddy in the driver's door pocket, so took it out and handed it to her daughter. Rebecca stopped instantly and played with it for a few moments before she dropped it down the side of her car seat, she then let out an extremely loud, high pitched, scream of temper. Corina leant over into the foot well to retrieve the teddy and went to give back to Rebecca, when she noticed that the traffic had come to an abrupt stop in front of her. Corina could see the back of a huge articulated lorry directly in front of her, but she had no way of stopping in time and she hit the back of the lorry at seventy miles an hour. The car crumpled up like a fizzy drink can that had just been stamped on. The sound of the wind screen, as it shattered into a million pieces, was the last thing that Corina heard. Everything had gone black....

Corina could hear Joseph's voice; he was frantically trying to wake her up.

"Corina, wake up, babe!" Joseph began to gently shake her "Honey, come on it's time to get up!"

Corina slowly opened her eyes and she looked at Joseph in astonishment. He was knelt by her side of the bed in their bedroom back home in Milton. He didn't have anything on apart from a pair of tiny white underpants that barely covered his manhood.

She suddenly bolted upright and desperately tried to get her bearings. She was sure she had just had a car crash. Where the hell was she? She was in a daze and couldn't think straight.

"Oh no, where's Rebecca?" she started to panic "Where the hell is Rebecca?"

"I don't know!" laughed Joseph "We haven't seen her in about ten years, she's probably hooked up with some girl somewhere!"

"Ten years? No, not that Rebecca, my daughter Rebecca!" Corina looked at Joseph, she was so confused "Am I dead?"

Joseph laughed so much, he could hardly reply "You are so funny, Cor. Of course you're not dead, and what are you talking about...your daughter? ... We don't know what sex the baby is yet, we said we would wait and have a surprise when it's born, remember?"

"Huh?" Corina looked down at her huge pregnant stomach, then she ran her hands over the bump to make sure it was real "Oh my god, I'm still pregnant!"

"Yes, seven months! You are hilarious when you wake up from one of your pregnancy dreams!"

Joseph got up off of the floor and then got back into the bed with Corina.

"It was a dream…. Oh my god, it was a dream!" shrieked Corina, the tears of relief began to fall down her cheeks.

She laid back down next to him and felt his face, she then lifted the covers up and put her hands underneath them to feel him up and down and all over, just to make sure he was not a figment of her imagination.

"Hey, stop that! …. we haven't got time for any crying or hanky panky!" exclaimed Joseph "I gotta get to work and so have you. You know how the Masshole gets if your late!"

"The Masshole can shove his job up his ass, I'm staying at home with you today. I'm not letting you out of my sight…. you hear me, Doctor Joseph Barsetti?"

"Well, if you put it like that, I suppose I can pull a sickie for my big, fat and beautiful wife!" he smoothed his hand over her baby bump and she quivered with happiness as soon as she felt his touch.

Corina couldn't believe he was there with her and she began to cuddle him tight, she nestled into his neck and smelt his unique smell. She didn't think she would ever smell that smell again, so she pinched herself on the arm, then squealed in complete joy when she felt the hard pinch on her skin. Her baby began to kick around in her stomach and Joseph could feel the baby's kicks against the side of his body.

"I am so excited for the birth of our baby, Cor…I just can't wait!" Joseph exclaimed "You should see all the baby things Mom and Dad have bought…. this baby is going to want for nothing!"

"Jo, you haven't been having headaches have you? …. or fits?" enquired Corina.

She looked him straight in the eye and waited anxiously for an answer.

"No, I feel as fit as a fiddle, and anyway, I would tell you if I was feeling ill…. just so you could put on your sexy nurse's uniform and nurse me back to health!" he winked at her, then held her close and kissed the top of her head.

"That was the worst dream I have ever had…I dreamt you had brain cancer and you shot yourself!" Corina couldn't help but cry at the thought of it. Everything in the dream had been so vivid and she could even still picture little Rebecca's face "Is it crazy to be missing your daughter that you gave birth to in a dream?"

"Ahh, Cor. Don't get upset. I wouldn't do that to you…. you do know that, don't you? I always tell you everything, because you are my life… and yes, it is crazy to get upset about a baby that you had in a dream!" Joseph chuckled to himself at how upset she was over a dream.

"It's not funny, Joseph. I thought I'd been killed in a car crash with my daughter!"

Joseph could not stop his laughter and the more he laughed, the crosser Corina got. When he finally managed to stop himself from laughing, he held himself up over Corina, so not to squash the baby. He looked at her face and felt an intense feeling of love that had begun to rush over him. He loved her so much that it made him feel all tingly inside and goose bumps started to appear on his skin.

Joseph began to passionately kiss her, he then moved his face slowly away from Corina's and was completely transfixed by her beauty. He knew he would never leave her on purpose, he loved everything about her and needed her way too much.

"I love you, my uppity English girl" he said softly to her.

Corina cradled his face in her hands and looked deep into his gorgeous blue eyes.

"I love you too… my weird American guy"

THE END

Acknowledgements

Heartfelt thanks to Dani, you are one very special lady with a wise soul and you mean a lot to me. I could not have finished this book without you, Thank You.

Special thanks to the wonderful Rachel for inspiration, and to my dear friend, Sue.... for quietly being there and listening. Also, to my lovely friend, Ali – The Tartan Widow. Stay strong and thank you for your support.

And finally, thank you to my beautiful children - for being quiet - so I was able to write this book in peace!